THE FECUND'S MELANCHOLY DAUGHTER

BRENT HAYWARD

ChiZine Publications

FIRST EDITION

LIBRARY AND ARCHIVES CANADA CATALOGUING IN PUBLICATION

Hayward, Brent
      The fecund's melancholy daughter / Brent Hayward. -- 1st ed.

ISBN 978-1-926851-13-6

      I. Title.

PS8615.A883F43 2011   C813'.6   C2011-900685-5

CHIZINE PUBLICATIONS
Toronto, Canada
www.chizinepub.com
info@chizinepub.com

Edited and copyedited by Brett Alexander Savory
Proofread by Samantha Beiko

Canada Council   **Conseil des Arts**
for the Arts   **du Canada**

We acknowledge the support of the Canada Council for the Arts which last year invested $20.1 million in writing and publishing throughout Canada.

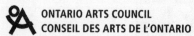

ONTARIO ARTS COUNCIL
CONSEIL DES ARTS DE L'ONTARIO

Published with the generous assistance of the Ontario Arts Council.

For mothers, especially mine, with apologies to Robert Burton

THE FECUND'S MELANCHOLY DAUGHTER

THE FIRST PARTITION

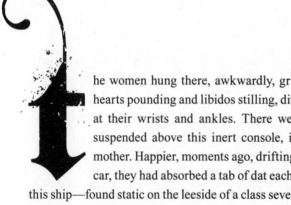he women hung there, awkwardly, grinding their teeth, hearts pounding and libidos stilling, ditto the tiny rockets at their wrists and ankles. There were three of them, suspended above this inert console, in the head of the mother. Happier, moments ago, drifting across from their car, they had absorbed a tab of dat each, to make entering this ship—found static on the leeside of a class seven moon while they killed time on a furlough—all the more of a rush. They had raced around, exploring, hoping eventually to fuck inside that great empty body.

Through the apertures of valves neither closed nor opened in eons, around delicate latticework of structural guy wires, through tangled cables and emptied conduits—a gloved hand almost grabbing a boot but not quite—to be suddenly silenced, bumping first into each other and then, entwined, up against the inside surface of the great, curved cornea. Game over. What had been a strange and unexpected discovery was now infinitely stranger.

Distant stars coldly watched reflections of the women shimmering in the giant slow curve of the lens and on the covers of the gauges as they disentangled, like chastised children.

"Holy *shit*."

"This mother should be barren." Voices hissed in each others' headgear. "I mean, she should be dead and fucking *barren*. You told us she'd be *barren*." Beneath them, arcing out of sight, a cloud-shrouded planet occluded space. "What happened here? These bodies, these exemplars . . ."

"Stop freaking out. And they're symbiotes. Ships this big needed symbiotes. Exemplars were on the broods. One on ones."

"We should leave. This is fucking creepy."

Crackling. The grey skin, open mouth.

"Nobody knows this mother is here, right? That's what you're thinking? That we're the first people here?"

"Take a deep breath."

"This isn't an abandoned wreck. Something bad happened here. Something killed all the symbiotes, or whatever."

"Maybe the supports went. The oxygen."

"Just like that? This mother's still alive, right now. Trapped in her own infrastructure. She's fucking alive."

"That's crazy. She's been here for hundreds . . ."

"Don't touch a thing. Let's split."

Yet the women lingered, watching corpses of the symbiotes move ever so slightly in the disturbance they had brought aboard. One body was still tethered to the console. These crew had died quick.

"Do you think she was pretty?"

"Who? The ship?"

"No, that girl, right there."

"Girl? That's no fucking girl. She's been dead ages. *Look at her.*"

"She's like us."

"You're fucking high. She was never like us. Groomed to live up here, serving."

"I'd like to, you know, really *see* her one day. You know? The way she was, when she was alive. Tell her it's okay. Maybe just, feel her hair. I heard they were all orphans."

"Jesus fucking Christ. Of course they were orphans. And things are not okay. There's dried up bodies here, forgotten on a long spacer, floating in the middle of fucking nowhere. Possibly intact. Something awful wiped the crew out. But hey, look, see? There's some hair floating by right now. There. Just reach out and touch it."

"That's not funny."

Slowly moving strands did indeed corkscrew the vacuum. Other clumps had twined in loose braids where two bulkheads met—joining Styrofoam chips, dust clusters, and sundry other debris—to make graceful yet chaotic orreries.

"All right. Happy now? Can we please leave?"

"Wait, though. Wait. Not yet. Let's stay for just another second. Really, what do you think they were like?"

"Sold their soul to rock and roll. Not real people. Spent most of their time plugged in, helping the ship to fucking *think*. You'll be asking about *her* next, the ship, the spacer. She's like us too. She used to be. And these symbiotes paid with their souls to work inside her."

"What choice did they have?"

"For fuck's sake, they would die if they were taken off. You know that. They were parasites. Barbaric practices back then. That girl fed her mother ship little bits and pieces of her own brain. And then the ships went mad. Their broods were even more fucked up. Why do you care what she was like?"

"I just wanna know, is all. Never seen one before."

"Plugged in, they were drones. Unplugged, they were morose. Lots of issues. Stunted and retarded, just like you. Now let's get out of here." Grabbing the suit of her friend.

But the third woman was down low, fumbling, pushing aside a tiny body with her elbow, searching in the console, muttering, "We're in the eye, right? Eye of the storm. Motherfucker. I swear, if she *could* be active, if we're the first ones—"

The other two kicked off from the lens, rockets ramping up again (but not arousal). They sailed away from the head, into the thalamic corridor, and from there down the passage of the ship's spine. In and out of shadow, illuminated by glowing ribs of light, while through their hammering veins—where hormones fueled by methamphetamines had recently raced—frustration and emotions closer to fear now jangled.

Moments later, the third woman, mask misted by hot breath, trembling in her suit, caught up. Her heart was pounding.

More dead symbiotes in what must have been a mess hall. These crew members, not strapped in, had floated free until contacting something solid, and there they gently rocked. The corpses had accumulated dull coloured collections of junk. Air must have lasted a while longer in here (there goes that theory), because decay had set in: sunken cheeks, pulled back from gums, exposed long yellow teeth; eyeballs gone altogether or shrivelled to the size of little black cocktail onions—

"What is *that*?"

"Huh? That? Broccoli. Let's keep moving. I don't wanna have to report this. Let's go back to the *Europa* and have a fucking beer. I need to meditate or some shit like that. Let's *leave*."

"Why so nervous? They've been here since before we were born. Nobody's searching for them. Nobody knows they're here. So what. They wrote all this off long ago. Program failed. Miserably. This is like a museum piece in the ideas we never should have thought up. For a fucking buck. Did people eat that green stuff?"

"I guess these spacers had access to real veggies. Hydroponics on board, probably in the stomach."

"What do you think happened inside this mother? The dead crew. The damage. You saw the damage coming in. Burns on her skin. What could bust up a ship this big? What could fool a system like this?"

"Maybe—"

"Movement." The third woman, who had had remained in the corridor, fumbling nervously with her pack, looked at her watch, about which glowing images and tables of numerals shimmered.

"Huh?"

"Just registered it. Outside. A craft's approaching. Slowly. Low frequency. Surrounded by drones."

"A *craft*? Surrounded by *drones*? Are you fucking kidding me?

What kind of craft? I'm not getting anything on mine—"

"It seems like— It's docking."

"What?"

"The craft is docking."

They heard then felt a faint shudder in the structure. The wrecked body of the mother trembled about them.

At dusk, from Black Fields, and coming slowly under the Talbot Lane Bridge, toward the opening that was South Gate—in the direction all flotsam must go, from mountain to ocean—the corpse floated, face down. Four kholics stood knee deep in the turgid water of the River Crane and watched. This was not an unusual sight for them. Paused in the task of skimming shit from the river, the men held their huge nets aloft, like pale flags. Light from a lantern, hooked on a pole, caught on low ripples in the brown water, and on debris, and then on puffy grey flesh.

The body was that of another man, naked and slim. He had not been dead for long; flesh did not last in these waters.

When the timing was right, one of the kholics waded out and extended the pole of his net to intercept, managing to hook the body by its stiff arm and pull it closer. Flipping the corpse was a struggle—a difficult task, but not impossible. Foul water and muck splashed the kholic. He did not flinch.

The dead man's throat had been cut, body drained of humours. Fat black leeches clung to legs, groin, torso. Across the man's face was a black tattoo, inked around both eyes and nose, extending— like the gash—back to the ears.

A kholic.

One of them.

Brief looks, exchanged: over the past few nights, working this bend of the river, the bodies of two other murdered kholics had been retrieved. The men knew these dead, had eaten with them on occasion, had cleaned with them, side by side, had stared at the ground together, to avoid the hemos' eyes.

As if the killer might be watching, they turned to scan the banks. There were a few people there, other kholics, mostly, labouring among the rocks. No one walked the promenade atop the embankment. Torches and street lanterns did little to the shadows of Nowy Solum, looming behind. Nothing in their city appeared out of the ordinary. The night, like most, was warm and humid, the river foul, the clouds close over their heads.

An upside of discovering that the dead man was like them: all they had to do was build a bonfire and toss the corpse of their brother onto it.

But as they began to pull the body to shore, a brilliant and terrible object hurtled across the sky, burning streaks through the clouds. Clay rooftops, mossy brick walls, buildings crammed together: all, for that instant, detailed more brilliantly than any day could ever possibly have illuminated them.

After-images trailed.

Smell of thunderstorms rained down.

The celestial object had vanished.

Warm dusk—for just a second—fell back into place, and as the men turned, frowning, to their work, the air was torn asunder by a roar so loud it seemed the world might have ended; now the kholics darted, clapping their hands over their ears. One fell headlong in the water. The lantern winked out.

Booming echoed briefly off the city, off the palace, off the towers and perimeter walls, off the markets and hovels, before all went quiet once more.

In this profound silence, on this profound night, Nowy Solum now seemed impossibly still, as if unchanged, as if nothing had happened. But the kholics knew better. Rules had shifted, fundamentals altered—

Concerns for the hemos, not them.

Without a word to each other about the incident, the men retrieved the body one more time—which had been trying to continue its way downstream, perhaps to escape—and brought their brother to the rocky shore.

Rolling lazily, laterally, the fecund let out a sigh. She half-closed one red-tinged eye. Her cascading body, strung with the weeds of her cell, was clearly swollen. Ready, it seemed, to burst. She said:

"I suppose we could begin at other points, if you'd prefer. Perhaps we could start with the chatelaine, finding herself, one morning, feeling strangely refreshed and clearheaded for a change?" The monster's voice could be very quiet when she wanted it to be. "But before we get too far with this story, I'd like to ask you a personal question, if I may?"

The trilling sound of frogs.

She cleared her throat, veiling lightly a sneer, and put on airs:

"Once-noble creature, marvel of marvels, viceroy of your domain—pushed forth from a thin caul into this shrouded world—what do you feel? Between trembling thighs, as you're pushed forth, or held aloft, above a steaming corpse, what do you *see*? Tell me, when you look out of those beady eyes?"

Stretching, like a huge green dog, butt in the air—and yawning while doing so—the fecund showed rows and rows of needle-sharp teeth. Then she settled, also like a dog, circling twice, and again, before finding comfort in the muck.

"I know you're nothing but bones and flesh, with various combinations of blood or choler or melancholy in your veins. And you're tiny things—mere mortals, as they say—subjected, from day one, to a host of calamities and infirmities. The list is endless. Pride, envy, desire, ambition. Plagues, insecurity. Raging disease. Loss. Factions and hatred among your own people! Ignorance and war. You humans fascinate me."

Still no response, save the thrumming of insects and the quiet splash of an animal—a fish, perhaps.

"And yet," the fecund continued, her unclear question devolving into a series of others, and from there into a customary ramble, "throughout these trials, time keeps moving, past your traumatic birth and childhood (which was most brief, spent hungry and snot-nosed in egocentric oblivion), past your self-indulgent adolescence (when you thought you could change everything, and that there was a small chance misery might pass you by), moving faster and faster, past your adulthood (if you were fortunate enough to make it that far), finally dragging the remaining few of you into old age and sweeping you along, toward eschaton!" As the last word echoed, the fecund shivered with what could only be mock dread. "Tormented race! Abandoned race! Oh, clouds have closed in, all right! (Or so they say: all I see when I look up is this damned stone ceiling.)"

Rolling again caused water to slosh against the walls.

"Do you know my opinion about this? Do you? Big deal, that's what. Twelve gods once descended from the firmament. I saw them arrive. From my verdant home, I saw crowds gather around them as they touched down. Gods can offer many things, including salvation. But how did you people react? With suspicions and pettiness and incessant questions. Constant doubts. Backstabbing. Granted, the gods acted little better, in the end. There was stiff competition and vying for followers. There were fights, divisions. People killed each other. And the gods began to fight among themselves, too, brother against sister, sister against brother. In fact, there are the dead bodies of two of them—at least two, possibly more—out in the great desert, to the east. At least, I assume they're still there. Long before the walls of your city were completed I saw them, scorched and pitted by sand, great polymer bones poking from the scorched earth.

"Who knows how many of the gods survived the battles? What was left of the pantheon took their cosmic balls and limped home, wherever that was.

"The bottom line is: humans had a chance to be spared life's ailments and you blew it. You fought, you killed hundreds, and you built this awful city."

Words faded softly down the long stone corridor. But the fecund's eyes were not entirely open, as if she might even have been talking in her sleep.

"Now you are free again, in this place you call Nowy Solum. Free to scuttle aimlessly about, with only small expectations to live up to, arbitrary rules to follow, no agendas of a higher power to fulfill. You are created, you suffer, and you die. That's it. Principal and mighty work—my little pink friends—you have fallen from the grace you so briefly attained."

Here the monster chuckled and quickly snapped at a haspoid unlucky enough to get too close. Licking her chops brought in crunching chiton, legs, wings. Thick ichors dripped from the scales of her chin.

"For me, though—" she burped "—and for every other unfortunate soul of a more, uh, sophisticated nature (shall we say), who find themselves here with you—those who don't fall into your rather rudimentary biological categories—we see things differently. Time, for example. Time could mean anything to us: the nightmare of an alien despot; cyclical, self-consumptive loops; a spectrum of theory existing altogether beyond your meager ken.

"Do you understand what I'm saying?

"Creatures like me are more—" a vague gesture with one clawed hand "—complicated.

"I mean, are we really in the same moment? Are we in the same place? Do we even speak the same language?

"And these gods, building up your hopes, coming down from on high and then battling it out, to leave you stranded, back you where you started. Who were they to me? Why should I care about them? Or about you?" She hissed and spat and blew steam out her nose.

"Because I don't. I don't care. So let's not even talk about gods. And don't tell me they're returning, or that they've been seen, flying overhead. This story is one of the last in your sordid history. Nowy Solum crumbles."

At the waterline, where paler scales stretched to near translucency, ripples on the swamp made duckweed ride up and down. Setting her jaw, bands of muscle hardened the angled jowls, though it was difficult to tell if the monster was truly angry or not.

"Now," she said, "where were we?"

The chatelaine reclined on her canopy bed, ensconced inside the palace of Jesthe, and decided, upon putting down her second cup of coffee—which was empty now, and clattering on her bedside table—that she would leave her chambers, go for a walk. *Perambulate.* Work the legs. She called to her women: fetch clothes suitable for outside, and fetch them quickly. Before she could change her mind. Lately there had been too many days of inactivity, laying about, drinking herself to sleep or staring listlessly out the window at the roofs of her city.

Out on the crowded streets, the day was gloomy, as most were, but it was not raining, at least, like it had been for the past fortnight. With almost a spring in her step, the chatelaine walked ahead of her servants, who awkwardly carried the various items they supposed a woman such as the chatelaine might need on a brief journey outside Jesthe. Servants were unaccustomed to any mood other than a somber one in their mistress and, frankly, they preferred when she stayed abed, moping.

Huffing and panting, arms laden, the women struggled to keep up.

Near the secondary refuse pile, at Hot Gate—a vast heap of steaming garbage against the sagging wall of an empty seminary—the chatelaine, who had been waving blithely to citizens, greeting them as they begged or jostled or otherwise tried to acquire food to feed their families, suddenly froze. She knew why she'd been impelled to leave her bedchambers at that particular second and go out, into Nowy Solum. The chatelaine was a woman who believed in destinies, and in the purposes of mysterious motivations, giving reasons to every gesture and idle action as if everything were ordained. (She had not always believed this, nor would she believe it for much longer, but on this day, the day of the walk, she felt sure that the mysterious and powerful forces of fate moved her and the lives of those around her.)

"I wish to speak to that girl," she told her servants, pointing with an unsteady finger. Her heart raced.

The women squinted, shifting their loads, making faces to indicate their confusion and distaste.

"I don't see any girls," one finally answered, either the boldest or stupidest of the lot. Certainly the largest. "My Lady," the woman added, as an afterthought, to try to make herself perfectly clear, "I see no girls."

The chatelaine, who had continued to point all this while, shook her finger. "There!"

"I see two, well, there are two *melancholics*, in the garbage."

"Yes, that's right. And one of them is a girl. I wish to speak to her. She's beautiful and I wish to speak to her."

The servants did not know what to say. They were very uncomfortable and getting more uncomfortable with each passing second. (Though, working, as they did, for the chatelaine, this sensation was almost part of their job.)

"In fact," continued the chatelaine, "I want her on the staff at Jesthe. Make sure she gets employment in my palace." This was an incredible statement, thought the chatelaine of Nowy Solum. This was bold, brave. The world was changing and she, the chatelaine, would drive these changes. Just a few nights ago, they said, there had been reports of a heavenly body over the city. A god, some said. The chamberlain had almost smiled. Yes, the world was changing. She filled her lungs. She felt very alive. She had not felt this alive in a long time.

"Employ— But, marm," complained the servants, "we need no more, not like her."

Without humour, the chatelaine laughed. "I want this girl working up on *my* level. I want to see her in the Main Hall. I want to see her in the Dining Room. I want to see that pretty, tattooed face in my bedchambers."

Silence again.

"I won't put up with this, you know. Approach her!"

"But," said another servant, very quietly, "she doesn't really, uh, exist."

"Nonsense." The chatelaine wheeled. "Of course she exists. We can all see her. She's right there!"

By this point, of course, the pair of kholics had taken note of the chatelaine and her entourage and had stopped doing what they'd been doing. They stood, filthy, knee-deep in garbage, eyes lowered, no doubt as uncomfortable as the chatelaine's servants.

Under their masks, the girl and the boy had identical features, and must have been twins, though neither the chatelaine, nor certainly her women, had the capacity to notice such detail.

A jolt passed down the length of the fecund.

"Who's there? Huh? I remember the cold vacuum of space, and a murdered body, floating face down in the river. Was the chatelaine heading out for a walk? Was I dreaming?" Her eyes flicked open. "These threads all drill into my head at the same time. What I'm trying to say is that there's more to a story than events taking place in one location, to one person. You need to look at everything, at the same time, in the entire universe. Look at every person, every creature. Turn over every rock.

"See? In one glistening instant, plucked from the stream of time as it passes by: countless episodes, from a myriad of human lives, all vital, all entangled in a shared moment.

"So many threads . . ."

A few heartbeats of quiet, then a sigh.

"But we can't follow them all, I suppose. You're right. Too many lives. And there is more than just one universe. At times I get so overloaded. Here, in Nowy Solum, in your city, there are masons, derelicts, housewives. Human, cobali. Dog-faced cognosci."

The fecund's eyes had begun to nictitate again. Her skinny tongue flickered twice. Breathing slowed. Both eyes closed. If the fecund had not previously been asleep, she sure was now.

Grumbling servants fetched the girl—the nasty kholic—and led her into Jesthe through the side entrance. From there, up the East Stairs. This chore was accomplished at dusk, on the chatelaine's order, when neither chamberlain Erricus or any of his palatinate were around, for their protests in the daily assemblies would have been most relentless and insufferably dull. As it was, in the days since the sighting of the celestial apparition, the smug attitudes and righteousness of the palatinate had been dreadful. But they were not welcome anywhere above ground level in the palace, and had not been welcome there since the chatelaine first inherited the city from her father; once the kholic girl was safely up in the living areas, with the chatelaine's staff, she was pretty much in the clear.

Would the chatelaine tell her father about bringing the girl inside? What would be the point? He had retreated long ago, in more ways than one, up the towers, to the dungeon. He had his own problems. He would never see the girl either.

Given a pallet to sleep on and a rough shift to wear, the kholic was (much to her surprise) more or less left alone. In fact, given menial tasks, like any other servant, she was soundly shunned and ignored. Only a few times over her first few days in the palace did the chatelaine manage to come by, to engage in small talk, or to half-heartedly admire the girl as she worked, but the chatelaine's moods had begun to swing again, as they often did, and she ended up spending most of the girl's initial fortnight in Jesthe nowhere near as enthusiastic as she had initially been, locked instead in her bedchambers with bottles of spiritus and a procession of nameless bedfellows, all in hopes of chasing away internal darkness, which inevitably slunk back, over and over, just as the chatelaine began to hope it might never return again.

The monster's outbursts contained nuggets of truth. They always did, if one was patient enough to sift. Twelve gods had indeed descended. The sky became obscured by clouds that never again parted. Now, in Nowy Solum, empty temples disintegrated.

And time—for people, anyhow—was a relentless river. Every citizen—except for the youngest of children, and those of infirm minds—knew this for a fact.

The monster snored. Parthenogenesis took its toll. Her sides rose and fell, rose and fell, in almost peaceful rhythm. Without a doubt, something growing inside that infamous womb kicked.

Had there been lies in the speech too, or speculation? Had words been said only for the sake of their sounds?

Most likely.

Moments slipped away, to become the past, joining millions of others mingling in the fading torrent. Only subjective memories would live on, and, even then, briefly, flickering in the minds of just a few.

Like the fecund had implied.

Elements of decay, elements of entropy. Now that the era of gods was over, taking with it the promise of eternal salvation, contaminants of impermanence and mortality had once again been integrated into each event, into each moment, into each human life. Thankfully, though, small fragments of beauty remained, entangled with the abominations. Laughter and music were inseparable from pain and injustice.

Grumbling, the fecund stretched again in her sleep, and let out a bubbling fart.

Night fell on half the world and day was about to begin in Nowy Solum. But there were in-between places even the fecund could never understand. Nether regions haunted flickering gaps between sickness and health, between gods and godlessness, between life and time and the inevitability of death. Nether regions straddled night and day.

The snoozing monster would never hear of this, even if she were awake; she would dismiss these claims forthright. Because, she would tell you, she knows everything. Then she would demand food. Or make lascivious comments. Or, in the particularly garrulous mood she had been in of late, lecture endlessly.

The fecund mumbled in her sleep. One clawed hand twitched.

Best tiptoe away.

Abandoned, the twin brother was, like the chatelaine, plagued by dark thoughts. Being a kholic, though, this was the expected state. All those like him, tattooed at birth, veins thick with treacle, were thus inflicted, to greater or lesser degrees—especially those whose hearts laboured to pump the thickest, blackest of melancholy. At this boy's birth trial, no fluids at all had leaked from the cut made by the palatinate physicker; the officer had squeezed the tiny arm, and squeezed it again, to finally reveal the slightest ooze of the pitch black humour that gave the baby life and condemned him, forever, to the ostracon, with the others of his temperament.

Naturally, the twin sister was also marked and removed, since they had shared a womb.

Their weeping mother was dismissed, empty handed, from Bedenham House.

Without his sister for the first time, the boy had slipped into an uglier and more self-destructive phase than usual. Seeing his twin led away by the chatelaine and her servants, without so much as a protest, or even a backward glance, had caused him, as the fecund would say in her vernacular, to *snap*. He howled, and he fumed, and he consumed vast quantities of ale and the hallucinogenic drug cultured from certain mould on stale bread, known in the streets of Nowy Solum as *bud*. He wanted to die. He got into fights with other kholics, wheeling through rooms and narrow halls of the ostracon, staggering alleys and streets. He blacked out entire afternoons. He woke up sick and vomited copiously in gutters. He stopped working altogether, letting garbage and shit and dead animals pile up around him while he glared at the silhouette of Jesthe, rising crookedly above the cluttered slums.

Because he was tattooed, his behaviour was tolerated, or rather, it was generally ignored. Perhaps even unnoticed, some would say. Kholics were known to be a morose bunch, prone to such outbursts. As long as the boy did not come into direct contact with a red-blooded hemo, who then complained to the palatinate, he could act pretty much any damn way he pleased, even dying on the streets with a mouth full of froth, for all anyone official cared.

But the boy did come into contact with a hemo. During this ranting and drugged-out stumbling around, cursing the clouds, railing against his lot, a beautiful and untagged girl watched from a market stall, on Tornblanket Street—which passed behind the ostracon. She circled closer, drawn to the suffering and low status of the kholic boy. To be succinct, this girl craved challenges and drama, and she was the sort who, like the chatelaine herself, had a predisposition for flawed lovers and doomed relationships. Nowy Solum was large enough, and decadent enough, to have many types. Of course, it helped that the boy (and his sister, who, at that point, felt rather surprisingly lonely in the palace) were also beautiful to behold—at least for those who took the time, or had the inclination or ability, to behold the tattooed outcasts of the city.

Bounding rabbit-like, braver children played in warrens that tunnelled into the rear of the palace, dashing out and then daring each other to go back in, farther and farther. One or two passages, children claimed—red-faced and breathless—led right into ramshackle rooms and cavernous chambers and larders stocked with dried foods. A few kids, mostly friends of friends, even returned with entire loaves of bread, or with actual stockings, but these treasures seemed few and far between, and the sources of the goods remained, predominantly, rumour.

Most tunnels ended at solid rock.

During the castellan's reign, before he retreated up the towers, into the dungeon, and handed Nowy Solum over to his daughter, children told each other that if they were caught inside Jesthe, they would be strapped to an operating table and vivisected, to be used in experiments. But when the chatelaine took over, well, stories changed, became more vague. There seemed nobody left in the palace to catch them, and what did the woman do in there, anyhow? People said she banned the palatinate from the inner halls and rooms of Jesthe just so they couldn't watch over her at night, and judge her. Many visitors, for certain, emerged looking a little worse for wear, into the cloudy dawn.

And there was talk, as always, of a monster living in a cell under the palace, the *fecund*, and of a strange menagerie in the chatelaine's bedchamber, beasts that she treated as if they were her own offspring, but no stories were passed down as clear and visceral as the tales of amputations and tortures done in the father's time, and from the even more barbaric times before that. Just what the chatelaine might get up to inside the palace was elusive for the children, beyond the grasp of young and healthy conceptions. They scared each other with stories about what could happen if they got caught, but, in the end, imagination failed them. This failure, of course, and the dim chances of being chased, diminished the thrill of trespassing.

That, and growing older.

Maybe kids still went into the narrow passageways, with exhilaration in their hearts and throats. Who knew?

Not the red-blooded girl, telling these stories to her kholic lover one afternoon as they lay on her thin mattress of straw while, outside, rain drummed on the packed dirt of Hanover Street. The boy had brought up the palace again, as he often did in their brief relationship, and he muttered about how his sister had been brought inside, and how much he hated the chatelaine for plucking his twin from the streets, as if she were a flower, a curiosity to be put in a vase and then discarded when she'd gone yellow and withered.

Lying there, listening now to the beautiful girl talk about her childhood—a red-blooded kid, playing in the warrens of Jesthe, like only red-blooded kids could—the kholic stared up at a moist stain on the ceiling. He chewed at his nails. He could get used to ticking as soft as this. One hand was behind his head. The beautiful girl held his cock, slowly making it hard again. He licked his lips, thinking about mattresses and monsters, thinking about experiments in dungeon towers.

He pictured the warrens, burrowed right into the foundation of the palace, and the nearly deserted hallways within.

He considered the chatelaine's beloved pets.

As the hemo went down on him, and took his cock into her hot mouth, the kholic had begun to form a plan, to try get his sister back, and to teach the chatelaine a lesson.

Grey rocks, grey clouds. Cold, grey rain. Father had gone inside, snoring loudly. No lizards here, in the rain. Very few birds. With an open mouth, head back, rain felt funny on his tongue.

In the distance, lightning burst.

His name was path. And he watched, squinting through the rain, listening for thunder, trying to remember what his father had said about counting the seconds. He smiled; path liked storms.

But as the rain intensified, and winds picked up, the smile faded. Storms were good when he was *inside*, not deposited here, in the garden. He had forgotten this distinction. His father had been drinking spiritus all morning and would not wake up, no matter how close the lightning came, or how loud the storm got, or if path started to scream at the top of his lungs.

Mud started to splash up the sling, as far as path's torso. Anxious, he wriggled his stumps, croaking, "Da? Daaa?"

Abruptly, the rain stopped.

Remote thunder, rolling overhead, a few drops pattering the puddles—which were rapidly soaking into the sandy soil—and the land around released its heat, once more, in a stifling surge.

Then path saw two lizards coming, sweeping low over the steaming rocks, heading for the small garden. Yellow lizards. He chortled, and was preparing to terrify the reptiles—as soon as they landed—when he saw another light suddenly appear before him; not lightning this time but a thin finger, pinkish, dead straight.

From above the clouds.

He cocked an eyebrow.

He quivered his stumps.

"*Da?*"

Slowly the finger of light moved toward him, stopping at the base of his sling. Looking down at it, path felt his body tingle.

When the light jumped, almost too fast for him to follow, there was a moment of exquisite pain—

And he was taken away. Other worlds filled him, other times.

Another life:

Born with healthy ovaries and bad prospects, she was registered, naturally, for the lottery. Before her first birthday, the State interned her in one of their hospices, Balhaven, just outside Newark, where she lived with other girls who shared her history. Her biological parents could afford neither the money, the time, nor the patience to take care of her.

By seven, she was a tall, gangly child. The birthmark across her cheek and nose darkened as she aged and added to her insecurities. She was sullen, and not very popular.

Her childhood in the hospice was like that of a million others across the

League of Nations, all of them born in the wrong place and wrong time, as most children were, it seemed, except that on her eighth birthday, she was selected by the Agency. The inconceivable. She had won the lottery.

When the news broke, she said nothing. Sat on the edge of her cot, staring into the face of the man who had knocked on the door to her dorm to tell her this information. She listened, wondering what the words meant for her future. Immortality? Death? She had heard these terms many times since coming to this place but she only knew what they implied, not what they meant. The end of existence, certainly, the end of being an unwanted little girl.

Such a fate could not be bad.

With two guards at the door, and the other girls cleared out, she hopped off her bunk and began to pack.

Doctors watched through narrowed eyes.

At best, dawn managed to tinge the bellies of the clouds amber. Beyond the thick mantle, the sun rose, unseen. Nowy Solum squatted in a fog that would never burn off.

Hard to imagine that, generations ago, the city—known then merely as *Solum*—had been nothing but a few huts and servants' quarters, a hamlet, sprung up around the palatial residence called Jesthe. Semi-cleared footpaths had defined the environs then, a few people within, humble homesteads, thin cows and sheep.

Remaining in the city's centrum, the original Jesthe existed still, but lost under additions and slums. Leaning tenements clung to the palace like barnacles, tried to climb her towers. Wings had been built, haphazard shacks raised, hovels and sundry other residences, nailed and wedged and otherwise anchored, both unsolicited and municipally approved—signed for by some castellan or chatelaine, long dead now—others appearing almost overnight, pushed the city and palace ever upward, toward these omnipresent clouds.

A smattering of lairs were excavated below, where massive cisterns had been discovered.

The perimeter walls of Nowy Solum struggled to contain almost four hundred thousand denizens. The census takers who arrived at this number included only the more productive and recognizably *human* residents, omitting those tattooed as melancholics by the chamberlain and his palatinate officers, leaving off the drifters and criminals who came through the gates (hopeful, desperate, and either quickly left the city or more likely perished there, in the streets). Nor were included those living precariously in innumerable crawl spaces, or the beasts, or monsters.

A few residents of Nowy Solum were well travelled, knowing there is but one continent, extending beyond the walls of the city, encompassing the surrounding desert and outlying forests, reaching out to the ocean. These people had seen windswept vistas and endured horrors and wonders in unmapped hinterlands.

Most citizens suspected, whether consciously or not, that the advent of Nowy Solum played a formative role in driving the pantheon and their respective congregations to a form of madness; even gods, apparently, cannot compete with the temptations of a city. Now, of course, all manner of immorality and decadence flourished there.

Days had passed since the commotion in the clouds, when the sky seemed to tear apart, and since the incident had not recurred, more traditional concerns returned to the populace. Officers of the palatinate walked the streets, adhering to their arcane lists of creeds, hoping their actions and faith would bring deities back, once and for all. Watched over by chamberlain Erricus, the officers circulated, collecting taxes. The one clear function left to them. The castellan, who had once given them instruction, was now quite mad, in their eyes, and his daughter, the libidinous and drunken chatelaine, seemed—not just to the palatinate, but to most residents of the city—equally or perhaps even more mad.

Without their gods, the palatinate were forlorn, clawless.

As filtered light slowly changed—illuminating the markets and streets and cluttered buildings with a yellowed, hazy quality—much of the populace, yawning, wondered about their next meal, their next coin, or if a knife might part their ribs in a tight alleyway before the concealed sun dropped once more below the equally invisible horizon. The steaming river, known as the Crane, cleaved Nowy Solum into unequal halves, turgid water as brown as the pall that hung overhead. Along the rocky shores, on both sides, ranks and ranks of public outhouses already started to fill. (Recently, clay pipes had been installed in a few of the wealthier dwellings, during a fit of inspiration on the chatelaine's part, mostly in higher locations—in the North End—and several so-called *toilets* connected. These mod cons, despite the brief excitement they generated, were basically chutes leading down to clay pipes, which in turn acted as simple conduits to the river, depositing the waste of the rich next to the waste of the poor, where the distinction was lost on the kholics, who attempted, each day, to clean it up.)

The stench of Nowy Solum grew to a palpable thing, an unavoidable miasma: not just the stench of shit, but of congealed blood from countless animals being slaughtered in the alleys and streets, for sale in the many markets, which were already open and bustling. Meat roasted over a thousand cooking fires.

Offal of the slaughtered was left, rife with maggots, to rot in the gutters.

This, too, the kholics cleaned, though some was eaten on the spot. Most they took back to the kitchens of the ostracon.

This was a time of illness and fevers. People died each day, on dry land, far from the ocean, with water filling their lungs. More would be taken today. There were poxes, skin rots, inexplicable swellings. There were possessions and infestations. Only half of the babies born in the city survived their first week, and a further percentage of these—careful numbers were kept in crabbed handwriting, in the chamberlain's ledger—got tattooed by the physickers, marked for the black humours that flowed from their spleens.

Shouts were heard from barkers at New Market, and from those at Horse Fair, joining cries from Soaper's and Candles.

At a temple abandoned by its congregation and main sponsor, Tiamat—the goddess who once promised to keep pestilence at bay, and whose body now lay dead in the great desert—bells tolled. A tenant there tended to his flock of poor and displaced.

Screams pierced Fat Man's Alley.

From the barracks at the foot of Jesthe, palatinate officers set out to make rounds. They were to visit the slums near South Gate, and so carried sacks to be filled with a variety of impoverished goods, taken in lieu of coin.

In the centrum, under the leaning palace, a line-up formed at the main well for bowls of water. There was a fight. The line-up extended all the way down the Street of Horses, lost finally under the houses that pressed up together, as if leaning in for a better look.

Before too long, most narrow streets and alleys—relatively still overnight—were busy. Prostitutes, bleary eyed and strung out, dreamed of sleeping for a fortnight, alone. Noblemen and labourers alike arose to knuckle their eyes. Underfed children kneeled, begging on corners.

Women shopped and gossiped.

A squalling child was born; an old lady clutched her robes and died, on her feet.

Kholics cleaned.

From everywhere, people emerged: from inside the structures, from underneath, climbing about on top.

The heat of another stagnant day grew and grew, trapped under thick, eternal cover.

And, in her bedchambers, buried within the rundown palace known as Jesthe, the chatelaine of Nowy Solum came awake, very hung over, to a pounding at her door.

Where the sun had not yet risen, icy mountains cragged. The River Crane was born in these remote glaciers. Past the mountains, the ocean extended outward, to plunge over the edge of the world and roil there, in the great abyss.

And, above the clouds, a man known as padre hornblower lifted his wooden horn to live up to his name. Hornblower also abided in a city of sorts—settlement, perhaps, would be a better term—but where he lived was not massive, nor congested, nor even built upon solid land: hornblower and his people had constructed their handful of huts high in the branches of a massive tree, a tree so tall it pierced the mantle of the world to brush against open skies.

The blast of hornblower's horn had been clear and loud and continued to reverberate his finely tuned tympanums. He felt a swelling of pride. Sniffing at the breezes, hornblower understood that his body was filled with potency and the strengths of his position. All was as it should be. He felt *good*. Cradling the horn, hornblower hardened his face and scanned the small crowd gathered on the branch before him, his gaze lingering on two girls standing near the front. Just this season the pair had reached the age of red sap. Needless to say, the girls stuck close to their mother's side.

Hornblower smiled. Moonlight was strong, the assembly silvered. All eyes were upon him.

Not one of these people—neither hornblower, nor the menstruating girls, nor anyone in the small settlement who had gathered here—suspected that they lived at the pinnacle of an oversized plant. Nor did they imagine that a place such as Nowy Solum could exist, far below, several hundred kilometres away. The citizens of this settlement, in fact, believed that the only thing under the clouds—which yawned, forever, and always, all around them—were piles of bones and ash, all stirred by poisonous winds. Great Anu, blind power of the sky, had told them this. *Only the dead*, he said (to their ancestors, anyhow), *emptied of their souls, can pass through the eternal mantle. Should any man with his soul intact penetrate the clouds, they would face torment for all eternity.*

Anu liked to talk in these terms.

A few fools still tried to climb down the trunk, never to be seen again.

If padre hornblower were to look up, he would see the firmament, which he tells his people should be both worshipped and feared, for in heaven Anu still lived. Hornblower had actually seen the power once, as a child: in his memory, Anu looked like a small, bright sun, but elongated, eyes dim as he moved slowly across the dusk. On all sides, the great power had been ringed by dozens of tiny ambassadors.

Back in the days of hornblower's grandpadre, Anu and his ever-present minions used to descend regularly, to assign quests and to kill heretics by making red sap burst from their ears and their noses. No one had seen the sky power in years. Nonetheless, hornblower often warned the population at his sermons about the very real possibility of angry visits. Frightened citizens maintained hornblower's own best interests, and were easiest to control.

Again, he looked at the girls.

Of course, many times the little ambassadors came down, to this day, relaying information, or merely hovering, watching the settlement. These visits hornblower had experienced on countless occasions. No ambassadors, unfortunately, had arrived on this night, the night of the funeral, but hornblower had not given up hope that a few might show toward the end, to add to the dramatic effect.

Never mind, he thought. The horn blast had been a good one.

And, when the service was over, visiting the girls would be a solemn pleasure.

Had everybody arrived? These dullards were so slow. Punishments would be meted for tardiness.

The growing wind caused branches of the world to whip the sky. When hornblower finally did cast his eyes up to view the vista that occupied his thoughts, and to add another accent to the faded echoes of his horn's blast, he saw—instead of the endless firmament, or mighty Anu descending, or even a cloud of his loyal ambassadors—the scruffy bower of the exile, Pan Renik. A small black void floated in the upper branches. Hornblower's eyes were drawn to the nest, this transgression, this gall among his people. Though the construction of the bower appeared tiny against the backdrop of heaven, hornblower scowled, and his momentum, for a moment, was thrown.

He cleared his throat and shifted his feet. He wanted to shout at all the people now, tell them to move forward, to hurry up, but padres should remain silent at such formal occasions—

Damn the exile!

He glanced up again.

Beyond the assembled populace were clouds, naturally, a thousand formations of clouds, sunlit by day, illuminated by the moon, or by a smattering of stars, like now, by night.

He stared at the girls a third time, but with anger. They cowered closer to their mother.

The last of the residents finally arrived, responding belatedly to hornblower's perfect call, wiping sleep from their lazy faces.

Another padre, bellringer, gave his signal, rung on high, and the funeral began.

Chosen exemplar of the most benevolent sisters Kingu and Aspu, who were in repose and had been for as long as time immemorial, bless them, was also resting, stretched in a hammock with his youngest wife, when he felt an acidic tinge abruptly mingle in his saliva. Surprised, he sat up, choking. The burning in his throat worsened and he began to cough. His eyes watered.

A summons.

The hammock had been set up in the shade, near the pepper fields. He looked out over the gardens, toward the ridge of hills. The day was mostly warm and breezy. Pressed against him, his youngest wife remained fast asleep. The exemplar tried to suppress his coughing, so as to not wake her.

Both he and this wife had spent a great deal of the previous night awake with their infant son, who was not a good sleeper, and who cried every time he was left alone. Maybe the boy was cutting teeth?

Seven years since the exemplar had accepted the host of the benevolent sisters, bless them, into his mouth. There had only been perhaps twelve previous summonses. Most of the time, the sisters communicated by the voice of the seed he had swallowed, talking softly in his head, but on occasion they wanted him physically at their side, as a witness, when they announced to him certain plans for the village, such as how to best cull ducks, or how to forge the sharpest of knifes. Once, the exemplar had to reconnect a damaged cable that had come loose from one of the goddesses' great flanks during a storm. (The exemplar had a hard time distinguishing Kingu from Aspu: the sisters, bless them, were *identical*.)

He hoped this summons would be for as simple a request.

Disentangling from his wife—who grumbled a complaint and moaned but did not wake—the exemplar managed to clumsily stand. He had never quite mastered getting in or out of hammocks and was satisfied with himself that he had not fallen or dumped his wife out on her ample ass. The burning in his throat had lessened but he knew this was because he had moved; if he were to lie back down again, try close his eyes, the discomfort would resume, twofold.

"Where are you going?"

"I thought you were asleep," he said. "I'll be back soon. The sisters are calling me. Bless them. Go back to sleep."

"The sisters?" She rolled in the hammock, face averted, hips rising. "Mmmmm . . ."

The exemplar blinked and, watching his youngest wife, adjusted his genitals beneath his robe. He had woken with a hard-on. When he returned, maybe they could make love? Being tired made him horny. So did warm days. And breezes. And hammocks. He smiled slightly, rubbing at his face, considering, just for a second, postponing his response to the summons. But that would be foolish: who in the world would ignore the call of their goddess?

"I won't be long," he said. "Hold that pose."

"Don't even think about waking me."

He could tell she too was smiling.

The exemplar had left his sandals at home, so he had to pick his way carefully, barefoot around the garden, heading toward the pad where the benevolent sisters lay dreaming. Keeping an eye out for snakes or thistles or anything else that could hurt his feet, he heard from beyond the trees the laughter of children, playing nearby, drifting though the walls of foliage. He was unsure if any of this laughter was from his own children, but the sounds helped relax the exemplar nonetheless.

Just for a moment's isolation he and his wives went to the hammock. For naps, and to maybe fool around. He touched his cock again through his robe, almost entertaining the thought that being an exemplar for his community was an imposition at times like this, but the sisters could read such thoughts, bless them, so he suppressed the idea as best he could, trying to hurry, and be devout.

Beyond the row of trees, he descended a path of black lava stones, which were sharp and further slowed his progress. At the crest of a second stony slope he cursed himself for not going back to his home to retrieve his sandals; he knew he must have looked ridiculous mincing his way down to where the goddesses slept.

If they wanted to, they could have seen him through his own eyes. They could watch this embarrassing display, if they chose.

Ahead, to the left of the great mountain, the dull ocean glimmered under cover of the clouds. A storm was picking up, far out over the water, angry and black. Even here, winds grew stronger. He sniffed the air. He would need to keep an eye on this weather, though the rocks that ringed the shallow crater where the sisters had instructed his ancestors to build sheltered the small community—

Like a stab in his throat, another bitter call came, a taste so sharp and painful that the exemplar groaned aloud and put his hands up to his neck.

Hurry. You need to watch us leave. What's taking you?

He was frozen with shock. Had the sisters said what he thought they had? *Leave? Was leaving possible?* The benevolent sisters, bless them, had *always* been sitting side by side, inert, on their pad. *How could they leave?*

Filling with foreboding now, regardless of the pain in his feet, the exemplar began to run.

At the northern extremity of the community, ringed by boysenberry bushes and clusters of red flowers, the sisters rested on their massive shale slab. Looking overhead, the mountain was craggy and dark green. When the exemplar got very close to where the sisters rested, he felt movement in the ground under his bare feet, and movement—not a wind, but a tremor, a *quaver*—in the air itself.

Coming over the final ridge, he saw them. The benevolent sisters, bless them, were shimmering. *Vibrating.* Garlands that had covered them—offerings he had draped casually over the past few days— fell from the smooth backs of the sisters to the rock. He saw the garlands wither with growing heat and, as he stepped up onto the shale, felt this heat himself, radiating from the goddesses like the blast of fires. There was a loud hum, and the smell of thunderstorms.

An eye cracked half-open. Never had he seen this before. Never had he seen the eyes of the sisters. The pupil was large and black and bottomless; terrified, the exemplar dropped to his knees, lowering his own feeble gaze.

Get up, the sisters commanded. *We shouldn't be gone long. Are you all right? Get up!*

On shaky legs, the exemplar managed to stand.

Unforeseen events have occurred, they told him. *We're needed elsewhere. You'll relay the story of our lift off to the people. You'll tell them.*

"Of course," said the exemplar. But what was lift off? What would he describe to the people?

If we haven't returned in two days, get everyone inside the cavern and remain there. Do you understand?

"Remain? But, but sisters . . ." His voice was as tremulous as the air and the ground. "Most benevolent sisters, may you be blessed and bless us in return, *where are you going?*"

Get everyone inside the cavern if we don't return. Do you understand?

He managed to nod, though all he wanted to do was weep.

When he looked up, more impossibilities unfolded: the sisters—each as big as a house—had spread out their arms, sweeping them over the perimeter of bushes, and now they hovered *over* the shale slab, a meter or so in the air. Their faces were alert, energized, their wings a blur. Muscles along the great spines bulged. They continued to watch him. They did not speak again.

Flowers that had died, and which he should have removed, and flowers that should have been replaced fresh this morning, all rolled from the shale, withering further or bursting into flame. The growing heat dried his skin and hot winds blew hair back from his face. He turned away, feeling small, ashamed of his weakness. He wanted to ask so many questions but was frozen dumbstruck as the sisters, bless them, rose even higher into the sky, turning their faces away from him at last.

Slow swells of water, as if the grotto had powers to alter viscosities of basic elements, such as thicken liquids or vanquish light, and the sound of distant dripping, had lulled the cherub into a deeper sleep. Little round face, pressed snug up against the gunwale, wings ruffled like a blanket over its pudgy torso. The creature breathed quietly. Watching the cherub in the dim lantern glow, the abductors had momentarily forgotten their recent disagreement. Adrenaline waned now, and exhaustion tugged at their nerve endings. Neither felt particularly fulfilled by their recent actions.

In the boat were a boy and a girl. A kholic and a hemo. The boy was the abandoned twin from the refuse station at Hot Gate, and the girl was his lover. After coitus in her room, they had dressed without speaking, a mood of solemnity following them from the tousled bed (he came; she did not). Leaving the room on Hanover Street, which the girl shared with three others, the couple walked to the centrum, paces apart. Nowy Solum was getting dark by then and the streets were nearly deserted.

Climbing into Jesthe by one of the tunnels in the stone foundation—which the girl had recalled so clearly from her childhood, and described in painstaking detail, with nostalgia a lump in her windpipe—was as simple to do as it once had been, yet upon entering, they both found themselves cramped and dirty and uncomfortable. Were these tunnels, wondered the girl, forcing herself forward, the tunnels of her memory? She tried to understand the difference between the tunnels of the past and the tunnels of the present but only managed to become saddened, having contemplated instead such things as time and life and her dwindling youth.

Though she had never been among the children to reach the endocarp in bygone days, nor see the fabled riches of Jesthe's interior (let alone return with a piece of salted meat or other treasure), accessing the interior of the palace now, with this kholic boyfriend in tow, was not especially difficult. Surprisingly easy, in fact. Certainly a journey without the myth and wonder of a child's perspective. She imagined the tunnels growing.

They emerged in dim, dusty hallways, empty chambers, dark cupboards. Peeked out, then withdrew. Cobwebs strung their faces. Creaks and footfalls echoed. After several wrong turns, and climbing a crude stone staircase, they ended up in a crawlspace, just beyond what could only be the bedchambers of the chatelaine herself. Through a dense grille, they saw the huge room, the canopied mattress, all illuminated by a pair of lanterns and a dying fire.

The chatelaine was there.

She was not alone.

Side by side the couple stood, cramped behind the false panel, for a long while. They watched, speechless, stricken, until at last the guests left and the chatelaine lay still on that infamous mattress, naked, face down and snoring.

What they witnessed was a series of drunken and depraved acts, at times involving as many as three men in masks, and two women. Bizarre apparatuses—the uses of which neither would have ever guessed had they not seen them employed with their own eyes— scattered the floor, like casualties.

The girl entered the bedchambers, emerging from behind a thick curtain, and crept through the dark, feeling rather foolish, nauseated by the smells, getting increasingly uncomfortable with agreeing to participate in this folly. There had been times, she knew, in the history of Nowy Solum, when a thousand guards would have raised their spears at her intrusion. Now, nothing of the sort occurred. The room was desolate and cold. The pale chatelaine lay like a bruise against the bedsheets.

After motioning several times to the kholic boy, who did not venture forth, the girl found the chatelaine's pets, caged individually, a dozen of them, in a mirrored alcove on the far side of the bedchamber. One pet looked like a cherub, and this was the only creature she could bring herself to touch.

From his hiding place, the kholic continued to watch. His limbs had frozen and his stomach burned with acid. He was horrified by his own fear.

When the girl pulled the groggy cherub from its cage—reflected dimly in the huge mirror against the far wall in the light of a torch burning low in its sconce—the creature came awake with a start.

Whispered and desperate assurances—for the chatelaine stirred on her bed!—caused the cherub, thankfully, to drift off again.

The girl came back, holding the creature to her shoulder. The feathers of its wings were grey.

He did not look into the girl's eyes.

They left.

Hurrying back, the abductors discovered that the corridors under Jesthe did web farther and in more convoluted patterns than the girl had described: they ended up, to their bafflement and disconcertment, not in the centrum at all—not even outside—but in the grotto beneath the palace they had both heard so many rumours about.

Awed by the size of this place, by the silence, by the darkness, they froze.

"You went the wrong way," hissed the girl.

"You were leading," said the boy.

She wheeled, thrusting out the sleeping cherub. "What do you want to do with this?"

He turned away. A large body of water, an underground lake, vanished into the blackness, as if swallowed whole. On the stone walls nearby, pale phosphorescence cast a greenish light. Four greasy flames burned in crude holders to either side of where they stood.

The boy took one of these torches and held it high, but the extent of the cavern remained lost, the wan hemisphere of light humbled by the dark.

"Let's get rid of it," he said, shrugging. "I don't know. Let's get rid of it down here."

From tiny caverns—places they had evidently found to settle—faces of people emerged, watching with interest. A child, naked, pale as a grub, stepped from the shelter of her home to stare; the girlfriend, with the cherub asleep against her shoulder, bade the child a quiet greeting.

When he saw the small skiff tied to a dock, the boy motioned toward it with his chin. "Here," he said.

So they boarded the boat, and again the cherub awoke, eyelids fluttering, muttering groggy inanities. This time the couple was far enough away from the chatelaine's bedchambers that there was no fear of waking anyone, let alone getting caught. Regardless, the girl quickly rubbed her nose on the cool, fat cheek, saying over and over in comforting tones, *There, there, hush little baby, hush, every thing'll be all right*, until a vacuous smile emerged, a pudgy white thumb thrust between pale lips, eyes closed in ignorant bliss.

The boy mounted his torch in the bow.

Pushing off, they knew their relationship was similarly cast adrift, threatened by imminent collapse, caused by inexplicable forces, risen up over the past few hours. Like the palace, their love was undermined.

The girl lowered her bundle to the wooden seat.

The boy poled the invisible bottom.

Neither of these abductors had yet seen out fifteen years. If either were much older, they likely would have settled on a less dramatic way of trying to ruin the chatelaine's day, or maybe they would have continued to lie there, after fucking, on the girlfriend's mattress, in her room on Hanover Street, merely talking, or falling back asleep, or otherwise letting inertia settle in. Idealism and naiveté were youthful cousins. Foresight and the considerations of age and experience often brought inaction, compromise, second-guessing; the ability to foresee the extent of actions—to understand implications of cause and effect—could effectively thwart spontaneous, if impractical, decisions.

Kneeling in the stern of the boat, the girl—who was named Dhuka by her parents but called herself Name of the Sun (because, like the rest of her generation, she had never seen this fabled orb, which burned, allegedly, above the clouds)—rowed, while at the prow, her paramour and the instigator of this misadventure, Nahid, the melancholic boy, steered clear of sharp rocks and the hanging masses of stalactites that threatened to brain them both from the surrounding ebon.

The weak torch crudely illuminated the immediate vicinity of the lake, an area not much larger than the skiff.

Grey aquatic creatures rose to bump oblivious against the hull, perhaps attracted to the glow, perhaps blind. Farther out, a monster breached, just keeping up with the boat—a string of sinuous humps—before slipping under the surface once more.

Then the ceiling of stone opened overhead.

This was *heard* by the couple more than seen: a gentle cessation of pressure, a change in the echoes that indicated the boat had moved into vaster parts of the cavern; beyond the glow of the lantern, fuligin depths remained absolute.

Turning in its sleep, the cherub snorted.

Both Nahid and Name of the Sun had been rendered insignificant, as if, in that second, their folly was exposed, the futility of their actions and the futility of their upcoming arguments, maybe even the futility of everything they have ever done or will do, was laid bare. They drifted, along with their victim, silenced.

Until Nahid dismissed all of this nonsense by shaking the cherub roughly by the shoulder.

"Wake the fuck up," he said. "Wake up."

All he understood was that things had gone wrong. The act was nothing like the foreplay. He tried so hard not to remember the crippling fear he had felt looking into the chatelaine's chambers. What had transfixed him? How would this deed bring his sister back, anyhow? Would it, for some reason, drive this other girl away, this hemo? Possibly. Maybe it already had.

Nahid shook the chatelaine's pet again, and it woke, turning its babyface toward him. Squinting against the light, the creature frowned. And blinked. "Who are you?" Sitting up on the worn wooden seat, knuckling its eyes. "Where's my mom?"

"Go," spat Nahid. "Fly away!"

"Am I in a *boat*?" The cherub smiled and appeared to be excited about its predicament; it stood on chubby legs to shake out its wings. Nearly as tall as the seated abductors, it peered around, into the darkness, not afraid at all. The boy suspected that the beast was too simple for sensible reactions.

"Fly away." When Name of the Sun spoke, she employed much softer tones than had Nahid. "You can go now. Fly away."

"But what about my *mom*?"

"Don't be a fool," said the kholic. "That woman wasn't your mother. Why would your mother keep you in a *cage*?"

The cherub only blinked.

"Nahid."

"Ever thought about that? You believe she was the mother of all those other poor creatures? In all those cages? Now go, get lost."

"*Nahid*," repeated Name of the Sun. Statements were implied in the way she said his name, convictions and condemnations both.

He scowled.

"She would sing to me," the cherub said, a far-away look in its eyes, as if it had not been listening (which, indeed, it had not). "Every morning, she would sing to me. If she was feeling okay. A lot of mornings she just stayed in bed. She would rub my back with her fingers, pushing them through the bars. She smelled of oranges and wine. Sometimes, when her sleepover friends had dressed and gone, and they had long-since finished the wrestling games they liked to play, light strained through the clouds—"

"Fucking go!"

With a start, the cherub lifted off, narrowly avoiding the swing of the shunting pole. Nahid's words echoed.

Name of the Sun cautioned Nahid yet again, disapproving of his methods, of his abruptness.

He had just hidden there, quivering!

Over the boat, staring down, the poor cherub continued to fuss and scold and ask in annoying tones about its mother until the pole whistled through the air a second time; only then did the beast circle—once, twice—flying higher, a blur on the far range of the light. Even the most idiotic of creations must eventually understand the obviousness of such situations, and soon it was gone, flapping away, flying its pudgy self into the eternal black of its new home.

Distant dripping.

The scent of sulfur.

Eyes watched, from the dark.

Feeling heavy and slow, wishing he could have remained forever in the streets, with his sister, Nahid ground his teeth. Name of the Sun, looking up, saw absolutely nothing. When she looked at Nahid, she still saw nothing, not in his shadowed face, familiar yet so strange to her now. Dark eyes floated over a darker mask. He would not meet her gaze.

What had they just accomplished? What was this ridiculous gesture? Name of the Sun had watched the chatelaine trying to get off, as attachments and devices were enabled, and clumsy companions tried various techniques, and she remembered looking down at her, passed out in her bed, an old and skinny woman, much smaller than Name of the Sun. More pathetic than anything else, a lonely figurehead in a decrepit city.

Taking a moment to inspect choices and actions that had brought her to this point in life, Name of the Sun was not happy with any of them.

About to trail her fingers in the water, she decided—as they touched the cold surface, and a darker shadow rose from the depths—against it.

Blades of the oars sliced down. The boat began to move once more.

And there came from the dark a series of cries, as if the tortured souls of the city had not, in fact, been taken by gods when they left Nowy Solum but had found refuge down here in the grotto, and had chosen this instant to wail.

Or, maybe, Nahid thought, listening closer, pushing forcefully against a column of sandstone to clear it, the souls were not wailing at all, but laughing.

Directly above, in a dorm in the East Wing, the sister, whose name was Octavia, suddenly sat up on her pallet. Rats scattered from where they had been watching her. She scratched at her latest fleabites. The darkness of the chamber caused Octavia to appear almost like the other girls, most of whom slumbered with more success on the pallets about. Though the large dorm room was cold, she smelled sour sweat. She shivered. Octavia liked this scent.

She had worked until long after dusk and needn't awaken until second breakfast, though it might have been close to that hour now. She had hardly slept all night. Whenever she did manage to drift off, her dreams, benign at first, became garish and loud and quite terrifying, waking her, though details were elusive when she woke.

Each night Octavia had spent in the palace had been like this: enough nights now that she wondered if one could die, or go mad, from not sleeping.

Exhaustion was dry pressure behind each eye.

She took a deep breath but could not fill her lungs.

At first, in the dreams, she and her brother Nahid were together, in one of the common rooms at the ostracon. She remembered her brother's hands, the veins like worms. He looked askance at her. "The womb," he said, "is reserved for life. Outside, all bets are off." She was not following. Nahid tried to explain further, but flames sprung up around them.

She tried to hold onto the parts where she was with Nahid, but these fragments became eclipsed by unnamed violence, obscured by the horrid acts that repeatedly woke her.

Coming here had been a mistake. She needed to get out of Jesthe. She had expected the chatelaine's bed, special treatment, a taste of privilege. Maybe even an opportunity to somehow help herself.

Not labour, and neglect.

Octavia lay back down, to try sleep one more time, even for a few minutes.

But she heard someone come into the dorm. She listened to the soft footfalls getting closer. She did not open her eyes. Whoever it was stopped by her pallet. And stood there. Still she did not open her eyes.

"Hey, sleeping beauty?" A woman's voice—Hetta, the night matron? "Hey, wake up. Our lady wants to see you."

A toe, prodding her, so Octavia could no longer pretend. She rolled over, glanced quickly up—and, yes, Hetta stood there in the gloom—and looked away. "Who wants to see me?"

"Who do you fucking think? You know where the sun is really hiding? Not above the clouds, but up yer kholic arse, that's where. It's a fucking disgrace."

"The chatelaine wants to see *me*?"

"Yes. And you'd better hurry. She's in a bit of a state."

Left with instinctual cravings and not much else, seeking concessions to dignity and a sense of peace, yet struggling with the means to accomplish this (let alone understand the drive), Pan Renik was more animal than man. From an early age, the situation of existence had been pretty clear to him: he could not live within the narrow parameters established by those who defined the norms of his society. Pan Renik had been an outcast even in his earliest memories. Now, in the treetop settlement, he was know simply as *the exile.*

He built his nest in the upmost branches, high above the huts and nets and concerns of the others, high above the padres.

Cut off from the hunts, without access to buckets of water patiently collected, Pan Renik was also desperate, hungry, and thirsty most of the time. Loneliness was a given.

Filthy, on skinny haunches he listened to the fading moan of the padre's horn. The instrument had sounded for the third consecutive night. Pan Renik decided right then and there that he would descend (albeit very cautiously, of course) to investigate.

The night was clear, with steady wind. Moon illuminated the cloudscape. Dreamlike. A triad of notes played over three nights indicated to Pan Renik—if memory served correctly—that an errant soul, teetering on the edge for some time, had now fled its corporeal home; the emptied husk could be sent on its way, to fall beneath the clouds, where only the dead could go.

Pan Renik, bug-eyed apparition, who once tore out his own matted hair, in dreads, to expose his white skull to the sky and unsuccessfully release unwelcome visitors from his beleaguered brain (and then lay bleeding and feverish in his nest, without help, for weeks), climbed quietly, hand over hand, lower and lower, nearer to the settlement.

Perched on a bough, body hidden by clusters of big leaves, he paused. A large crowd had gathered on the main branch. He hoped for an easy opportunity to rob an attendee or two—dash in, maybe get a few nuts or other treasures, then scurry off and up—but there were far too many padres and citizens on the branch for that: almost everybody in the settlement had gathered. Rows of people lined the bough, mostly on this side of dead man's run, extending out to the end of the huts, their hollowed faces illuminated by well-guarded candles, and by the moonlight as it filtered through the rarified mists blowing overhead. Surveying this, Pan Renik grunted. Decrees must have been passed. Padres had wanted, for arcane reasons, full congregation.

Pan Renik wondered, for the first time since hearing the horn, who might have died.

Glimpsed between the forms of the citizens, he saw the corpse, tethered to a raft. No details. Pan Renik waited. He was good at waiting. That was another of his gifts. His life, it seemed, had been nothing but waiting.

Finally, caught in the orange glow of the guttering candles as they flared in the wind, he discerned the profile of the dead man's face and he understood the turnout, the decrees.

The oldest man in the world had finally died.

While winds picked up, Pan Renik hunkered against the bark, clinging tight, not sure what he felt. Remote memories churned, memories of when he had still been a citizen, when he had known this dead man and had lived in the settlement, among his people. (But already an exile, he reminded himself: already stared at, talked about behind his back, mocked and derided.)

Back then, Pan Renik had slept in a forked branch, not too far from the dead man's hut. Images rose and burst in procession. Once, he recalled, as punishment for a forgotten transgression— for breaking some ridiculous rule—he had been forced by padres to clean out the dwelling of the oldest man. Pan Renik remembered the stench of dried garbage, caked to the woven floor, and chunks of yellow phlegm, hardened at the side of the man's cot. Even in these memories the old shitheap had been ancient. Yet padres, of course, loved the man, then as now, in death, because the dead man had been a toady, devout and unquestioning, a symbol of the padres' success.

Pan Renik spat between the gaps in his rotten teeth.

As a young boy, he had heard that the oldest man in the world was born before the great branches of the world first kissed the sky—

Thwack!

The swing of the settlement's sole metal knife caught Pan Renik by surprise; one of the attending padres—ironuser, it looked like— had cut the raft free.

Pan Renik craned to get a better look.

The old man's lemurs, clearly terrified—not yet ready to leave this elevated plane of existence—huddled low against the corpse, growling and staring about wide-eyed as the raft began to roll down dead man's run.

From the crowd—most holding candles aloft—came muted sounds of encouragement.

Beyond the limit of the last hut, where the great bough dipped and the safety nets ended, the raft picked up speed. Light of the moon was strong enough beyond the canopy that the shroud of leaves over the corpse seemed to glow with a light of its own. Despite his disappointment at the lack of opportunities here, and despite the sour sensations remaining from his reflections of the past, Pan Renik's mood was briefly distracted, buoyed almost to amusement by the spectacle of the raft as it launched over the edge of the world, hanging there, suspended for a moment against a backdrop of night and endless clouds, small lemurs pinwheeling slowly out, shrieking into open air.

He grinned and bobbed his head and scratched at his scalp (which was and forever would be patchy, scarred and itchy).

Distant lights flickered under the clouds, illuminating the skeletal ghost of another treetop a great distance away, though Pan Renik saw this apparition as the fiery hand of a man who was trying to wake up before sinking under the poison for a third and final time.

He made a low hooting sound, like a little monkey he had once seen, as the death raft plummeted out of sight, lost forever—

But here came padres, walking the branch in two groups of three, chanting and swinging their braziers. Tiny red eyes glinted inside their cowls. They scrutinized the gathering. Maybe they were looking for him? Pan Renik sniffed the wind. Dawn approached. He lifted his eyes skyward, saw his lonesome nest.

Sun started to limn the clouds.

Reluctantly, Pan Renik clambered back up, empty-handed, his brief enjoyment gone, replaced now by the more familiar longings and sparse trappings of his solitary life.

THE FECUND'S MELANCHOLY DAUGHTER

In times of crisis such as this, the chatelaine found herself wondering about moments immediately before and after tragedy. Though her world had crumbled this morning, and she was distraught, she managed to cast her thoughts back to her waking moments, just before *the discovery*, to see if there had been a clue that the burgeoning day would soon take an awful turn. Had there been portentous dreams? The fecund, rambling about time and the city from her cell? No images lingered or stood out. Certainly nothing that would make the chatelaine reach bedside for any cotton wadding.

Regardless how much she reviewed the early part of her morning, it seemed there had been no hints, nothing amiss. Just aches and dull pain and the regrets of a regular hangover. Minor issues, quotidian and insignificant—no longer of any consequence—had nagged her when she opened her eyes at the door's knock.

The day someone was to die in an accident, did they have premonitions? Seconds before a huge chunk of stone, say, fell from an archway overhead to crush a man where he stood, was he *truly* unsuspecting? Or had this man, for that second, given up, surrendered to his fate, knowing that inevitable destruction hurtled closer?

For the chatelaine, the idea that tragedy could strike without any indication, no matter how subtle, must be impossible.

But she'd had none she could recall.

She took a deep breath, thought for a second that she might cry. She did not.

Her morning, thus far:

A lifetime ago, she'd been awoken by knocking, both at the doors to her bedchambers and from within the confines of her own skull. Her muscles and nether regions throbbed. Her mouth was very dry, sinuses swimming with the fumes of her dirty room. Without opening her eyes or even moving, she had done a quick inventory of her body, as was her norm on mornings after such excesses, searching herself for injuries other than the usual, such as sprains or cuts, or ruptures and other sources of discomfort that might run even deeper.

Then she'd cracked one eye open, examining the bed for guests. Seeing none—nor any on the floor—she felt a moderate sense of relief.

Her chambers were a disaster.

Banging again at the door.

Memories of the previous night were incomplete, but physical evidence of her activities had left her with a strong need to remain alone for as long as possible. Yet she was never allowed to stay alone for long. There would be parchments to sign, meetings to attend, her father and the citizens and the entire damn city to worry about.

She sighed.

Noises from Nowy Solum came muffled through the parchment over her windows. Judging by the light, it was well past dawn.

Banging, a third time, at the door.

Then the squawkings from her pets. Was that the sign things were amiss? Had her creatures been more upset than usual, or were these regular cries for food and affection now they knew she had woken?

"Please," the chatelaine had whispered, holding onto her forehead, where an invisible knife twisted. "Please, my little babies, please. Momma has a *splitting* pain. Give me a second . . ."

Breakfast was pears and quince jelly, a croissant, black coffee. The tray was left abandoned in the doorway, on the wooden planks of the Great Hall. Nobody around. A glass of fizzy water for her stomach, which she sipped before returning with the tray in one hand to her bed. Once there, picking at the meal, propped up against her pillows and listening again to the sounds of the morning outside and to the protests of her pets, she tried hard to recall details from the latter parts of the night—faces at least—forcing herself to steer away from further guilt or regrets, or at least staving off these feelings for as long as possible. Clinical, she told herself. Be clinical. This is your science, your study.

Several people had been in the room. Evidence was widespread: empty and half-filled glasses; a broken bottle; discarded garments. The son of a barker from Soaper's and Candles, a man she had taken a liking to—Jonas, was it? And maybe he had brought a friend. And a dark-skinned girl, from goodness-knows-where, possibly outside Nowy Solum, who had sat on the mattress for the longest time, fiddling with her hair and frowning before finally crawling over. Her lips and tongue had been black, rough. There were oils flowing, endless spiritus, the smell, and crack, and taste of leather.

At one point, two cobali had watched the activities—she remembered an isolated and crystalline image—laughing at the exertions from the foot of the bed.

Then the chatelaine lay thinking about the kholic girl, the one from Hot Gate. She pictured her pretty face. The poor thing had been brought inside with the best intentions and then left, alone, somewhere in Jesthe. Was she still in the palace? The chatelaine had no idea. Not that she ever wanted to involve the girl in an orgy, but neither did she intend the child to become lost in the huge halls and empty rooms of her home, just another servant. Today, she vowed, on this very day—or perhaps the next, at the latest—she would seek the girl out.

Almost ready at that point to throw off the cover and call for a bath, the chatelaine looked into the large mirror—which took up most of the west wall, and in which she discerned the row of her beloved beasts, stirring in their gilded cages—and, for the first time, saw the door to one cage hanging open.

That was the moment her day, her world, her life changed.

Agitation was clear in the faces of those remaining creatures, at least those with eyes. Fearful expressions, not understanding what had happened, brimming with hurt and betrayal of what they had seen in the night. The cries had been much more than hunger: they were of *betrayal*.

Why had she not looked earlier?

Heart pounding, the chatelaine stood for a moment, dizzy, naked except for the band of flea fur around her upper arm. She held onto the bed for support. Tiny stars spun about her head and drifted, falling, across her vision.

Her cherub was gone.

She glanced about the bedchambers, a slight twist of anticipation on her face, as if maybe an obscure joke had been told, one she didn't quite get. Or maybe she was hopeful that the precious creature might be watching her, perched on a curtain rod, or on a statue, but she saw nothing of the sort and her wispy smile faded as quickly as it had come, replaced by apprehension that was like a rag pushed into her throat.

The cherub had never before been out of its cage.

Oiled parchment over the windows remained intact and the door had been closed when she awoke. Had one of her guests taken the poor thing during the night? Had a guest done unspeakable acts with her beloved pet after she'd passed out? She recalled, before the evening had really fallen apart, an image of herself and a man called Zoran, from the kitchen (bearded, skinny), standing in the alcove, drinks in hand, laughing while she introduced, one by one, her menagerie.

Had she taken other guests over there later?

The chatelaine stumbled over to the alcove. The beasts, looking away from the mirror to see her physically enter, let loose with shrieks and twitters and grunts, feathers flying or fur airborne. Only one or two remained inert; they had no choice, created immobile, twitching with pent emotions. She had caused this hurt, had torn apart their safe and pampered world by acts of irresponsibility.

How *could* she have just lain there?

The lock to the cage was scratched. Part had been bent. Picked, no doubt. Really, though, the quality of the lock was embarrassing, little more than an ornament.

Biting a knuckle, she stifled a wail.

Her poor cherub. Her poor, poor cherub.

She was a fool and an idiot and a terrible mother for getting herself into the state she'd been in, for letting strangers into her room every night, for drinking until oblivion put her to bed. The pets were right: she had done this with her own hands.

Two things became certain to the chatelaine as she stood there, breath coming in ragged gasps: first, of course, for the sake of Nowy Solum, she had to replace the cherub as soon as possible. Second was that she must tell the chamberlain of her mistake. Erricus and his palatinate officers already called her all sorts of a fool. She knew of their profound disapproval, for just about every aspect of her lifestyle.

They were right, it seemed.

She took another deep breath and began to pace.

As a young and anxious girl, the chatelaine had been handed control of Jesthe. Now, after years of decline, she had finally proved herself unworthy. There need not be a lecture from the chamberlain about priorities and her lack of security, and respect for the palatinate; she was all too aware that they had warned her of this very thing, as far back as the day she had first banished them from her wings of the palace. Erricus would imply, as he had back then, that she actually harboured a wish for someone to come into her bedchambers and cut her throat while she slept. She was lucky this time, he would say. This was a warning, a wake-up call.

The chatelaine did blubber a bit then, because she hated platitudes, especially when they were called for.

She offered hysterical apologies to her remaining pets.

Painful to admit that the chamberlain had been right all along. She sniffled.

Where was her little baby?

She made a fist.

During today's conference, she would tell Erricus that the palatinate could return to all halls and chambers of the palace. She would admit defeat, and be humbled before his smugness.

Would this make her father happy? She was sure that the castellan worried about her, without protection down here, but in his current state of mind it was hard to be certain of anything.

She ground her fist against her palm.

Searching the floor for clues of any sort, she saw the signs of struggle and distress, but nothing unusual. Could she recall *nothing*? What was the matter with her?

Maybe a person other than a lover had come into Jesthe during the night, from the slums outside? Might even a servant, one of her own women, have done this? Almost anyone could enter the bedchambers on nights like the previous one. The palace was riddled, like old cheese.

Were there people in Nowy Solum who wished her ill-will? This concept was always a bit hard for her to get her head around. Why would people want to hurt her? The biggest crime she'd ever committed was sloth, or disregard. She was not malicious, nor had she ever harboured any ill-will of her own to force upon the citizenry.

She wiped her nose on her sleeve. "They should receive steel," she told her pets, who raised a small furor at the sound of her voice. "Or burn in eternal fire!"

The chatelaine could trust none of her staff. Not one of them. They were all backstabbers, harpies vying for attentions and favours and—

The kholic.

This time, thoughts of the girl stopped the chatelaine in her tracks. Even her pets fell suddenly silent. The first kholic ever to be in these parts of Jesthe and the chatelaine didn't even know where she was or where she had been. Could the kholic have taken the cherub?

Surely the girl was as innocent as her pets?

But what did the chatelaine really know about kholics? They were taken away from their mothers at birth, raised in the ostracon. Everyone knew that much. They had black fluids in their hearts and could get no pleasure, save from cleaning up the refuse of hemos—

If Erricus and his officers were allowed up here again, on this level of the palace, what would become of the melancholic girl? They would encounter each other at some point. What then?

If the kholic was still around.

The chatelaine dressed quickly in a long chemise and threw open the doors to her room, standing at the threshold to the Great Hall. Crooked Greta, the candlemender, was, by a misfortune of timing, passing by at that precise moment.

"Fetch the new girl," demanded the chatelaine.

Greta frowned, twisting her entire upper body to make eye contact. "What?"

The chatelaine did not yet even know the kholic's name. But today she would. She promised herself. Today. Today was a new day, a new start. "Fetch me the kholic."

Scowling, mumbling, Greta shuffled away.

Recalling then, as she waited for the girl to arrive, the pretty, tattooed face, and the fabulous body hinted at under the shift that the kholic now wore, the chatelaine had to admit that there were elements of spite in the attraction and lust she felt, a distant but gnawing jealously of the kholic's youth and beauty. She tried to tell herself this was a foolish thought: she was the chatelaine of Nowy Solum, after all, and the girl was just a kholic from the streets outside, but the chatelaine knew all too well on this morning of truths that her own youth had dwindled, her vitality faded. Exposed here, in her new skin, she also understood that beauty and youth were the reasons she had solicited the girl in the first place. Beauty, youth, and novelty.

"You are a fool," the chatelaine said to herself under her breath, almost smiling. No, she did not suspect the kholic of misdeed: she *needed* the girl, more than anything, to be with her now, to make her pain go away.

A second later, miraculously, the chatelaine found herself staring down at the kholic's face, a face even more beautiful than she recalled; the girl had appeared in the broad doorway to her chamber like a seraph.

Without hesitating, the chatelaine reached out and touched the kholic's hair, which was brown and matted and greasy. The girl's blue eyes did not quite meet the chatelaine's own, but were nonetheless a startling colour against the black tattoo. The chatelaine wanted to embrace and be embraced in return. She cleared her throat. "Thank you for coming." The girl was *truly* disarming up close. The chatelaine's heart raced. "I would like you to call me, er, Terra Bella. That's the name that the castellan—my father—gave me when I was born. Though no one is really allowed to call me that. I want to tell you, I've been robbed, and I need you to do me a favour."

Those averted eyes, set off so gorgeously by the tattoo, did not appear to react in the least.

"Last night," continued the chatelaine, quietly, reluctant to invite the girl in, for she did not trust herself at this point and felt, somehow, that if she did let the girl come in, the servant might get put in as much jeopardy as the pets (which were making a ruckus yet again): the chatelaine's environment, and maybe even her own touch, were unsafe around any innocence. "A cherub, my beloved cherub, was taken from my chambers."

"Winged baby?"

The kholic's voice, too, was exquisite.

"Exactly. Yes. A winged baby. Can you hear my other darlings? They are in mourning. As am I. They are all I have, and I am all they have." Now she could not stop herself from brushing a knuckle against the kholic's blackened cheek, though she made a lame effort to fight the urge.

"Sorry to hear that."

"I thought of you." Her fingers went up to the matted hair again, twined. "You must forgive me for bringing you into my palace and then abandoning you. I had become, well, distracted. What's your name?"

Octavia told her.

"You know, I feel I can trust you, Octavia." The chatelaine smiled, but it was a pained smile. "Though you might find this impossible to believe, I think we have much in common. I feel it in my heart. We were meant to meet. Tell me, Octavia, have you ever heard of the fecund?"

"My Lady?"

"Of course you have. Even you." This didn't sound right at all. The chatelaine plowed on. "The fecund is my associate. My familiar. She belongs to Jesthe, rather. To whomever lives in this room. She was my father's and now she is mine."

"I've heard stories."

"Well, the fecund is real, let me assure you. And you will meet her soon."

The girl said nothing.

"She's locked up, you see, in a cell, below the palace. She's been there almost forever. I want you to visit the fecund, and I want you to give her a message. I am too ashamed to go myself. She already believes me unworthy. But she can be a powerful friend, you'll see. She'll meet with you, Octavia, and will listen to you. She'll like you, I'm sure."

Now the girl looked beyond the chatelaine, toward the rumpled bed, toward the harnesses and attachments abandoned on the crude side table, still smeared with fluids from the previous night. If Octavia was shocked by what she saw, she gave no indication. Her nostrils flared, sniffing.

"I don't know what the fecund'll make for me this time," said the chatelaine, in an even quieter voice. "Probably not another cherub, not like that one. They're all different, you know." She put her hand on the girl's taut shoulder. She could not stop touching her. "Listen, Octavia, I would invite you in but the place has not been cleaned, and my fire has almost died. I must see to that."

"I understand."

Was there a heat radiating from this girl? The chatelaine ran her fingers down the brown, toned arm. "Maybe you'll come back later, after your task? Tell me how it went?"

"Sure." There was still no expression on the tattooed face. "I'd like that."

The chatelaine excused herself to fetch the small wooden box from her bedside table. When she returned, she displayed the contents to the girl. After a long moment, during which neither chatelaine nor kholic moved, she said, "You must choose one."

"What are they?"

"These are my dreams."

Hesitantly, the girl's fingers rose.

"She feeds on dreams, you see." The chatelaine whispered now. "I mean, she eats food, like me and you, but a dream gets her started. The fecund makes my pets, inside her, around these dreams, like pearls around a grain of sand. These are not from last night, naturally, but from several nights ago, from when I had an almost pleasant sleep. I was holding my baby in my arms while she rested against me. And when I awoke, I saw her on her perch, in her cage, looking peaceful and sweet. She sang me a little song that morning. She could talk, you know? The only one of my pets that could ever talk. Oh, Octavia, my heart has broken!"

Eyes downcast, looking at their feet. "What shall you have me do?"

"Do? Well, yes, of course. Please select one of these pieces of cotton and go down there right now. My chances are good, I think, to have a new baby similar, at least, to the gentle cherub. Will you go, Octavia? Will you do an old lady a favour?" She dabbed at her eyes with her fingers and felt moisture there.

The girl inspected the damp waddings and lifted one from the box.

"Be careful. Hold it in two fingers. Don't get it all sweaty. With that in your hand, you'll have no problem finding your way to the cell. I need not tell you directions. She'll guide you, she'll pull you there."

As the kholic turned to leave, the chatelaine took her by the upper arm. "Your face is very pretty," she said. "I have to tell you that." She did not know how to continue. She knew absolutely nothing about this girl. She did not understand the kholic's boundaries or sensitivities and felt that, already, she might have gone too far.

THE FECUND'S MELANCHOLY DAUGHTER

Were they all this damn stoic? There had been one or two in the past—strictly men, as far as she could recall—but subtleties of their demeanour were lost in the haze of spiritus and fervour of the moment—

Those blue eyes never once looked up.

The chatelaine straightened, trying to slough off this mood and appear, belatedly, to be the persona she was meant to be, whoever that was, certainly not this moping, awkward teenager. She cleared her throat again. "We need to descend and ask the crabby old fecund for another miracle." But could she press her face into that neck, just once, lose herself in it, draw even a small portion of the girl's youth into her aching lungs? "This is very important for me. You might think I'm a heartless and ugly old hag who wants to replace her pet on the morning it has gone missing, but there's more to this than I can possibly explain to you right now."

"I need no reasons. I'll go see the fecund."

"Well. Well, all right, then. That's fine. I won't hold you back any longer." But the girl had not said, *You aren't ugly, Terra Bella!*

Turning away at last, the chatelaine held her hands together in front of her, to remove them from the situation. Tears were coming now. She did not want to cry in front of this girl. "Of course, we will find who took her. We will have the city turned upside down. Now go. Please, go. I don't want to lose any more time. We'd best begin."

Octavia bowed.

The chatelaine watched the girl as she walked the Great Hall in retreat. "Come see me after," she called, blurting the words out. "So long." And then she chastised herself for sounding too desperate and adolescent. The chatelaine wondered if, of all things, she might be falling in love.

Up from the shallow valley, as if regurgitated in desiccated forms of sand and the harsh battered shapes of burnished wood and tin and other detritus—perhaps even imagined by the lakebed dry these many seasons—there rose piecemeal into view a series of what could only be the dwellings of people. Dull, scoured from rocks and desolation, all bespattered with dust and shit and pocked by endless storms, these were nonetheless homes. *Homes*. Perhaps two dozen or so of the structures clustered together, extending into the near distance where mists began to claim their details.

So incongruous and shocking was the sight of this ramshackle village—after travelling two full days now through deserted and unchanging badlands—that path's father stood silent atop the hillcrest for a full minute, perfectly still, regarding the apparitions while hot winds plucked and pushed at his own tatters, urging him onward, and down.

His son, path, groaned and craned his neck just then, grumpily peering past the fabric ridge of the sling he rested in to see his father's face; the boy had been dozing and felt shudders pass through the familiar, skeletal body that supported him, a trembling in the sternum always pressed to his own spine. This shudder had been followed by the cessation of movement; he woke from sleep to see tears streaking the grime on his father's cheeks.

"Now what?" He ground his little teeth together. "Father? Are you listening? Will you please keep moving?" But by then the boy had also seen the structures out the corner of his eye and, as he turned his head, implications of what they might mean settled over him. A few moments passed before he found words again.

"All right," he said, finally, reverentially, more like a breath than true words. "We can start here. Maybe this is what we're looking for." Path's small heart pounded in his ribcage like that of a bird.

His father wiped at the dampness on his face with a shaky arm and, abruptly, as if suddenly disgusted, removed the sling from around his neck. He held the contraption away from his body, suspending path mid-air. He turned to the boy, to look into his eyes. "You told me you wanted people. I see lots of houses, son, but no people."

This was true. Path frowned.

"Or it could be," his father continued, "that they ain't no people *alive* here. Could be something else. Not people, I mean. Other things. Hiding in the buildings."

"Put me down."

So path was placed, unceremoniously, onto the hot ground.

The sling had a rigid frame, clamped to path's torso, and three short, strong legs that locked into place, enabling him to rest in an almost upright position. He could look around, at least until his neck became too sore to hold up his heavy head. More or less propped upright, he peered over the top of the sling, watching eddies of sand dance with the silent structures.

"Goodness knows what could live here." His father held a hand over his eyes as a visor, though there was no sun and had not been any sun in his life or even in his father's life. "I've heard stories."

"Will you just go down there? Find out."

"Likely kill us for trespassing just as soon as give us water or listen to any words you got to say." Path's father licked chapped lips. He was haunted by this adventure, by leaving his home, by what his son had become. Without looking back or saying another word, he suddenly turned and walked the grade, awkwardly, all elbows and knees, like he always moved when he was without his cumbersome burden.

Path closed his eyes, just for a moment. His lungs ached. He tried to control his breathing. The sounds he heard with his eyes closed were old bones tumbling against each other. He tried to recall details of what he had been like before the light had stricken him, transforming him, but he felt nothing inside. Nothing much remained from that time. Vignettes, tastes, an isolated cry. He knew only that he could never return to his old life or to his father's house.

When the winds died a little more, path opened his eyes again. The only thing moving out there—other than his father, of course, who was still walking away—were flies: hundreds of the insects, in thick masses, hovered over the huddled houses like irritated spirits. Had they been there before? Path was unsure, and this unsettled him.

His father meandered, nearing one home before veering off toward another. A painful display to watch. Path looked away, in the direction from which they had just come, where the shapes of rocks in the badlands were being relinquished by the receding night: to path, squinting, the formations seemed to be giants, once stalking the landscape in great strides but frozen now, in place, by the advent of this day.

Yet rocks, he knew, were as incapable of walking as was he.

Until this point in his life, path had never seen so many huts. Not like this. Not in one place. His own home had been mostly cave, with several crude partitions to keep out blowing sand. There were a handful of people living in the area he came from, maybe seven or so at any given time. Mostly men, living alone, in similar caves. No children that he knew of. Ever. And women seemed to have been sucked empty, as if the land was so devoid that it stole any form of essence that could either give or sustain life. His own mother had withered to nothing, just a husk of skin and bones, losing her flesh and then her mind until at last she roamed the yards, a hollowed spirit, staring at path when he was left outside, or shrieking silently at the clouds. Eventually, she faded away to nothing, tattered on the winds.

What was left of path's mother they buried in a jar: a handful of grey parchment and slivers of yellow bone.

He could remember her.

The spot throbbed where the light had touched him, the mark on his forehead, as if the luminous finger were still pressing hard against him. He had awoken from fourteen years of sleep with the burning desire to leave the desert, seek out people—not people like those who lived in the rocks near his home, or those weathered relics who gathered at the local market (which was really just a few blankets of junk set up a day's walk to the north)—but *thriving* people, mercurial-minded people, living together in much bigger numbers than the sand-blasted ghouls he knew.

But his father was right: there were no crowds here, maybe no one at all.

Standing by one of the nearest huts, after having completely circled the silent community, path's father was apparently still searching for a door or other means of egress. Path watched the clumsy movements with his small stomach gone sour.

"Knock," he shouted. He was not heard. "Will you just knock?"

Suddenly batting at a dark cloud of flies—for the insects were upon path's father now, and biting at his flesh—the forlorn man looked over at his son for a second, despairingly, hoping no doubt that path would call this whole thing off.

"Go!" Path's voice was the creak of desert rats. Flies would find little succulence in his body. "Knock on the door, will you! Tell them we're here!"

His father abruptly vanished.

Somewhat shocked, path wondered if his father had gone inside the hut. What else might have occurred? And who knew what his father would say, if indeed he was in there.

The heat sung. Path waited in this growing heat as best he could. Without options. What if his father was killed? How long would he remain here before dehydration killed path or a beast came to investigate?

Sand stung path's face and he turned away.

Later, reappearing from the house, walking briskly, narrow head held down, his father did, however, return.

Path had to prompt the man several times to discover if anyone had been in the hut, and why his father had chosen that house in particular, and what had happened within, because his father would never think to volunteer such pertinent information.

"Yes," answered his father, finally, "they was people in there. Well, one anyhow."

"Just one? In the whole place? Was he human? Like us?"

"Well, he was like me." Their eyes met.

Path tried to ignore the implications of the comment but his stumps twitched. "And?"

"I told him you was waiting outside."

"And?"

"Well, the man—cause it were a man inside there, a sickly man, and old, too—told me they ain't no people here. Used to be, but no more."

"What happened to them?"

His father pointed with a trembling hand, one boney finger indicating the direction they had been headed. "Out there, he says, just a few hours walk, or maybe a few days, is a place known as Nowy Solum. He said this place is where all people went, including his own three daughters, who left him alone and never paid him no visits nor ever bring him food. Out there, he says, in that direction. Out there what he called a city."

"Pick me up," path said, stricken. His forehead throbbed. High-pitched sounds played in his ears and images flickered behind his eyes. He could almost recall the epiphany that had changed him, and why the desire to leave home had been so strong. "That's where we'll go," he said. "Pick me up."

His father looked down the road. "No. We shouldn't go there. We need to turn back. Go home."

"We had no home." Path was alarmed by this vehemence in him. "We never did. Just a hole where you drank yourself to sleep every night." He watched the expression change on his father's face—a draining of resistance, a slackness that set in, as if a shadow had fallen; his father bent slowly and put the sling around his neck.

"Look," path said. "I'm sorry, but it's true."

THE FECUND'S MELANCHOLY DAUGHTER

Without further protests, his father stood and began walking, heading toward Nowy Solum.

Path strained to see anything up ahead, any detail of the upcoming city, but he could not—only sand and low clouds, and the last of these few deserted huts that had, just moments ago, seemed so monumental.

When he closed his eyes to rest, perspective shifted:

Wrapped in lengths of cloth, he lay on his shelf where he always lay, near the firepit. The dried fruit salesman, who had unluckily been passing through the arid area where path's family had dug their hole, sat cross-legged on the packed dirt floor, sipping weak tea. This was clear: the man's scarred face; the hair on his hands; the smell of his cheroot as he smoked. Mention of Nowy Solum had brought this image back, like a form of sorcery. Prone on his shelf, path was invisible to the stranger. His mother and father listened to the stories that surely could not be real, stories of a fabulous, teeming place, stories that trailed off when the salesman realized path's father, drunk on spiritus, was a lost cause, a waste of breath.

But this traveller had lived in Nowy Solum. Had lived there for some time. He described all manner of people and creatures, pushed together in the thronging streets, for better or worse. Anything, the salesman said, could happen there. A man could die in his tracks and be stepped over by all that passed by, or a man could grow rich beyond his dreams. There was food, so much food: fish from the distant ocean, and herbs and roots and spices, giving out such scents as they simmered that they could transport anyone who breathed them. Jewellery. And women, too, like you could never imagine. (Pardon me ma'am.)

Physickers and splicers created life with their own two hands almost as easy as they might remove it. A palace, and a beautiful young chatelaine. Officers, without gods to lead them, and fecund monsters hiding in underground caverns.

Exemplars of the gods had once led congregations there, swallowing their host, or touched by the light of the deities.

Touched by gods.

Path's forehead throbbed.

The smell of the cheroot stung his sinuses.

He saw scars on the man's face and the way the salesman stared at his mother—lusty, through half-closed eyes.

At the time, path could retain nothing, had no framework on which to hang these stories, no references. He had imagined, as the days passed, that the words and images had been devices, illusions meant to impress his mother, who was very much alive then, and still plump, human, and warm (though by no means could she ever have been considered beautiful, like the chatelaine the man mentioned).

Path had also seen the way his mother silently regarded the salesman as he spoke, peering from her shadowed corner of the living area: like a shrike watching a mouse.

But the salesman finally did leave, unscathed, without a sale and, because his father had managed to stay awake the entire time, without his mother's full attentions. Path's mother, therefore, was in a foul mood when the door finally closed. No one ever really knew or cared that the boy had lain there, listening, first to the fabulous stories, then to the argument, then to the sounds of fists striking flesh. Familiar cries filled the hovel: pain, and frustration, and the isolation of their parents' desiccated lives.

Drooling, an idiot, path lay on his shelf.

Yes. These were the memories that could come back now. He would need to be careful.

Temples, path thought. And being touched by the light of the gods.

Could his father recall these events, the salesman? Preoccupied, brooding over the curse that was his progeny, no doubt his father did not remember the encounter, or the fight with his now departed wife.

They continued along the road, which became more and more defined—more and more like a road with each step—both of them aware that Nowy Solum had called to them, and that the city was, and possibly had always been, their destination.

THE FECUND'S MELANCHOLY DAUGHTER

Beyond the vaulted stone ceiling of the grotto, where Name of the Sun's eyes had earlier failed to discern anything of note, and where the liberated cherub soon came to roost; beyond the stalagmites and lime deposits and the blind white cave beetles that fed on the guano of blind white bats, was a corridor, and a series of holding cells, used for prisoners of castellan and chatelaine alike, throughout the ages. There were four cells. Currently, three were empty, sealed, and had been this way for centuries. The fourth was occupied.

Forever ajar, hinges crusted with buboes of rust, wood gone soft and black and pulpy, the door was a swollen affair. Dank vegetation from inside the cell spilled out through the narrow opening and, in many places, through the rotten wood itself, to die there, in the unlit corridor.

Approaching, a smell of mould and rotting vegetation, of stagnant water, became denser and denser, but there was another scent, almost indefinable—sweet, not altogether unpleasant. The young servant girl, the kholic named Octavia, nearly choked on this brew. She filled her lungs again and again, eyes watering. She had missed such pungency.

Octavia held her lantern out, staring at this partially opened door, or what was left of it. Strangely, there was another light, dim and green, coming from inside the cell. These plants by her feet, dying or not, defied nature.

She hung the lantern on an iron sconce.

Stagnant water pooled the worn stone floor, staining the rough corridor for some distance. Her flat rattan shoes were quickly black and befouled, but until a fortnight ago, she had never worn any.

From inside the cell erupted suddenly a bray of laughter, followed by low, muttered phrases Octavia could not catch, though she was sure she heard her name.

There was just enough space for her to squeeze between the stone doorframe and the rotten wood of the door, which pressed against her body, soft as flesh and almost as warm; with the stench and heat of the cell filling her lungs, dense against her face and hands, Octavia stepped forward.

And she looked in.

First she saw a portcullis, within arms reach, though not at all as rusted or old as she would have imagined, if she had imagined a portcullis. Beyond these bars she saw no creature, no fecund, though just how this beast might appear she was not entirely clear. There was only a lush habitat of startling green, a riot of growth, as if the source of all life were crammed into here.

Was this a joke? An initiation of sorts? Those stories from her childhood, tales and rumours passed down in the dorms of the ostracon, untrue? Maybe the chatelaine was playing a trick on her?

She stood upon a thin strip of wet rock. On the other side of the bars, vines spilled down the walls and over the floor. More vines hung in verdant cascades from the ceiling, which was almost totally obscured. The more she looked, the more vegetation she discerned.

Tiny lizards hovered over the flora, and black beetles rustled through the humus strewn by her ruined shoes. She frowned. She even smelled traces of the outdoors here: soil, smoke, and a struggling breeze. But from where? That greenish light seemed to emanate beyond the lianas overhead, as if there was a source up there, but none of this was possible because she had travelled down several flights of steps, and down many sloping corridors in the bedrock—tugged along by the chatelaine's dream, which she held clenched in one sweaty fist—to get to this subterranean room.

In a quiet, quavering voice, Octavia called out, "Hello?"

That breeze, rustling, was her sole answer. Followed by the hum of bumblebees. She could not really tell how big the cell was. When she established a wall, and then tried to see the wall opposite, they seemed to shift.

THE FECUND'S MELANCHOLY DAUGHTER

Was a pond covering most of the floor? The surface had become so thoroughly choked by arrowheads and duckweed and algae that it almost appeared to be comprised of the same greenery that overhung the cell and draped the walls, and when one first—

The pond *moved*.

Octavia stepped back.

Solidifying, massive and green, rising up before her, what else could this be, emerging from the water? As if the pond was metres and metres deep? What else but the fabled fecund? Octavia steadied herself against the wall. Had the monster been lounging, camouflaged in the shallow water all this while? Or maybe, Octavia thought, there was no floor at all in there, and the fecund had come when she had called, swimming up from a water-filled tunnel below the palace—

The monster filled the cell now, turning her long face slowly toward Octavia, revealing through this movement the undeniable fact that all of this was *extremely* real. Their eyes met. Octavia could not look away, though she tried. Evidence of the fecund's gender was certain, locked into those little red eyes. Though difficult to admit, Octavia felt an unspoken bond tremble between them, a connection that was like a faint shock through her body; she tried to step farther back but the wall prevented her.

"My my my," said the monster, in a strangely soft and motherly voice (though Octavia had never heard her mother's voice). "What have we here?"

Rough skin, tinted like the water in most places, but mottled with brown, as if by disease. Those eyes were like a snake's, with vertical pupils. Clearly no human emotion had ever been portrayed there. Predatory teeth, hundreds of them, all exposed in what might have been a smile. And a black, forked tongue, flickering, tasting the air.

"Speak up, child. What do you want? Why did you call me? I don't have all day."

The voice was tremulous in the air, hissing inside Octavia's skull. "I'm sorry to disturb—"

Quickly, from that long tongue, the fecund spat several small, dark items, two of which hit the bars of the portcullis, but one hit Octavia wetly in the face and then dropped to slide slowly down the front of her shift. *A tadpole.* A fat brown tadpole. Octavia brushed the larvae off—maybe frog, or toad?—as the fecund tossed her head back to laugh the same laugh Octavia had heard while approaching.

Then the monster said: "You didn't wash before coming here?"

"I beg your pardon?"

"Your face. Your face is dirty."

Octavia would not let the fecund bait her.

"Did the chatelaine send you? I see she's scraping the bottom of the barrel. Or is visiting me only fit for untouchables?"

"We're not called that. Not any more. We're kholics. Melancholics."

The fecund laughed again. "Oh, I've touched a nerve! How clever of me. *Melancholics.* But really, you humans are so predicable and boring. I don't care what you have on your face or what you force others to put on their face. You're all the same to me. Let me guess. She's adopted you?"

"What do you mean?"

"You're her latest project. Or, if you're not now, you will be soon."

"I work here, in Jesthe."

"Really? Doing tasks other than wiping asses?"

"Yes."

"Are you sleeping with her?"

"No."

"Shame. But my goodness. Social changes! Marching forward and all that. Bravo! What does everyone else think? The staff? Do they treat you nice? Do they welcome you to their bosoms? Do they play cards with you? Share gossip? What does the chamberlain think, for goodness sake?"

"I've never met chamberlain Erricus. He doesn't go to the floor where I work."

"The floor where you work. That's rich. From what I understand, he would remain unaffected by your marred and somewhat offbeat beauty. He might not even see you at all. Or perhaps he would see only your mark? That would be enough for him. I'd love to know what he would think if he knew you were here! And what would his predecessors say? They would gut you like a rabbit."

"How could I know the answers to all your questions?"

"These questions are rhetorical. You're so serious. Do you know what rhetorical means? I don't need you to answer me. But you say that the chamberlain knows nothing about you? No one has told him, I'm sure." She tilted her head, squinting at Octavia. "Maybe you would charm even the cold palatinate. What do you think?"

Octavia shrugged. This reek, she realized, was not the smell of rancid gardens, or of the river that bisected the city, but was mephitic, a perfumed corpse, preserved forever by unnatural means, forever rotting.

Her legs trembled. The fecund seemed to know everything. Octavia squeezed the dream in her fist and tried to clear her head. Surely the fecund could not see her thoughts, flicking unwittingly through her mind, like birds? "The cherub," she said quietly. "The pet you made for the chatelaine—"

"*Made*?" Moving so fast that her great body was a blur, spraying water, the fecund wheeled, algae pendulous from her torso. The swamp seemed to be a mere puddle. That grin was long gone. "What happened to my baby?"

Octavia stammered nothing coherent.

"*What happened to her*?"

The monster's stomach distended in muscular rolls and her green breasts hung heavily, two either side. What looked like smoke came from her nostrils as she levelled an accusing finger at Octavia as big as the girl's forearm. "And I didn't *make* that cherub." The monster moved her rear quarters, lifting them so they cascaded. Octavia saw the green vagina, opening between scaly thighs. "She was my *baby*, my child. Tell me what happened."

Emerging fingers spread apart the grey labia from the inside: a nose poked out, briefly, twitching, and glittering eyes glanced at Octavia before the face withdrew, though whether by its own volition or if it had been sucked back in by contractions of the infamous uterus was impossible to determine. Octavia felt dizzy.

"Will you answer me, kholic? Can you tell me? Because that *cherub*, as you insist on calling her, was my *child*. Now what has happened? Is she alive, at least?"

"Uh, the chatelaine, that is, she's not sure. I don't know much. Your child was stolen."

"Speak up!"

"Stolen."

"*Stolen*?" The fecund's voice changed, deep enough now to shake the stone walls of her cell and reverberate the very bedrock of Nowy Solum. "People are such hopeless fools! How could someone have *stolen* her?"

"I don't know any details."

"What? I told you to speak up! Thieves, you say? Thieves in the palace?"

"Well, in the chatelaine's bedchamber."

The fecund made a loud hissing sound, no doubt of disgust, and slopped back down, splashing water up against the walls. "Now I understand why she didn't come down here herself. She got you to do the dirty work. Was the stupid bitch drunk again last night? Drinking spiritus and fucking animals?"

"I'm not sure," Octavia said, lamely, but of course she knew the tales of indiscretions and self-abuse; these were common knowledge in the city. Even in the ostracon. Until not long ago, Octavia couldn't have cared less about the chatelaine's behaviour, but now she had stood on the threshold of the bedchambers, had felt the gaze of those eyes, the dry heat of the chatelaine's fingers on the nape of her neck. She had seen the devices and smelled the scent of stale sex. She cleared her throat. "The chatelaine told me she needs another cherub, for her collection."

"Oh? For her *collection*?" That tongue came out again, coiling, accompanied by yet another low hiss. Several black worms fell from the fecund's gums to quickly dive for cover. Yet the monster seemed to have partially resigned, or at least had let go some of her anger. "But I have little choice, right? I must submit, for I am but a slave. Do me a favour, kholic? At least tell your boss this for me. No more. Tell her that. My babies are not playthings. They live and breathe like all little babies." The grimace forming now on the fecund's face might have been a different form of cruel smile. "They are children, as I've said." She cocked her head. "Well, what are you waiting for? You must know what I need to get started? Have you got the stuff?"

Octavia nodded. She opened her fist and held the batten out.

"Throw it."

Octavia hesitated.

"Go ahead, throw it, girl."

So she tossed the cotton at the monster, who caught it with a snap of her jaws and a grotesque wink.

"Thanks, sweetheart." Swallowing.

Octavia waited, afraid she might pass out from the tension that tightened in her chest.

The fecund squinted, chewing. Paused. "Hey, that tastes a little funny."

"What?" Chills ran down Octavia's spine.

But the fecund laughed. "I'm kidding. Jeez! It's yummy, as usual. I can't wait to see what this one's all about. Now run along. Let me gestate. And bring me what else I require. *Soon.* Has she told you about that?"

"No."

"Ha! Well, she will. The old lady isn't through with you yet, I assure you. We'll talk again. Hey, are you all right? You seem a little pale. In a few places, anyhow. I hope I didn't frighten you. I get a little angry, that's all. I'm bored. I like to make jokes. I'm actually very maternal, you know. Which is an understatement. But maybe next time you could find the key for that gate and come sit right here, next to me?" Patting a mossy stone. "Then you could hold my hand while I deliver? That would be *so* nice. Nice to have a visitor. *Especially* one as comely as yourself. Really, with that nice tattoo all over your face. It's been many years since I've been close to a young girl as beautiful as you. I used to have quite a, well, quite an affinity—a taste, shall we say—for girls as attractive as you." The monster licked her scaly lips and smiled again. "You'd better go. Let me sleep on this." She burped.

As Octavia turned, a large salamander, or similar such amphibian, mostly pale green but with fat red spots, appeared on the shoulder of the fecund, grinning, and its face—or so it seemed to Octavia— bore hints of her own features, including the black kholic's mask, which arced over the snout, mocking her own.

Nahid walked a few paces behind Name of the Sun, on Listower Avenue, between the ever-leaning structures. A chicken ran between them, pursued by a lone, sluggish cobali. The sound of the blacksmith, and the smell of his forge, was in the air.

They were going for a beer.

Bland-faced moon, sinking, peered down upon Pan Renik. He was very near his nest and out of breath. His failure to bring anything back from his expedition stung inside. Within the thin limbs of familiar territory, here at the top of the world, more expanses yawned than either branches or leaves: the dome of the open sky was so close. Winds became stronger, too. Crisper gusts reached Pan Renik's lungs, more fragrant and liberated than those stifled ones puffing in the stinking settlement.

Pan Renik imagined he could detect hints of impossible reaches. From where, he wondered (for perhaps the thousandth time), could these winds originate?

Before long, powerful yearnings to be elsewhere—somewhere other than this world—coursed through his blood, taking him over, inflaming him with the thwarted desires he could never explain (had he ever anyone to explain anything to). Was there more to life? There had to be, to continue. More than just branches and the open sky and poisonous clouds below.

Looking directly into the waning night, frowning, Pan Renik suddenly paused. Intangible masses of billows extended out to the horizon, of course, dusted white in places by the waning moon and, from underneath, by occasional flashes of far off lights, but there was . . . something else? A new scent? A sound he had not heard before?

He strained to hear, to sniff, to discern.

Nothing.

"Galls," he swore, though he did not himself know to whom or what he referred.

Small evidences of life arose from the settlement below—a faint, chanted prayer (for the dead man, no doubt), and a child's brief cry. They were returning to their beds. Wind and the creak of limbs joined with the voices. Belly full of wistfulness (and that's about all), Pan Renik gave in to the profound wave of futility that suddenly washed over him, draining him of the small hopes he had detected on the night breezes.

Once in a while, like now, he deliberated opening his veins with a sharp piece of wood, spilling his thick red sap over the people below—

A loud wail brought him out of self-indulgence.

From above.

He looked up.

From his nest.

Pan Renik's body went cold: he was utterly at a loss. The wail had not been the caw of a lemur or the scream of a nighthawk. Maybe he'd misheard? Had gliders arrived, in his absence, to romp with abandon on the woven leaves of his bower? No. The cry had been from none of these sources: it had been from a person, a person in need, a person in distress.

A person in his nest.

No one could ever have climbed up while he was gone. No other citizen came here. There was not one in the settlement who could climb as well as he, none brave enough to leave the nets and webs and safeguards they all pathetically clung to down there. Not even padres had the balls to come up.

He made a few low hooting noises, to relieve his anxiety, and bobbed his head.

Who in the world could be up there?

After a few beats of his heart—wondering for just a moment if he should wait until the sun rose farther, so he could see the situation better—Pan Renik forced himself to subdue his fears and climb higher. Still, to his shame, his limbs shook and his bladder tightened as he circled underneath his nest. (Was he weak, like the rest of them? Surely not: he was a brave, exiled warrior!)

Crouching, much nearer, Pan Renik was still unable to see the full extent of his bower—

Then he heard the person in his nest again, weakly calling out.

Unmistakable.

Followed by what could only be the rustle of something heavy and unseen crashing through foliage—

A startled glider flapped noisily away from where it had been hiding, making Pan Renik nearly fall to his death: heart pounding, he watched the skinny body silhouetted against its own wide sails, flying down, toward the low moon.

Now came a moan of pain, or maybe pleasure, raining through

the sparse twigs as if it were substance; Pan Renik cowered and looked back up at his nest in time to see a form moving there, a hard-edged shape, rising from his bower—

Sudden images of his club and handmade mace lying abandoned, useless, stung him like slaps across the face: whoever was up there had access to his weapons.

He was unprepared.

To squash the growing feelings of uselessness and self-condemnation, Pan Renik had to act. "Hey," he said, keeping just a little hushed, so that padres would not hear, "who's up there? Who goes there?"

The response came, reedy and pained, in a strong accent that made the two words very strange—hard, for a moment, for Pan Renik to recognize. But a human's voice. The voice of a woman. "Help me," it said. "*Help me.*"

Pan Renik stammered, almost in a panic, "Look, keep mum, mum, for goodness sake. Padres could hear you. I'm coming up."

"In the . . . branches down there. Please. You must help . . ."

How did he manage to climb the last few metres, so familiar, yet, on this night, so strange and alien? How? He did, though, arms and legs moving of their own accord.

After drawing a deep breath, and then another, he pulled himself up, into his bower—

She lay on her back.

Sprawling, body flattened, dark and dully glinting, as if oil from a squirrel's body had been spread across his nest. At first, he thought—for just a moment—that the woman was a form of creature he had never before seen, but this was a device she lay on, an invention, not a part of her at all, flickering highlights of silver. Her shape covered his nest, drooping off the far end, into the night.

She was in the centre, sheathed from toe to head in the complex, deep red garment, integrated into the device, but even without the tubes and membranes and shiny structural frame that seemed to bind her together, Pan Renik knew that this woman, though human (he decided), was nothing like him. Not like anyone in the settlement. Beneath the clinging layers of the outfit, so tight over her skin, and beneath the mask covering most of her face, this woman was not like anyone.

Dark eyes, buried in the shadow of the headgear, moved. Their gaze was sharp, suspicious, watching him as he leaned closer. Her mouth, obscured within the mask, twisted.

"They shot me down."

"Who did?"

"They shot down our car. And when I came up . . ."

"Came up?" He frowned at the clouds, then looked back at the woman's face. What was she saying? That she'd come from *below* the clouds? She was madder than him.

There was so much pain in those eyes, an unfathomable amount. More pain than Pan Renik's. This realization, for reasons he did not want to think about, made him angry, as if he had sole rights to such despair.

"It's cold up here," she said. "My legs are not . . . good. No longer function . . . No air up here, and cold. Are you not . . . cold?"

Pan Renik said nothing. He was staring at the device again, mesmerized by the glints. These tubes were *metal*! Like the padre's big knife and a few other artifacts padres kept in their trapeza— gifts of the sky power. These tiny objects in his nest were metal. Scattered, several fragments lay between the woman's legs, several more to the left of her torso. Only padres could touch metal. Metal was what made padres padres. Pan Renik's mouth had gone dry. Reaching out with one arm, entranced, he could not quite bring himself to lay his fingers on the glinting shapes. Would metal burn him? Or would Anu suddenly descend, to strike him dead, if he touched this sacred material?

He spat off to the side.

What the woman lay on, he saw, in the pre-dawn light (which was creeping across the clouds in his direction with slowly increasing intensity), appeared to be a blanket of sorts, a greasy membrane, spread out across the twigs and branches. The woman's thick arms, trembling in spasm, were bound within the structure by straps.

He saw the whites of her eyes now.

Her back was broken. He knew. He could tell.

Then, suddenly, Pan Renik understood something else, understood something as clearly as he had ever understood anything in his life: the woman had *flown* to his nest, like a glider, through the skies. From another place, from another world. The device that lay broken in his nest had caused her to fly.

She had dropped into his home. *A gift*.

"Where you from?" he asked, awed. "Where do you come from?"

"Hypoxia." The woman's chest seemed broad and strong, yet struggled to rise.

"Hypoxia." Repeating the word, tasting its magic, Pan Renik could not help but think that hypoxia might be the place the winds came from, the place of his imagination, and to conjure in his mind this other world, one where he would be able to come and go without fear of being chased away, where his past would be forgotten and forgiven. A place where he would not be an exile, nor ever be hungry or lonely. There would be riches there, too, metals of all sorts, and food to be taken by handfuls and stuffed into his face until his belly was finally, once and for all, full.

Through the visor, Pan Renik discerned the altering expression on the woman's face as he climbed carefully up onto the rim of his nest. He crouched over her, making sure his toes curled on branches and not on the giant membrane, protecting it from his long toenails. She looked at him, perplexed. Concerned. Maybe even a little hopeful? He took great care, as he moved closer, not to damage the frame of the precious device.

Beneath the woman's shoulder protruded the handle of his wooden mace. He had made this weapon himself, using bark and cloth to smooth the wood. Touching the mace now, rubbing the shaft with his rough fingertips, he said, "And where were you going?" He almost asked, *Who knows you are here?*, but decided, at the last moment, to shut up.

Holding the shaft of the mace made him feel stronger, confident; he ground his remaining teeth together, recalling (with great distaste and shame) his earlier fear—fear that this woman had caused.

Meanwhile, she coughed, and continued coughing for some time, unable to offer any response. When she did speak again, Pan Renik no longer understood the words she used, for they were not in his tongue.

He began to work the mace out from under her heavy body.

"Rescue," she said, suddenly, her voice dry and weakened, struggling to lift one hand toward him. "My friends are still there. I must tell someone. Listen. If they come looking for us. We found a ship. In stasis. A mother. We boarded her. But she wasn't discarded. And I took her seegee from her console. I stole it. And when I touched the surface, I felt the connection, the jolt. She used me. She was waiting for someone, someone like me, for ages. Her symbiotes had all been killed. But there was a brood ship. And when we tried to get away, we were shot down." She licked her lips. "It's insane. This world. We crashed . . . But I came up again, to send for help, because no transmissions get out from these horrid clouds. My friends told me it was crazy but I insisted. They were waiting. The drones. They saw me. And now I can't move."

She had begun to weep.

Against the dawn's light, Pan Renik slowly raised the mace above his head. Too many words, he thought. Just like a padre. Too many words, spinning around. For an instant, the briefest of hesitations, while he tried to consider options, he paused. But he came up with no options. There were never options. He felt only vague remorse as he brought his weapon down, with all his might and frustration, trying to destroy what was left of his fear, smashing the woman between her shocked eyes. A little remorse, but not much.

Looking down through the parchment, shacks and cluttered markets appeared heaped, as if thrown from the window and abandoned before the slightest logic and pattern could be imposed. Beyond them, the River Crane seemed blurry and a more uniform sepia than usual, most likely due to her hangover and the dampness that sprung to her eyes.

Outside, there had been rain.

The chatelaine waited for Octavia to return. Her bedchambers felt colder than usual. Because she had not yet ordered it cleaned, the air was still rank with scents: stale wine gone acrid from half-full cups left in the corners of the room and on the few available surfaces; bodily fluids from countless bodies, passing through, essences of which rose above the heaped bedclothes and the strange, scattered devices like spirits of her lost evenings; decaying crusts of food, desiccated and rotting on plates forgotten under the bed. She felt quite ill. Buried like this, in her own city, as most of the palace was—quite literally—allowed the standard brew of city smells to infiltrate from outside, and at times penetrate her room, but the chatelaine had added her own contributions to the mix from within. These combinations nauseated her now.

Most pungent of all was the smell of fright, from her menagerie.

Her poor, poor pets, traumatized by the intruder during the night. Now they were tired from their displays of fear and merely quivered, silently.

What was left of her menagerie, anyhow.

The chatelaine knew she was a leader wont to excesses and, as such, existed in a world filled with the residues of her indulgences. She lived with this knowledge every day. Could the kholic help her change? She imagined scenarios of the two of them together, sharing absurdly mundane domesticities.

Rustles from a rat or other vermin caused the chatelaine to turn from the hazy cityscape: a beast ran across the reeds that carpeted the central part of her timber floor. Not a rat. A faster creature, on two legs. Reddish. Long tail. A jinn, perhaps? Too fast for her to be sure. Some new, unclassified beast, escaped from the dungeon, or even created up there?

The creature vanished behind a curtain.

She sighed.

Just like she had told the pretty kholic, the chamber's big fires were nearly out. The fireplace itself, which was as tall as a person and two such lengths in width, held but a few sad, smoldering logs. No wonder the pervasive chill. During the previous evening—flushed, eager, much too drunk—she had dismissed her servants, including the fire-tenders. (To their great relief, no doubt.) Though this was a usual call, it was also a stupid one; often these fires expired; often her chambers became cold. All the stone, she imagined. But did it seem strange that, beyond, the city sweltered? Perhaps it was she who radiated this chill?

Regardless, she was a bad mother.

When Octavia returned, she would tell the girl how she felt.

And then visit her father.

Turn over a new leaf.

Be forgiven.

She put her fingers together, raised them to her lips.

Surprising, sometimes, that servants ever returned. Then again, what choice did they have? They surely must be afraid of what they might see.

The chatelaine nearly smiled.

A void had been left when the cherub was abducted. Out in the city, there would be suffering: the void must be filled.

Even from where she stood she saw, in the large mirror against the far wall, the reflection of the gallery of cages, and—near the centre—the empty one, the glaring space.

Her missing cherub represented the Main Gate—the bridge leading into Nowy Solum, and South Gate, spanning it, welcoming or threatening all those leaving or visiting the city. From her window, the chatelaine could not see these parts, but she had an awful feeling just then, a crawling on her skin, and she wondered if someone or something unpleasant might be arriving just now—or would arrive shortly—through the unprotected gates.

"We came over the sand for two days. We left our home 'cause my boy was not right in the head but then a light come down and touched him, changed him, put ideas in him. Only he don't know what they mean and he needs someone to unlock 'em. Or explain 'em. See? A light come down from the sky and we needed to leave home."

Path's father had paused to take a sip of murky water. Then he choked for a while. In the lantern light, his skin appeared pale. His hands shook. Path was perched on the table, in his sling. Because of his position, he could not see much of this hovel, nor of their host— just a wall of dry reeds.

"A finger of light touched him?"

"Yes." His father wiped at his chin. "That's what I said. Didn't see it happen, though. He was outside, in the garden. Watching for lizards. He would scare lizards away. That's what he did." Another pause. Father glanced at son, who stared back, unblinking. "There's not many people where we live. After this here light hit him, he was a new boy. Smarter. Not like the boy we tried to raise. I didn't believe him at first. But he was different."

"You do now?"

"What's that?"

"You believe him now?"

"He talks in his sleep. Says things no one could understand. Words no one knows. He's changing every day. He speaks in a voice I don't know. He talks about places I don't know. But I guess that ain't saying much. We're stopping in almost every home, to see if the right words will come, but he's said nothing so far."

"Any women travelling with you?"

"Women? I don't see why . . . My wife, you see, she got ill a long time ago."

The stranger chuckled wetly.

"Stop talking," path said. "He's making fun of you. I'm not getting anything here. This is not the place. So just stop talking."

His father, who looked as if he had run out of oxygen, acquiesced.

Then the man who owned this property, and who had reluctantly given them water, said, "Your boy's right about one thing. You talk too much." He spat on the floor of his own home, which was not dirt, like the floor in path's home had been, but a sheet of real tin. "You talk and talk."

Path craned his neck again to try see the stranger. Fragments of the vision had begun to flicker once more in the perimeters of his mind but no directions or clarifications were presented. He saw a girl, alone, and then crowds of vague people. He saw a vast, cold void where surely nothing could live. What had his father been saying? Did he truly talk in his sleep? Everything seemed like a dream now—

Abruptly the homeowner's face loomed. He was grinning. He had a hole where his nose should have been and only one eye. He said, "You don't look very capable. If you're heading into Nowy Solum, I give you a day, at best. Now get your dad to hold your cup up, drink yer water, and get on out of here."

Path said, "We were thirsty."

"Show yer gratitude, boy." A knife appeared in the man's hand. "You're done here."

Path's father swiftly hoisted path. "We'll be going," he said. "Thanks for the water."

Later, at another house, a large and ugly woman told them her husband was out back, and that he would eviscerate the pair of them if they did not get off the property. From the wedge of gloom behind the woman's huge body, a child watched with saucer eyes.

The door was slammed in their faces.

All these people regarded path and his father with overt hostility. A few asked gruffly where they were from; most shoved weapons at them. They should get lost, never darken these doorways again.

"There's something wrong," path said, after yet another rebuke. "There's something wrong out here . . ."

The dirty road they followed was fully defined now, and packed, the surface marked by the passage of both wheels and feet. They had passed several groups of people, heading the other way, into the badlands, and other groups had passed them, heading at a quicker pace, toward the city, which was still hidden from their view but palpable, a presence in the vicinity. None of these people had wanted to speak either, and path received no more of his visions.

Clouds overhead were the full amber of day. Path squinted. Heat grew but was not yet unbearable. Craning, as he had all morning, to look into the distance, where the road dwindled into haze and shimmering illusions looked like water, he finally became convinced that he could discern shadows and hints of spires, the minarets and fabulous structures that the salesman had once described. Fading in and out, the details did not become clear.

Yet more groups of pedestrians approached, driving animals ahead of them: sheep; a bird, flying at the end of a thin chain; a dog, erect on two legs, squinting with suspicion at path before curling one black lip. There were dirty families and wary men, travelling alone. Most, if they saw path, head bobbing above the fabric ridge of the sling, looked away. His father stumbled and bumped path hard against his sternum. Here, vendors had set up haphazard stalls, either side of them, selling sundry and sparse items. A whiff riding the breeze was suddenly rank and exciting.

And then Nowy Solum appeared from the mists, undeniable, unavoidable.

They stopped, awed.

The sheer size of the apparition had helped obscure it. Stretching across the horizon—defined by the sheer cliffs of its surrounding wall—the city dwarfed them, dwarfed the road, these homes. Ahead, a sluggish river merged with the road to enter the enormous main gates, bridged by a stone arch. Path heard his father gasp for breath, felt his father's heart pound.

There was a singing in path's mind, and far away voices. Before a nearby stall, in which a bearded man presided, small crowds had gathered. "There," path said, mouth gone dry. He saw flashes of white from the counter of the stall, and these flashes seemed to be trying to relay information to him. "Go over there."

Path's father stood, swaying.

"To that vendor."

As they neared, path saw that smooth, pale forms had been arrayed, like alien patterns, symbols on this parched road made from another time or from materials so rare that no pedestrians or itinerants should ever be allowed to stand there, gawking at them.

"Push through," he choked. "Closer . . ."

His throat was closing. He gasped and quivered. At that moment, how path wished he had arms, fingers. He needed to touch these items, to rub against them. He would have licked the pristine objects, placed them in his mouth, received sensations from them, for there was a connection here: they were messages, chunks of a puzzle, keys to his new identity.

"Put them near me," he told his father. "Rub them on me."

But as the scrawny hand of his father touched one of the pale forms, the seller, who had been discussing price with a strikingly beautiful woman accompanied by two fat, well-armed eunuchs, spun and grabbed path's father firmly by his elbow.

"Watch out, mano. They're seventeen small coins each." The voice was grated, rough, his face hard. Bearded, glassy-eyed, the seller glared. His long, tangled hair hung in clumps. "And they're *genuine*. So don't touch them."

"Genuine what?" path asked. "What are they?"

Now the man looked down. He had obviously not known path was in the sling. He stared for a long moment. Path stared back. Others in the crowd were also watching. Someone whispered. The beautiful lady made a sign with her fingers, holding them at her chest, and backed away. Her eunuchs blocked.

"Let me touch them," path demanded.

"Why would I do that?" The seller wiped his mouth with the back of one hand. He spread his other hand on the counter and glared. There was something wrong with his eyes. After a long while, he looked up at path's father. "What you got there, anyhow? What is this thing you lug into the city?"

"My boy."

"*Boy*? Is he for sale?"

"I'm not," said path.

The man grinned. "Know what these are? I'll tell you. What you have in your palsied hands are parts of a celestial body." He raised his voice, addressing anyone who would listen. "That's right, folks. Genuine parts, from above the clouds. Come and see! Step up, step up!"

Despite his loud barking, no new customers approached. The seller scowled and presently turned back to path's father. "Know what I'm saying, old man? These fell from the sky, a few days ago. I'm not one who says gods are coming back, like some do, but something is happening up there. You heard about the sighting over the River Crane? There was a fight. Pieces rained down. What you hold is a tooth or part of a polymer bone. You got any small coin?"

"No. I don't even know . . ."

"Let me touch it," pleaded path.

"There was great thunder," said the man. "They clashed, and a streak come in from the west. But they're all mine. I have a license to sell them, signed by the chatelaine herself, so unless you got the money to buy them . . ."

"My boy wants to touch them. That's all."

"Shit," said the man. "That'll cost you. Where you two from?"

"Please," said path, "let me touch one . . ."

"What's in it for me?"

"We'll leave and not scare away any more customers."

The man laughed at this. He nodded. "All right, then," he said, and he quickly grabbed one of the artifacts, pushing it against path's neck, though he did step back and drop it when path began to thrash violently in the sling.

Path's father shouted. But the shout was faint, far away, much too late to accomplish any purpose:

Taken by train to the lottery headquarters, she saw the ocean for the first time, grey out the window. Sheets of rain streaked the glass. At the horizon, it appeared as if the water ended abruptly, falling over an impossible cliff.

When she arrived at the building, and was admitted, she discovered that a total of four girls had won. Like her, they were eight years old, and from hospices. They waited without speaking, in large plastic chairs, sitting as far apart from each other as possible in the large room.

An intern came, spoke to each briefly, and led them away, one by one. She was last. She never saw the other girls again.

Later still, sitting with an administrator, she signed reams of contracts and releases, marking them with her thumbprint after they had been read and briefly explained to her. The doctor, sitting with them, smiled and nodded, indicating the plate each time: she should touch it and move to the next document.

There were tests. She was prodded and scraped and attached to all manners of machine.

Did she understand the program?

Yes.

Was she aware that her current housing would cease to exist?

She blinked and looked up to meet the gaze of the administrator. The administrator had blue eyes and seemed tired. She wore a pink lab coat.

You mean my body?

Yes. Your body.

I understand then. It's okay with me.

The administrator leaned back and glanced at the doctor.

You are a brave girl. You will be assigned to a long spacer. A crew of fourteen hundred symbiotes. It's an important job.

A long spacer was one of the biggest ships. She felt her eyebrows go up, impressed, flattered.

There will be twelve associate crafts, grown in twelve gestating tanks. Do you know what this means?

I will be a mother.

That's right. You will be a mother. You will have a brood.

Finally, in a white, steam-filled chamber, she was instructed to undress. A tub of milky liquid gently roiled, inviting. Music played a soothing tune.

She took off her clothes. On the ceiling was a large mirror. She did not like to see her own gangly body or even her own blotched face. She was not a brave girl. The administrator and the doctor were wrong. She was not brave at all.

The liquid in the tub was room temperature. She was able to float. Her skin tingled. Presently, though, she fell asleep, and was pulled under.

"Three things elevate our life from the shit we clean up. One is the struggle, and not just with fists and teeth, like an animal—though that has its place—but against things you can't hit. Like what we just did. Against this." A movement of his hand, rotating on his wrist to indicate, perhaps, the city and everyone who lived in it. "Number two is getting high. Ale and bud." Nahid raised his glass and nearly peered directly at Name of the Sun through the cloudy beer within. "Number three is fucking. Coming. Because there is truth in fucking."

"That's very enlightening. Reassures me a great deal about our future." Name of the Sun had folded her arms long ago. "But I don't see all kholics fighting. Only you."

Nahid took a long, slow mouthful. The reaction from the hemo was not what he had wanted. Even his own words, to his own ears, had not come out as he'd planned. He had meant his list to have an ironic edge but knew there was vitriol in his voice. He certainly did not believe that the entire sources of potential fulfillment—even for those such as himself, with the blackest of melancholy in his heart, and tattoos over his face—were limited to the three acts he had mentioned.

He put the glass down. He was tired.

Did he want to provoke Name of the Sun? He considered this possibility and decided that he did. But what was the point? She was already angry and could only get angrier . . .

Well, the point was that Name of the Sun—maybe even since the second she first touched the cherub, back in the chatelaine's bedchamber—no longer wanted to be with him.

Her glare radiated, like heat. He did not react well in such situations. She claimed to know what his problems were? She claimed to know what the problems of all kholics were. It seemed to Nahid sometimes that Name of the Sun claimed to know what everyone's problems were, kholic or not. How could she possibly understand what his life was like?

He drank deeply. Beer ran down his stubbled chin.

Fuck her for these doubts. Fuck all of them.

His own solution, for now, was to get messed up.

Holding warm, cloudy ale in his mouth, Nahid looked away from the table, at other people in Hangman's Alley, where they had stopped for a drink. During the night, by crawling into Jesthe and successfully liberating the chatelaine's cherub, he and Name of the Sun had contributed to the first of his three criteria. And, by draining four pints and swallowing a bud (when Name of the Sun had gotten up, to walk down to the nearest outhouses, at the end of Sandripper Row), he was well on his way to achieving his second. Unfortunately, Nahid knew for certain that he was moving swiftly away from the last item on his list. Which was too bad: in his buzzed and tired state, Name of the Sun looked incredible. He had imagined—if they pulled off the cherub plan—that they would go back to her room for a victory fuck, a celebratory tryst, but she was so remote to him now, so cold. He could virtually see the wall that had descended, altering her face, hardening it like crystal. At times, over the past fortnight, he had learned to feel sorry for people exposed to this disdain: he knew the withering they must have felt inside. Now, for the first time, he felt the sensation himself. He wanted to kiss her on the mouth, to get up and walk away, to lie with her and sleep for ages, pressed up against her. He wanted to throw his beer down and smash his glass.

Hard to imagine (he remembered to swallow the beer) the acts they had done together, even as recently as yesterday, or follow in his mind the trail of mundane events that could lead to such explosive and decadent abandon. He tried to avoid memories of specific details but a barrage of raunchy images made him grimace.

(He recalled, for a moment, the chatelaine's drunken romp, the procession of positions, the shouted commands. Did his own couplings look as absurd?)

He tried to regulate his breathing.

What was Octavia doing in the palace anyhow? Sleeping with the chatelaine? Living the high life? She had not been among those deviants in the bedchambers last night—

In the flow of Nahid's veins, mixed with traces of adrenaline, still waxing and waning, and the thick pitch of his humours, the bud raged full force. He had almost reached the point of no return. Images stuttered in the periphery of his mind. His hands left traces of motion. He heard the tide of melancholy in his veins. He ground his teeth together and tried to stay in control. The drug was trying to convince him that he didn't need anyone, ever, not even his damned sister.

When he attempted to speak, his tongue did not cooperate. He tingled all over. He shook his hands loosely. Movements left shadows that continued to dart about when he looked away.

Name of the Sun was a glaring statue with a face of uniform tones. "All right, Nahid," she said. "What the fuck. You're just going to sit there in a trance" —with perfect fingers she pushed to one side the greasy leaf that had wrapped her food—"I'm going home."

Remnants of meat crawled with tiny insects. Nahid tried very hard not to be afraid but this took considerable effort. Name of the Sun's half-pint glass (with which they had initially used to toast) stood full. His own empty glass, along with several other empties, were stoic monuments. But to what? The future? For Nahid, it was impossible to conjure his future self, waking up in alleys, alone, going by himself to the ostracon, averting his eyes from every hemo he saw, cleaning up their shit.

He curled his lip. Why did he get involved with this girl? Smart, unmarked. Sanctimonious. He should have remained celibate or found a nice kholic. With his teeth exposed in a grimace and his heart skipping beats, he wondered if he would continue to get even higher or if this bud would start to level off soon. Terrified, he leaned back in his chair.

Hangman's Alley thronged. The activity seemed to suddenly snap into place, vibrant and vital and loud. Vendors stood at booths, either side, trying to draw the attention of potential customers. No one paid much notice to the couple—the kholic and the hemo—sitting there, tiny among the looming structures, wreathed in grey fog. Mostly a forgiving place, backing onto the ostracon, Hangman's Alley was a refuge not only for melancholics but for outcasts and criminals and deviants of all sorts. Local barkers had interest in getting passers-by to stop, purchase their cakes or cheeses or useless trinkets, and passers-by wanted to continue on, anonymous.

Beyond a nearby wall, someone began to kill a goat; the scream of the animal rose above the din of the city and Nahid smelled fresh blood spilling. He also smelled shit that the animal released upon death. He breathed his lungs full. "I'm thinking about last night. I'm thinking about the chatelaine's face when she woke up." Bands of steel winched tight in his lungs. "No one cares any more. The chatelaine is a disaster. The whole city is. You saw her, flailing away?

How could we just walk in like that? To the chatelaine's chambers. With no one stopping us."

"What are you talking about? Would you rather go back to a time when I would get lashed for sitting here with you? Anywhere in Nowy Solum, let alone a place like this. And if they knew we had slept together? I'd be kicked out of the city. Or maybe drowned in the Crane. You would be dismembered."

His fists clenched under the table. "You know, I've fucked other hemos before. You're not the first."

There was a moment of terrible silence.

"You're such an ass," she said. "I don't care about any of that shit. For fuck's sake, Nahid, tell me what we did, exactly? What did we accomplish? I'm tired. I'm going home."

"You said that already."

"Why are you being like this? What's your problem?"

"Me? It was you all excited about the idea of going into Jesthe. You approached me in the first place! Don't tell me you weren't excited to go into the palace."

"It was juvenile. I don't know how you convinced me to go along with that. And anyhow, *we* went in there? Me *and* you? That's not how I remember it."

Then he understood. She thought he was a coward. He bridled. "I couldn't go into that room. You know that."

"Why not?"

"There are limits."

"Can't you even look me in the eye?'

He did, for a full second, but her request made him furious. "You don't know anything about me. About any kholic. We're not just tattooed versions of you. We can't do the same things and we don't fucking want to! We're not the same."

Name of the Sun sneered and managed to look both gorgeous and utterly out of reach at the same time. Her hair, messy and heavy with oils, hung before her face.

"You know," he continued, "there's always girls hanging around the ostracon, with lame pretenses, looking for a forbidden kholic to fuck. To make their dads mad. And red-blooded men raised to not even notice kholic girls, lurking outside to offer them money. Or just take what they want for free. You know it happens all the time."

"You're drunk."

"Like your idiotic roommates." He could not stop now, though he knew he should; words spilled out. "They're titillated by me, not because they like me, but because of what I am." He touched his own cheeks, the inked skin. "You too. You march me around like a prize."

"*What*?"

"You like what I am, what I stand for. A conquest, an experience."

Name of the Sun's eyes flashed rage at him. They both knew the truth in this statement, and they both knew that saying it out loud meant Name of the Sun really did have to get up now, and that they could never again have a shot at sharing what they had briefly tried to share.

During this argument, the owner of the tiny stall where the couple were sitting, Hakim, who had left his cooking fires to clean adjacent tables, moved nearer and nearer, trying to mind his own business but also, by his proximity, trying to remind Nahid and Name of the Sun to keep their discussion hushed. At the advance of his big hands, offended flies rose from remains on the big, curled leaves he served his food in. Nahid nearly looked straight at Hakim. He wanted to tell the man to stay out of it, but that would be adding insult upon injury: the stall was one of only two in Hangman's Alley that served kholics, and it was the only stall in all of Nowy Solum that served kholics sitting with hemos. Despite relenting (or collapsing) mores, Hakim's business was slow, vandalism frequent, and harassment concerning municipal codes or any other violation that the palatinate might be able to lift from the books relatively routine.

A large man, gruff and loud, with a huge stomach and scars either cheek, Hakim was not tattooed, though no one had seen him smile. First impressions were invariably that Hakim was mean, possibly a killer; the man had several grown children and numerous grandchildren, who clambered all over him when they came by, as if he were a rock. Patrons knew him as the source of sage advice. Sometimes Hakim let patrons eat for free if he saw they were skint and hungry or desperate enough. Nahid—who had been coming to Hakim's with Octavia regularly, whenever they had any small coins, since they were old enough to leave the ostracon and work the streets—knew, even in his current state, that it would be foolish to lose a friend like him.

Instead, he motioned for another pint.

"If you drink one more beer," said Name of the Sun, "I will truly leave."

Between two structures just then, coming into Hangman's Alley from across the way, a chanting song arose, getting louder: all three looked. Nahid, whose veins were positively singing with the combination of drugs and anger now, felt a small sense of relief at the distraction.

A group emerged from behind a stall on the opposite side of the Alley, all of them men, bare-chested. Crowds in the market parted to let the procession through. There were perhaps five, leading two cognosci in collars and muzzles. The shaggy beasts looked dazed, and over the muzzle of each was inked a parody of Nahid's tattoo. Blood—hemo blood—trickled from numerous wounds on the stocky torsos of the creatures while, behind them, coming up the rear, a tall, narrow-faced man bearing a whip—who was leading the chanting—lashed out.

Hakim was there to place a heavy hand on Nahid's shoulder, keeping him seated.

"What is this shit?"

"They circle Hangman's and the ostracon each day. You've been busy. They're confronting kholics that get in the way."

"Confronting?"

"Don't do anything. I'm warning you. This guy with the whip, he claims to be cleansing the city, so gods can return."

"The gods?" Nahid spat. "Gods have nothing to do with me. What does he want with kholics?"

"He wants them to leave Nowy Solum. Or die."

Nahid stared the group down, forcing himself to look directly at the man who led the chanting, draining his glass as they went by. He slammed his empty on the table. The man with the whip paused directly in front of Hakim's stand and their eyes met. There was a quick jolt that passed through Nahid, almost physical. A hush fell over Hangman's Alley. Nahid tried to stand but Hakim's hand remained on his shoulder. The man facing him was thin but banded with hard muscles. His face seemed equally hard. His head was shaved and his cheeks smeared with streaks of red. Nahid held his gaze.

Others in the crowd, seeing this boldness, this transgression, and recognizing the potential confrontation, began to clear away.

Hakim shook Nahid, hissing as the man with the whip slowly raised his free hand and pointed a long finger. Then he brought his hand up and moved his finger across his own throat. Between the two, the marked cognosci danced nervously from paw to paw.

"You fool, Nahid," Hakim hissed. The stall owner's hands were huge and powerful; Nahid could not break free. "You're lost in your own world. You have no idea how the city has changed."

Nahid's palms had gone cold. Had changes happened to Nowy Solum because of his actions? Would he never look at Name of the Sun's face again? His gaze began to burn with tears.

Was he truly a coward?

Across the Alley, another kholic—a young boy with long hair and a broad, dark tattoo— cleaned the gutter. Nahid felt as though he had betrayed this boy, and all the others working the streets.

Then he found himself wondering how another full glass had arrived so fast. And, when he turned to Name of the Sun, to share with her a new theory about why the time was so right for the actions they had taken, and why he had to stay behind the curtain, she was no longer sitting at the table.

Nahid was stunned. How long had she been gone? He drank half his pint in big gulps. He was not a coward. He was not. And he would prove it. He would return to Jesthe right now, alone, to enter the cavernous chambers, to walk the hallways of Nowy Solum's rundown palace.

The chatelaine pulled open both doors as soon as the girl knocked. She had even tidied the room herself, perfunctorily, putting away her devices at least, and telling herself as she did so that she would not retrieve them again for some time.

On the threshold, Octavia looked small and even more lovely than earlier.

"How was your visit?"

"I did what you asked." The girl's blue eyes, collarbone level with the chatelaine, seemed out of focus, swimming in the tattoo, as if she were trying to conjure some remote memory. "How long has she been down there? The fecund?" Her eyes flickered up, and away. "She said strange things to me."

The chatelaine laughed. She touched the girl. "Oh yes, you get used to her. She says all kinds of things. She's never the same twice. Sometimes she knows the future and other times she's afraid of her own shadow. She talks about aggression but I know for a fact she can do no harm. She's not like us, Octavia. Now, did she ask about me?"

"In a fashion."

Again the chatelaine laughed. She felt *so* much better. This girl was a veritable *tonic*. "Won't you come in? The room's still a bit of a mess but please, come in, sit down. I've lemonade ready. Do you like lemonade?"

Octavia let herself be steered into the bedchambers. She sat on the end of the bed, where the chatelaine patted, and took the cool glass of lemonade. She held the glass between her knees, in both hands, but did not drink. She looked down at the straw matting on the floor.

"Well, did the fecund like you? Was she surprised to see you? Did you talk for a while?"

Octavia looked up warily but stopped short, as always, from looking the chatelaine in the eye. "I think she, uh, I think she liked me. Like you said she would."

The chatelaine clapped and released from her lips a strange exclamation that neither acknowledged. "Who wouldn't like you? My goodness. Tell me, what did she say? Or you can tell me later, if you'd like. Look, I'll show you my pets. Would you like that? Drink up."

"If it's all right with you, I'd rather just sit here for a while."

The chatelaine hoped that neither her disappointment nor her nervousness was obvious. "All right, then," she said. "All right. Another time. I know how tiring it is, going down there. Positively draining." She bit at her thumbnail. "But are you okay? Did she upset you? I should have told you that she likes to say, at times, outrageous things. She can mess with your head. You know she won't hurt a fly? Well, maybe a fly. But that's about it."

"I just need to rest for a while."

The chatelaine moved closer to the girl. She thought about kissing Octavia, maybe pushing her back, gently, onto the bed.

But then the lemonade would spill.

As if sensing the growing energy, most likely trying to postpone the chatelaine's advances, the kholic said, "I guess you could show me your pets, if you'd like."

Relieved at having a goal—back on track—the chatelaine gestured for Octavia to stand. When the girl did so, they walked together to the alcove, the chatelaine's hand propelling Octavia from the small of her delightful back. Reflected in the huge mirror that covered the entire wall, the creatures, and indeed the women's own reflections as they approached, were distorted by flaws.

Watching their mistress, watching the stranger—those with eyes, at least—the pets began to get excited. The chatelaine frowned, thinking for a second that they might have recognized the kholic.

In front of each cage, the chatelaine gave a short introduction to the beasts within, which peered out or drooled or huddled away in fear. They were formless monsters. They hissed and burbled and chirped. Those she could reach, and which were benign, the chatelaine touched, rubbing their skin or scales through the bars with a crooked knuckle.

"This one represents Soaper's and Candles, and the Horse Market.

"For Torchmere Lane, and the homes of North End, on the hill.

"This one is for Hangman's Alley, and your ostracon."

A beast uglier than the rest.

Octavia stared, unblinking.

"Child," said the chatelaine, after a while, sidling closer, "Nowy Solum was not always the way it is today. Even during my father's brief time as castellan, the city was different; it changes, subtly, with each leader. Chaos in the city, if there is chaos in Jesthe." The chatelaine frowned at the intent expression on the kholic's face. Was she even listening? Her pets seemed to be entranced by the girl. The chatelaine shivered. "The fecund," she said quietly. "Do you understand? The monster takes what we give her and gives us back in return. She can change Nowy Solum. The colbali, for instance, when my father was down here. They appeared then. Me? Oh, I don't know. My babies, and maybe even you, coming here!"

Octavia glanced at the chatelaine and then continued to the end of the alcove, where three paintings were hung in a vertical pattern, each illuminated by a torch, either side of the ornate frames. Then Octavia asked about the large iron key, hanging on two hooks above the wainscoting.

"That is the key to my heart," joked the chatelaine.

The girl took a sip of her lemonade and put the glass down on a small ledge upon which the chatelaine usually kept water jugs to quench her pets' thirst. She glanced at the floor for a moment but when she looked back up, her eyes met the chatelaine's and burned with an intensity that made the chatelaine look away this time, breath catching in her throat.

"My— my father, painted these pictures, and he is also somewhat of— of a physicker, a splicer. I'm sure you know he's up there, in the dungeon?" She pointed self-consciously to the wooden ceiling. "Self-imposed isolation. He's afraid of ailments, you see, among other things. He once explained to me about the four humours, the biles. And the elements of fire, and water. Air, of course." She had almost told the girl, right then, that the castellan often accused his own daughter of having traces of melancholy in her blood, so prone was she to gloomy moods, but the chatelaine managed, at least, to not blurt this out. At a loss for further words, however, she stood awkwardly, regarding her pets, feeling like she had already said too much. The empty cage taunted her. Something had just happened here, in the alcove. Something had shifted between her and the kholic. Then, as soon as she accepted once more that she really didn't understand Octavia at all, the girl leaned forward and kissed the chatelaine on the lips. When the chatelaine opened her mouth, their tongues twined. She pulled the girl closer, ran her hands down Octavia's back to her buttocks, where they stopped. The chatelaine was already wet. She tried to lift Octavia's shift off, but the girl, breaking away, did it herself. As the garment rose, exposing the stunning body, the chatelaine's breath was finally stolen.

She raised shaking hands, worshipping.

Her pets again went mad.

THE FECUND'S MELANCHOLY DAUGHTER

Ambassadors buzzed Pan Renik, lashing whenever they could at his exposed face and hands with their wire tails. Unable to defend himself (and knowing enough in his state of delirium not to even make an effort), the exile lay on his side, in his nest, moaning as he struggled to hold onto his rather limited senses. When he opened an eye, just a crack, wire tails caught at his skin and made him whimper.

One ambassador hovered a few centimetres before his face. Wings a blur of silver, it was there every time he looked, as if studying him, or maybe waiting. He peeked: still there. The tails beat at him. Never before had Pan Renik seen a single ambassador this close—usually only hordes of the messengers going about their business on high, or giving padres instructions from the sky.

Sap trickled his forehead.

If he had not known better, Pan Renik would have been certain that the ambassador was made of metal, for it shimmered, and reflected his marred face. But padres told the people that Anu and his countless minions were composed of *polymers*. Bio-engineered polymers that even—

Look what have you done.

For a second, Pan Renik thought the voice might be his own conscience; his conscience had spoken to him in the past, in various voices and from several sources, internal and external. But this voice was somehow different.

Do you have any idea what you've done? Everything was calibrated: her crash, her wounds. She was meant to remain alive.

The ambassador, he realized, addressed him: this voice was no conscience. But ambassadors only spoke to padres—and to Anu, of course. Yet what other explanation could there be?

Humbled, Pan Renik accepted the pain and asked, "What did I do? Why are you here?"

Small fissures and cracks in the little round face, but no mouth, no feature at all that could be considered a mouth. Several wings on the back end. Sharp, dangling legs. The size of his fist.

The ambassador did not respond.

Pan Renik struggled, without much success, to sit up.

Perhaps a dozen of Anu's emissaries had gathered in the air about him, including the one facing him, the one that seemed to be communicating. Others worked on his limbs, slashing at them. His arms and legs were covered in growing welts. His face burned.

When the ambassador spoke again, it radiated a mild heat. This heat was, in its own way, like another wire, twisting in Pan Renik's brain:

Anu is interested.

Each syllable stung as the ambassadors circled around, no doubt to get better shots, to strike at his forearms, his forehead, the bottoms of his poor feet.

He tried not to flinch. "Interested in me?"

Yes.

"How can that be? I'm the exile."

She came up from the clouds.

"What?"

The one you attacked. She came up from under the clouds.

"That would be a miracle."

Yes. A miracle. Exactly. A miracle, until you killed her. Now Anu is coming. He is far away, but he is coming here.

"Anu? For me?" Pan Renik saw now that the woman's body was there still, in his nest. He touched the corpse with his toes. The metal also remained. He could not imagine how he could have been left alone with these treasures, or why.

Now the power was going to visit.

Nor could he imagine a way out of this situation.

Though Pan Renik knew he had not been unconscious for long, daylight had grown stronger since he had cracked open the woman's skull. Black sap marred her face. Her mask was broken. In this early sunlight, all metal tubes and the remains of her flying device glittered more than they had before, when he had first laid eyes on them. He reached out toward one of the rods but instead, trembling, his grubby fingers came to rest on his mace, still sticky with the woman's fluids.

Circling ambassadors renewed whipping his exposed skin.

You need to tell us what she told you. We saw her speak to you. Anu needs to know.

Those wire tails inflamed the skin on the back of his hands, on his face and neck. "She said nothing. So leave me alone. I mean, did she do this to me? Or did you? How did I get like this?" He wiped sap from his face with one hand, then looked beyond the ambassadors, toward the horizon, where it was already full day.

Idiot! She tried to defend herself. What do you think? Her suit gave off a jolt when you bludgeoned her.

A pause just then. Silence. The wire tails froze in mid-lash so that only the very low buzz of the ambassador's wings could be heard. Pan Renik's wounds during this interim stung with renewed throbs of this intense pain. Could he fight the tiny emissaries of Anu? Polymer, the padres said, was tough. And there were so many! If he did fight, would that assure his own death? Either way, he could not take a renewed round of lashes.

We would like to inform you, the ambassador said, *Anu approaches the vicinity now. Prepare yourself. You'll be interviewed, and recycled.*

Refraining from defending himself had achieved nothing. He would be *recycled.*

Far below came faint shouts of the padres, rising from lower branches, as if they too had heard the proclamation. Had padres watched all the while? No doubt they had grown more and more concerned. Why were ambassadors of the sky, they must have wondered, talking to a citizen? To the *exile*, no less! And attacking him? What in the world had Pan Renik done? How had he messed up this time?

Managing to sit, then, smeared by his own sap, condemned to die,

Pan Renik suddenly smiled; ironically, he had found an inadvertent way to get revenge on the settlement, to spoil the lives of the padres. He felt a surge of energy, and he used this energy to stand.

Take it easy, said the ambassador.

So, Pan Renik thought. He would be *recycled*. Life was over. Everything was over. If not killed by Anu, then killed by padres. All for stupid pieces of metal.

He reviewed, briefly, his impulse to bash the women's head in and could see no good way the scenario might have ended. Perhaps he was an idiot. He had been called this many times, for sure. He looked at the corpse. All he had ever wanted was a chance to improve himself and to own shiny things. Were these the crimes of an idiot?

His eyes burned. His skin, stung over and over by lashes, seemed to scream. Snatching up his mace, Pan Renik tried desperately to formulate an additional step, one last step, or to see if one were possible, but the tails beat his face, his neck, his shoulders. "Leave me alone," he shouted. "Leave me alone, you lousy galls!"

He saw more ambassadors approach from above, through the red haze of sap on his face. Dozens of them, coming to get access to him, to contribute their bit to his punishment. Exile, condemnation, existence: all unfair!

As a tail caught Pan Renik across the cheek and he felt hot fluids burst on his face, his strength and anger and energy suddenly exploded: he spun the mace without further thought, knowing full well he could never hit an ambassador, for they were invincible messengers of a higher power, of the mighty Anu, but to his shock he heard the mace connect, heard the buzzing clip: the ambassador spun down, fizzling, crippled, to land on the twigs of his nest, near the woman's corpse, where it flopped about and emitted a high, keening wail.

Other ambassadors backed off a few metres, en masse.

Pan Renik stared at the crippled messenger for a second. Incredulous. Then he looked up, beyond the masses of hovering ambassadors, at the clear blue sky. There was no entity visible, no sign of Anu coming out of the sun to kill him.

Not yet, at least.

He smashed the broken ambassador again as it tried to lurch away. Sparks sprayed from a crack in its back. He hit the device one more time, a mighty two-handed wallop that smashed its carapace, and again, until the ambassador stopped twitching and lay in shattered fragments.

"Galls upon you," he panted. "Galls!" A spring popped up from the wreck: the trajectory took the spring over the side of his nest and down, beyond the clouds, out of sight.

Pan Renik's breath came in ragged gulps. He tightened his grip on the mace.

Then a distant rumbling, as if of thunder, emanated from the firmament, building slowly. Pan Renik only saw the calm blue expanse of the morning, stained along the east cloudline with brighter light.

But something was coming.

Faster than his eyes could follow, the ambassadors vanished.

All of them.

Something was coming—

Scrambling over to where the dead woman lay, Pan Renik madly searched the black outfit. There were strange seams, confounding him, a variety of studs, clasps, all foreign to his clumsy fingers. Several openings parted easily, others he tore, but he managed to completely strip the sap-covered corpse.

Naked, the woman seemed less alien. Smaller, somehow. He tried not to wonder what her laugh might have sounded like. He tried not to think about lying with her, like a padre, and how her body might have felt against his, if it were not cold and hardening.

The rumbling from heaven continued to build.

He saw, next to the woman—so black it looked like a hole in his nest—an object the size and shape of his forearm. He thought of starless nights. Hesitating, stooping, his fingers almost touched the object, but not quite, because a faint voice started to whisper in his mind.

But there were no living ambassadors around.

He grabbed the treasure, which must have rolled free of the outfit, grunting as his hand closed over a surface so smooth and cold against his skin he thought he'd been seared. When he lifted and cradled it, the whispering grew louder and louder, and he wanted to throw the thing away but literally could not. Voices reached a crescendo in his head, then just the sound of wind.

He pushed the object back inside the suit, then put his own limbs into the sleeves, under the straps. He fastened clasps he had previously undone. He pulled material tight over his body. Pan Renik had no way of knowing if he had put the bizarre costume on in the correct fashion but he could not wait, not for anything. Not anymore. Waiting was over.

Sounds from above made the thin branches quaver.

Metal rods that the woman had died for extended out either side of Pan Renik's body, trapping gusts of wind. Strung between the rods, the black blanket stretched, filling, pushing him forward. He looked like a glider. He looked like a gall-licking glider. He hooted and tried to make a rude gesture in the direction of the settlement but his movements were hampered. The rods were lighter than Pan Renik had expected. He braced himself on his haunches, shrugging, even dancing a bit, and discovered that he could unlock the frame; pressure from the wind suddenly decreased; he was able to fold his arms.

The broken mask, streaked with the dead woman's sap—and by drips of his own—covered Pan Renik's eyes, mouth, and nose.

And here they came! A mass of ambassadors, approaching directly from the sun. More than he had ever seen before: a thousand, ten thousand. Behind the myriads, some bigger shape shimmered into view. The intensity of light made him gasp. Around the form, sky broke up into scales of light that made it difficult to focus. He saw a large torso with a fiery tail, and an elongated head, eyes dim with blindness.

Ambassadors were leading the sky power to him.

Massive hands grasped the air, tentatively, spread out to soar—
Anu was coming.

THE FECUND'S MELANCHOLY DAUGHTER

The end of the world. The end of everything. Looking down at the distant settlement, Pan Renik spat (but the spittle caught the wind and smeared his own cheek), shrieking, "Rotten galls! Aphids! Tumours!"

Taking an awkward run at the corpse, keeping low—rocking from side to side—he used all his strength and what little momentum he had to roll the woman, moving her body toward the edge of his nest, pushing with his shoulder, straining with his legs. Garbed in the outfit, shifting the corpse was difficult and the woman's naked limbs were rigid and unyielding. Outflung arms crashed down against the twigs, impeding movement. Once, twice. But he flopped the body over. There were metal studs down her blue flesh and these flashed patterns of dull lights at him. Tattoos on her palms. Tattoos on the bottoms of her feet. Hairless legs, vagina, head. But he could not look at that face any more. Glassy eyes watched him. Black crust of sap, silver teeth, exposed in an ugly rictus.

The rods over his back clanged against each other. The blanket flapped taut against him.

Then the body tipped over the edge, catching for just a second on twigs before plummeting down, away, toward the clouds. He heard faint but rewarding screams of the padres, no doubt trying to protect themselves from the blasphemy falling at them from the sky.

Pan Renik stood on the precipice. Above, Anu, moving quicker now, guided by his phalanx of ambassadors, was about to take his life. Below lay endless, poisonous clouds. He held his arms out, fighting for balance, staring down as the winds roared, eager to pluck him away.

For just an instant Pan Renik lifted his face, one last time, eyes nearly closed, and let out a scream of defiance.

Then he launched himself over the edge of the world, arms held out like wings, like a glider, in hopes of soaring into the morning, leaving all this behind, but instead he plummeted, faster and faster, shrieking down, past the padres—who stood open mouthed in shock—entirely out of control, toward the clouds.

Afterwards, she lay on her bed and might have even dozed. The girl had quickly departed. The orgasm had not been as exceptional as she had hoped it might be, though it had not taken the kholic long to achieve. Truth be told, when sober, little effort was required to get the chatelaine off. Plus, Octavia could make almost anyone come by just standing there. Her body had been taut, pungent, lithe. Her skin was grimy. People in Nowy Solum that were able to look right through Octavia, as if she did not exist, must suffer from dementia.

The chatelaine rolled onto her side and looked in her mirror, upward, at an angle, so she could only see the wooden ceiling of her chambers. She wasn't ready yet to meet the gaze of her pets. There was always a tiny element of shame she harboured whenever they had witnessed her shouting and thrashing about during congress. Sometimes she wished that when she came she could retain more decorum. Be discrete. Absurd that she lost control like that. What did the girl possibly think? Octavia had been utterly silent throughout, even as the chatelaine went down on her. What did any of her lovers think during sex? The chatelaine knew that citizens talked about her, chuckled about her antics. Octavia had even paused at the worst possible moment, looking up from between the chatelaine's thighs, probably to see if the chatelaine was okay or not. Embarrassing.

Yet she smiled at the memory.

The chatelaine tried to gauge if fucking the girl had changed what she thought about the kholic. She did not feel *more* in love—if these emotions were indeed burgeoning love—but neither did she feel further distanced, as sometimes happened after the mystery of such attractions was, well, consummated. One thing for certain: her day had begun to look up.

Octavia did make several flattering, if deadpan, comments during their lovemaking.

And, of course, the girl had initiated the sex. That was a compliment the chatelaine would not soon forget.

She rose, arranging her clothes, checking herself in the mirror to ensure everything that was supposed to be covered stayed covered, and left her chambers.

The nearest access to one of the towers that supported the dungeon was across the Great Hall, in the corner of the room her ancestors once used for dining. Fires here had not been lit in years and the great table was furred with dust. Mice scurried as she entered, and a larger creature, unseen, thumped wetly to the floor to drag itself off. She had brought a lantern, but even shadows crept slowly away.

The chatelaine had climbed this spiral, the Northeast, countless times, since she was a little girl, but never once had she been able to count the actual number of steps. Even now, ascending, as an adult (albeit an adult in fairly bad condition and somewhat preoccupied with events of her day), the chatelaine tried to count them. Of course, she had the capacity to reach higher numbers than she had as a girl, but seldom did she pass three hundred with any confidence of accuracy, and this number was reached perhaps a third of the way up—still well below the level of the highest rooftops outside.

The stairs themselves were barely wide enough for her feet, and the torch the chatelaine carried illuminated only the nearest of the steps and the immediate curve of the adjacent wall. She was very careful to make sure her footing was secure on the damp and worn stone before moving upward; if she hurt herself here she might lay for hours, or tumble head over heels to her death. Servants seldom came up, the palatinate never. Not anymore. Thanks to her. Food for the castellan was delivered via a system of pulleys, through a long shaft from the kitchens. There was one old man, Tuerdian, who lived permanently in the dungeon with her father, in tiny chambers of his own, employed to tend to the castellan's fires, arrange his meals, and draw the old man's infrequent baths, but Tuerdian spent most of his time sleeping or sitting in his cot, hacking up his lungs. Thinking about the man now, the chatelaine realized she had not seen him in many moons. She would ask her father about the old servant's health, when and if she finally got to the top.

Moments later, glancing out one of the tiny apertures in the tower wall, the chatelaine sighed at the clutter outside. Perhaps, she thought, walls surrounding the entire city should come down, to let Nowy Solum spill forth. There had been times when the chatelaine had ordered the destruction of makeshift homes, which appeared— seemingly overnight—hastily built in such a way that access to one of these windows was compromised. Whenever she gave the orders, she felt bad, for a little while anyhow, and even considered offering the displaced families compensation—though she had not done anything of the sort so far. Shacks and hovels would completely smother both her and Jesthe, if she let them.

Resuming her tedious climb, around and around, the chatelaine moved above the last of the rooftops. Her mouth was gummy, her tongue sticking to her palette. The taste of the kholic was on her lips. At the highest window, the chatelaine paused. The parchment cover was torn, and it crumbled when she tried to move it aside, to get a better view. She was far above the city now. Only the other towers remained, and the mists. A small flock of brown lizards flew by. It was starting to rain again. She thought about her father, emptying his chamber pots onto the homes below. There were no pipes up here, and the castellan balked at the idea of having them put in; he claimed they would make him ill. Symbolism of her father's act was so obvious that the chatelaine, thinking about it now, smiled sadly.

A breeze murmured in low tones, as if mad. Nowy Solum extended, cluttered and dark, the rooftops muted tones of rust and brown. She saw the River Crane, and the parapets atop the perimeter wall, where it arched over South Gate.

As she began going up again, pigeons erupted from a hiding spot very near her, in a panic, preceding her and leaving behind a small storm of feathers and debris. She put a hand on her aching heart to calm it. On this day, it had seen such extremes.

When the storm had passed and waters were relatively calm, the women tried to repair the mast, which had snapped and trailed in the sea. All they had to work with was the clothes on their backs and the salvaged remains of the second flight suit. But stiff oceanic winds made short work of their splicing attempt; the frame of the suit, which they had used as a splint, bound against the shaft of the mast, quickly bent; the sail remained useless.

So now they sat, peeling and reddening and blistering, as the raft drifted, uncontrollable. Yet these issues seemed insignificant compared to dehydration and imminent starvation.

Shoulders touching, the women watched the horizon. Clouds sometimes reached out to smite the water, as if in battle, and occasionally the water leapt up to retaliate. Once there had been an island—small, inviting—but this too had drifted past. They had wept then, silently, for hours.

There were gulls, too, and the women had briefly seen the floor of the ocean through gorgeous water, long weeds brushing the surface.

They were astonished by faces on the fish that rose to watch with eyes like their own, looking back up at them.

They drifted close to the edge of this world. They heard the crash of the waters, falling into the abyss. When their crippled car had been shot down by the brood craft, and had plunged through the atmosphere and clouds, they had desperately sought a place to come down. Just enough time to register a desert, and a city—like a sudden scab—then the impossible cliff of water. Banking over the abyss, holding the car aloft for as long as possible (though the engines were smoking and debris broke away), they wheeled back over the ocean, to strike the water—

They ejected the raft, the suits.

All three had survived, with only cuts and scrapes.

The brood craft did not pursue below the clouds, which, they soon discovered, blocked all efforts to get any signal out.

Without a sail, or oars, the plunge was inevitable. An end to this ordeal was something to look forward to.

The third woman had vanished so long ago now that she must be dead, though it might have only been two days since she had left. Their co-worker, their friend. Their lover. She had taken a flight suit and a transmitter and gone up, to fly above the clouds, to send for help.

She never came back.

Any form of rescue seemed impossible now. Their associate had not made it. They would never hear her laugh again, or her foul mouth, cursing them as they played and drank and worked.

The two remaining women said nothing to each other. Peace would come soon. They would expire together. They watched lights moving above the clouds. From here, these lights seemed almost pretty.

Screaming, Pan Renik fell. There had been branches at first, then nothing but vapours. With no choice but to suck in the mists, he was shocked to discover he did not die right away. He imagined his inner works filled with poisons, damaged beyond all hope. Or maybe he was already dead, and the transition to death had been painless—

As the suit also gulped air, and flapped loudly, turning him about, the vista cleared, intermittently, affording moments of nothing but whistling wind and the sight of another bank of rapidly approaching clouds.

Once, a pack of startled gliders!

Then amber again.

Pan Renik grew tired of screaming and sucking in poison and wondering if he was dead. Wind burned his exposed skin and stung the welts the ambassadors had raised. Could he fall forever? Were the clouds of infinite thickness?

This was an oddly pleasant afterlife; he felt moments of surprising peace, such as he had never before known.

With his shoulders he clicked the rods over his back into rigidity, extending the blanket until it was taut: he was propelled forward. Clicking the rods once more enabled him to slow forward movement. Hunching his back, first one way, then the other—forcing his elbows to bend—caused wide, slow turns.

These clouds, poison or not, were wet, almost refreshing against his face. Pan Renik spread his arms as wide as they could go, closed his eyes, and let himself soar.

Spluttering awake, path sucked in fluids, filling his lungs. As he sank, dying, light came dwindling through the milky liquid. He did not want to drown. He did not—

"Son?"

His father was shaking him; he was not immersed in liquid.

Groggily, he said, "I am a mother . . ."

But, blinking away the dream, another vision faded, joining the first to lie mingling inside him.

They were stopped by the side of the road. His father peered down at him. Others, curious, gathered around. Path shuddered. His mouth was very dry and he felt sweat trickling his forehead.

"You all right? You was flopping about. Then you went all still."

"I'm okay," he said. "Let's go . . ."

The stall of artifacts was no longer at the roadside; either the business had relocated or, he thought, had never existed.

As they moved again, scents such as path had not before encountered, and residues of the vision, made him cough, feverish in the damp sling. His imagination flared with virulent but elusive images. As far as he could see, in both directions—even upward—extended the massive perimeter wall of Nowy Solum. The road they were on led over a stone bridge to huge, opened gates, through which he could now see the forms of structures. Above the top of the wall, several towers were visible, high enough to penetrate the clouds, where a stone room perched in the haze.

His stubs twitched. What would he find here?

Who he was becoming?

Path's father also seemed to be experiencing distress now; path felt tortured heat from the scrawny body pressed against him. Together they were a furnace.

He hissed encouragements from low in his sling as his father stumbled up the incline, toward the bridge. Here, vendors manned small grills, selling food, or blankets of products were spread out. Clearly, even to path—who had only ever been to that one wretched market before, where a handful of desert merchants had set up—the items available here were substandard: rotten things, half-eaten or broken.

He and his father had no money to purchase anything, no matter what the quality, and no things with which to trade. The only food they had was bread and a skin of water—which kept path's belly satisfied for now, as they walked the bridge—but then what? He would not beg in this place and he did not think people would donate food, no matter what stories he might eventually tell them.

During his life in the desert—certainly before enlightenment—he had never thought much about money, nor, he knew, had his parents ever possessed any; people where he came from bartered or traded, yet as path and his father passed through this aisle of desperate commerce, not having money, or a way to get money, was clearly an oversight in the hasty plan they had made to leave home. Path sensed how people with money could live inside the city, and he sensed the hunger for it in these people at the gates, who had none. Want of money was one of the scents this close to Nowy Solum, another stench in the air.

Along the stone wall of the bridge, families lived in primitive tents or slept directly on tarps right on the wooden slats. Beggars, kneeling, averted eyes. Path saw dirty children running with their siblings. Filthy, but intact. Children with the ability to be independent. He had never seen anything like this before. These were gangly, awkward creatures: loud, their motions swift and constant. He blinked, for his eyes had grown bleary. He had to turn away when he could no longer bear the sight.

Onward his father tottered, walking a gauntlet toward the gates.

Passing below was a wide, brown river. The smell of the slow water as his father looked over the edge made path gag; it seemed to be a current of waste, bleeding sludge from the city.

From shadows inside the gates, the definition of individual structures rose over heaps of tumbled masses; he saw chimneys, roofs, sagging walls.

And people in there, throngs of people.

Cresting the bridge, path and his father passed under the stone arch, between the great doors, and into Nowy Solum.

Red-robed guards eyed them as, buffeted, his father lurched to a stop in the broad terrace.

Path saw a creature he never could have imagined: two hands high, bluish, with eyes like a woman and a laugh, when it saw him gawking, that could have broken glass. Children, faces marked in black ink, dressed in rags, scrubbed at a gutter. Beyond them, a small group of hairy beasts lingered, shifting by the mouth of an alley—

"Go on," path said, trembling.

"But *where*?"

His father's heart pounded so hard that path moved rhythmically in his sling.

Streets led away crookedly between buildings, like arthritic fingers from the palm of an old man's hand. Behind them, the massive arch of dark stone, ornately carved with icons and gargoyles, loomed. Down each of these streets, crowded and noisy and terrifying, worlds of unknowable options.

As path's father hunched over, the fabric of the sling rode up and obscured path's view, so path shouted, "I can't see! What are you doing?"

His father lurched, one step, two, and then they were falling. Immediately, path spilled painfully from the sling, tumbling across the cobblestones like an offering to Nowy Solum. He banged his shoulders and head, tasted blood in his mouth. He was kicked twice before he came to a stop. Looking wildly around for his father, all he saw was a patch of clouds, a leaning wall, legs.

A child with a black mark on his face peered down at him quickly, did not meet his gaze, and moved away once more.

"Help me," he said. "Please . . ."

But the boy had gone.

Sure that he was bleeding, and that his bones were broken, path tried not to panic. What if this entire situation—the light, the visions, the knowledge that had changed him—had been a ruse to get him to this point, so he could lie, humiliated, injured on the streets of a foreign and hostile landscape?

People stepped past without so much as a glance. He might have been garbage, discarded there. He recalled what the salesman had said: one could die in the streets of the city and no one would take notice.

What had happened to his father?

A deep voice said, "Well, well, well, what we got here?"

Without a chance to react, path was roughly hoisted by a set of huge hands and stuffed into a rough and stinky sack.

THE FECUND'S MELANCHOLY DAUGHTER

Nahid fought, which—as he'd said to Name of the Sun—was number one on his list, and so seemed inevitable. The fight was brief but left him leaking melancholy from his nose, and somewhat sobered, for the fight had been with a hemo. Nahid was pushing his luck. Being with Name of the Sun for a fortnight had changed him. Or maybe watching his sister being led away by the chatelaine had changed him. Either way, he took too many chances, pretending to lead the life of someone whose fluids were not black and thick as treacle. He looked hemos in the eye. Now he had grappled with one.

Surging through the crowds, to get away from something he suspected he could never get away from, he wondered almost hysterically when the last time was that he had skimmed the Crane or cleaned gutters. He missed his old life like a throbbing, constant pain. He had been severed in two and was afraid he might never be whole again. He wanted to gather washed-up weeds and decaying garbage from rocks of the river. He wanted to pile offal at Hot Gate, and return to the crowded ostracon.

Neither kholic nor hemo, but a creature between; he no longer belonged in Nowy Solum.

To fight on a crowded street—with a red-blooded boy—was incredibly stupid. Fortunately, the grapple had ended quickly. During it, Nahid had kept his head down, so he would not draw too much attention (but thus had sustained three stiff uppercuts). At least the pudgy boy—who had been sitting by the curbside with his pudgy girlfriend—had seemed unlike the type to file any sort of complaint with officers of the palatinate.

A comment about Nahid's mark had made him look up, directly at the boy, who was taken aback by the transgression of this kholic returning his gaze. Then Nahid looked straight at the girlfriend's fat face.

The boy, unable to ignore this violation, of course, yet somewhat unsure and clearly shocked, rose.

Nahid grabbed him. The boy was shorter but broader, with blond hair and an upturned nose. Nahid threw the first punch. For the hemo, this was unthinkable—attacked by a kholic! But Nahid's punch glanced off the side of the boy's head as he turned away, and the boy threw several wild roundhouses of his own, hitting Nahid in the chest and, finally, in the face. Only when Nahid's nose began to slowly drip black fluids did the boy back off. Hemos were afraid of melancholy. Nahid flung congealing shapes of fluid from his throbbing hand and lurched away—

Fortunately, no palatinate had been in the area, and none of the other hemos in the vicinity tried to stop him from leaving. But surely there would be questions at the ostracon this evening, a visit by the palatinate to interrogate the senior kholic on duty.

He held his shirt up to his face, heart still pounding. At least the melancholy had stopped dripping; it clotted almost as soon as it touched the air.

With ghosts of Name of the Sun and Octavia following him, haunting him, he could only eat more buds. The alcohol had receded, but before the next wave of his high ramped up, he rested briefly on a patch of loose gravel, sitting under a downspout. Reaching out, he made a few lame attempts to remove a rotten and festering thing from the nearby curbside but ended up flinging it away when he saw the maggots beneath. He sniffed at his fingers, licked them, and rocked forward and back, hurting from head to toe.

When he glanced up, he saw the dungeon's towers high over the rooftops. Shapes shuddered toward him, broke apart in the air. The castellan was locked up there. And, in the rooms beneath—rooms he had recently seen, but had not stepped into—dwelt his daughter, the chatelaine of Nowy Solum—

He was not a coward!

Nahid felt his mouth hanging open, dry, and he vomited

suddenly, twice, into the gutter, leaving it there for one of his brothers or sisters to mop up.

He drifted past Kirk Gate and the teeming livestock markets, past the slaughter and the bleating and the flies, toward the river. He would find his way inside Jesthe again and return once he'd found his sister. The time of pranks was over. He would bring back Octavia where she belonged.

Grinding his teeth together, Nahid toyed with the buds remaining in his pocket. They were soft and damp. He passed under the overhanging homes of the Merchant Quarters, onto Red Cross Street, and from there into the city centrum.

Anu, the almighty power, trailed by ambassadors, hovered in all his fearsomeness over Pan Renik's abandoned nest. Beyond the glow from his skin, even the firmament seemed pale by comparison. Ambassadors dove, momentarily lost in his light, then flickered away.

Anu was the size of five huts pushed together.

His roar shifted, lowered.

Hornblower watched fires burst from the mighty loins; along the great back, several sets of wings blurred with heat of their own. Staring up, the padre trembled. His heart thundered. He was close to expiring right there, on the main branch. He wanted to run but was afraid running might attract attention. Even if he tried to run, he doubted his legs would obey.

All other padres on this lip of the world—ironuser, leafjoiner, ropemaker, plus three or four junior leaders whose roles were not fully assigned yet—stood likewise trembling, no doubt in the same awed state.

They had expected the exile to be executed.

That had not happened.

Because Pan Renik jumped.

Now Anu, mighty and fearsome, had arrived.

Were all dreaded things about to come true? Anu—whom hornblower had spoken about so cavalierly his entire life, and whose name he had used so many times to achieve what he wanted, to get what he desired—was real, right here, and no doubt angry.

So easy had it been to interpret and shape words passed down from generation to generation, to visit girls, claiming the visits were on Anu's behalf, to instruct people, to lead people, but in the power's glow, hornblower now felt transparent and as mortal and flawed as anyone else in the settlement. Should he stammer an explanation? Beg for forgiveness?

What explanation could there possibly be?

Crazy Pan Renik had jumped into the clouds.

Anu's hands brushed against the upper branches as he turned. Ranking him, ambassadors zipped frantically, whirrs audible over the thrumming roar of the power. Once clear of the branches, Anu descended, blowing hot air and stirring up leaves, making the padres robes tug and crack like whips.

Of course, Anu knew they were there; he had known all along, despite his blindness. Ambassadors had told him.

The power glowed with a light that was impossible to either look at or look away from, just like the stories had said, just like hornblower's father had told him in sermons. The light illuminated hornblower's inner self, his secrets, inside and out—illuminated secrets of all the padres. None could ever look away again.

His eyes watered. The roar was like a throbbing heart. On the power's long face, the large eyes were cracked and dim. Anu's fingers, the size of branches, flexed and trembled. Close enough now that hornblower could have hit his flank with a stick, had he been so foolish, Anu slowed.

Ambassadors touched Anu's skin, lingering there for a second, then darting off. Hornblower saw seams on the body of the great power and a series of darker marks, splayed in streaks toward Anu's outstretched legs where his smooth skin seemed scarred and dented.

The hum rattled hornblower's teeth.

Next to him, a padre began a sermon: "Decayed friends and awful neighbours . . ."

But his voice trailed off.

Damn Pan Renik! The exile should have been thrown off the edge of the world at birth!

"Anu," cried leafjoiner, unable to withstand the pressure of the situation any longer, "tell us your intents!"

Renewed gusts of hot air came from under the entity as it shifted, turning away from hornblower. Ambassadors circled in another flurry of activity.

Hornblower muttered a prayer. What else was there to do? Was there the slightest chance that Anu had come down from his skies on a visit of commendation and reward for the devotion of his padres? This did not seem very probable. He thought again about getting to his knees to praise the almighty, and he tried not to think about his indiscretions, or how much pain he might feel if the power finally decided to punish him.

Anu slid through the air until he was only a few metres away, filling the sky. Hornblower reviewed what his own padres had taught him, looking for a maxim to cling to, to save him, or at least give him small comfort in these last moments.

Words seemed so futile now.

Then, suddenly, to his left, padre firelighter dropped to his knees. From the corner of hornblower's eye, he saw the man pitch forward, face down onto the bark of the great branch. Hornblower could not stop himself from turning, just for a second, to get a better look: red sap leaked from both of firelighter's ears.

The padre twitched and went still.

Dead.

"Please," hornblower whispered, unable to keep his silence, "please spare me. Great Anu, power of heaven and the sky and all that is overhead. Please, *spare me*. Firelighter was weak, it's true. But I was always speaking for you, in all that I did. Always. I obeyed . . ."

An ambassador appeared instantly, close to hornblower's face, and froze there.

Anu, it said, buzzing, *chooses you*.

"Me? For what?"

To retrieve.

Hornblower was stunned. Surely the ambassador was not talking about retrieving Pan Renik? But what else could it mean? The phrase was like cold metal in hornblower's head. He did not look to see if other padres could hear this, or even if they remained alive. Now he knew the madness of what the power wanted: he had to go beneath the clouds, never come back. He would follow Pan Renik into the afterlife. "Ask Anu not to make me go down there," he said quietly. "Ask him . . ."

Anu has not taken a human exemplar in a hundred years. But now he chooses you. He can't go alone. We can't go. So you will guide him.

Below the ambassador, behind a hundred of them, Anu hovered, stoic, arms out. He did not seem like anything that was ever alive.

The one that jumped took with him a device that belongs to Anu. Anu wishes to get it back.

"But not into the clouds . . ."

You will be Anu's eyes. Your hands will be his hands. We cannot follow him. Do you understand? You will guide the power down there.

"I can't go. I can't."

Tastes of agony put an abrupt end to further protests. Hornblower closed his eyes and hoped he would never open them again. The pain was worse than any pain he had ever before felt. When it lingered, he put his hands up to his face, expecting to feel sap gushing from all exits, but there was none springing forth from his ears, or nose, or mouth. And, in his chest—at least so far—his heart still pounded.

Taking a chance, he glanced at the other padres.

Dead, all of them, leaking their lives out onto the branch.

He could not resist Anu. He could not do anything. Just like old times, the great power of the sky had come down from the firmament to deliver his wrath, and to assign to an unfortunate padre a divine and impossible quest.

Rubbing both palms over her eyes, and holding them there for a moment, as if she hoped reality might alter when she finally lowered them, Name of the Sun said, "I did something stupid last night."

They sat on damp and filthy rocks on the shores of the River Crane, by New Market quay. For Name of the Sun, the ambient stench was anathema, but because her friend was a kholic, the smell of the river was a form of comfort. Name of the Sun tried her best not to show her distaste, but she had never been able to get accustomed to certain of the kholic predilections, no matter how often she associated with them.

Nowy Solum rose like ragged cliffs. A few boats struggled on the Crane, beyond where several people stood in the shallows, with nets or poles, looking for anything they could eat or sell or clean—not all out there were kholics, though several tattooed children clustered about nearby outhouses, lean bodies spattered.

"I went with Nahid." Name of the Sun watched the children. "We did something crazy."

Her friend, Serena, looked down at her own knees.

Around the girls squatted several cognosci. Two of the beasts gnawed bread crusts. A third, as Name of the Sun turned, lowered its paws from its muzzle, then showed teeth to her, massive and yellow.

A moment passed before Name of the Sun understood that the creature thought they were playing a game, peek-a-boo, initiated because she had been holding her hands up to her face. She tried to return the distorted smile. Cognosci were ugly by any standards, their doggish faces compressed, their skin sagging and grey. The beasts made horrible growling noises when they breathed, as if with each breath they were about to expire from a painful ailment. Yet she knew the creatures were oblivious in their ignorance, unrelenting in loyalty. "Last night," she said, "Nahid and I did something I regret."

Serena said, "Are you going to tell me?"

Still watching the cognosci, Name of the Sun hesitated. She recalled Nahid's drunken list, the so-called pleasures in his life. Why had she expected more from him? Kholics were restricted by training and culture and history. Like these simple cognosci, rooting for remnants on the beach, they were damaged by the city.

The brains of these creatures, low functioning at the best of times, had been fried altogether by bleach, which had been served to them by the madam who had captured them, and knew how to permanently pacify them. Serena had found the cognosci discarded behind a whorehouse; fucking the creatures was popular among certain deviants in Nowy Solum.

How different, Name of the Sun suddenly wondered, was the fetish of fucking kholics? In the eyes of some, no different at all. She shuddered. Just to entertain these thoughts was horrible. Nahid had put doubts in her with his hurtful words.

"We used the tunnels," she said, "to get into Jesthe."

"From the centrum?" Now Serena seemed alert.

"I hadn't been inside since I was seven. Nahid had never been in there."

"Why would he? Kholics can't go in. That place is for hemo kids."

Name of the Sun frowned. "I told you his sister works in Jesthe? His twin sister—"

"Octavia. Sure. Everyone knows that." Serena made an expression that was hard to decipher.

"We went to where the chatelaine sleeps. We went into endocarp."

"Endocarp?"

"The inner sanctum. Heart of the palace."

Serena almost looked up. "I know what it means. You went there with Nahid?"

"Yes."

"And was she there?"

"Octavia?"

"No. The chatelaine."

"She was." Name of the Sun did not want to tell Serena any more of story. This had been a bad idea. She said, "Have I done something to upset you?"

"I'm not upset, it's just that there were these men who came by the ostracon—"

"Maybe I should just go."

One of the cognosci, which had been looking over its shoulder, started to make a nasally whine; people nearby—three male hemos—were moving among the rocks, carrying fishing poles, making it nervous. The cognosci were accustomed to Name of the Sun being around, but men terrified them.

"Let's both go." Serena stood. "I need to get these guys back up. You can come back, too, if you'd like."

Serena ran a shelter in a shed on Red Cross Street. There, she had taught herself rudimentary physicker training—enough, anyhow, to mend the most obvious of ailments. The creatures followed her wherever she went. But the invitation to return to the shelter had been cold, hollow; Name of the Sun did not feel welcome. She was so tired anyhow, and she had a shift at the end of the day. "I should get some sleep."

They walked the embankment and Name of the Sun glanced up to see a man wearing only a loin cloth, holding a crop, staring down at her. She froze. The man's chest was streaked with welts. He pointed toward her with his whip and she looked away for a moment, breathless—

When she looked back, the man was gone, but the cognosci huddled by Serena, baring their teeth, piddling where they stood, and would not budge.

Lingering in the narrow archway at the top of the stairs, the chatelaine watched her father. Her lungs and legs were sore from the exertion of the climb, and from the recent sex, both this afternoon's and the debacle of the previous evening. She should have brought water to drink.

Or started to act her age.

She hooked tabs of a gauze mask behind each ear, pushing the fabric against her mouth, making sure it was snug; some days her father demanded this and would only greet her if she wore the mask.

He stood at his work table with his back to her. He seemed smaller than he did the last time she'd been up here, which was a fortnight ago, maybe a little more. As he worked, his narrow shoulders rose and fell. He was naked, as always: ribs prominent, hairless buttocks clenched. On the table, something she could not see squealed; her father lunged, grunting, to subdue it, or catch it, as it tried to bolt.

The dungeon was colder than her own bedchambers; there were no reeds on the floor here, no wall hangings, no sparks remaining in the cavernous fireplace. Smiling grimly, the chatelaine recognized a definite familiar bond: neither of them was able to keep a fire lit, even with a city of resources and servants at their command.

Lanterns cast dim light over the dungeon chambers from sconces angled either side of the room, but since there was no parchment over the windows here, the dim yellow light of day also fell across the worn wood of the floor; the room was generally brighter than most. But no window covering also meant that the dungeon was abuzz with insects, mostly swarming the table where years of blood, choler, and melancholy had all drained from a central funnel to collect and congeal in a stone trough on the floor.

Somehow, in the castellan's fractured logic, this situation was not an issue. The chatelaine had long ago abandoned attempts at seeing logic up here.

Out in the streets of Nowy Solum, the old castellan's reputation was worse than the chatelaine's own. His reign had been brief and tumultuous before it was suggested, in many counsels, that his young daughter take over. The chatelaine had been a child when her father retreated to this room, just a small girl, left alone in a great palace, with monsters and silent palatinate for company.

Would chamberlain Erricus agree that there had been an improvement after the change of power? She doubted this; both her and her father pursued passions and lifestyles that the old man could never approve of.

For a moment, the chatelaine continued to watch her father torture the poor creature, striving as he did to discover unknowable secrets.

Then she stepped into the room.

He did not turn. Over his shoulder, she saw the small blue body now, limp in his hands, but still breathing, heaving, partially strapped down to the table and twitching spasmodically. Against the far rim—which was made of hammered tin—two similar bodies huddled close to one another, staked together and making low moaning sounds.

She stopped, shocked. "*Cobali*?"

Arrayed on the table were various implements, mostly stained with red blood. Her father appeared to be trying to push a thin metal rod into the forearm of the hapless beast.

"Where did you get those from? Who in the world gave them to you?" She felt a surge of nausea. "That criminal, Tully? My goodness . . ." But she was too tired, too dizzy, too occupied with her own tumultuous day to make much of a protest or sustain her repulsion; another time, maybe. "What are you doing to that thing?"

The castellan turned now, frowning at the interruption.

He did seem older, if that was possible, his face gaunt and drawn. Was he shrinking? Aging faster than most? The chatelaine was not even sure he recognized her. One of his eyes was shut, and in the corner of that eye dried blood had welled, as if he cried it, like tears.

"I'm trying," he said, "to make the world a better place."

"I don't believe you. You just like to torture things, make them scream."

"Terra Bella. How could you say that to your own father? This is not torture. It's progress." He smiled, but with no conviction.

"Is that—?"

He had an erection.

Trying not to look down, the chatelaine cleared her throat. "Your eye. What have you done to your eye? You've hurt yourself."

He shrugged.

"You are aware that cobali have families?" She could not help but glance again at his bobbing cock. "And that they mate for life? Raise their young. Like I have heard *some* mammals do." She looked away, anywhere but toward her dad. "This has been decided by committee. A council I hired. The beasts are intelligent and I signed the decree. See? You think I do nothing down there."

Now the castellan actually laughed. "Lucky for the cobali to have you on their side. You are like a carnivore, my Terra, who bemoans the slaughter of animals yet stuffs her face with chops at every opportunity. You are an inconsistent girl. I think you should peer into a looking glass before you accuse me of torture. Hypocritical, if I may say so."

"What do I torture? I embrace *living*, not illness and dying. I'm a lover. But I thank you, father, as always, for your sensitivity."

He turned his back to her again. "May I ask why you're here, sweetheart, so early in the morning?"

"It's midafternoon."

"Still, early for you. Do you wish to ask my advice about mundane tasks? Are you going to convince me again that it's safe to come down and take over the city? Or maybe you wish to confront me about stories you might have heard?"

"Stories? What stories?" She bit the inside of her cheek. "Gods have flown over Nowy Solum. There were reports. Celestial beings appeared, they say, over the river. Erricus is beside himself. But listen, father, I want to talk to you. Not about stories. I've made a few decisions."

The castellan was becoming lost in his task again; the cobali shrieked as the rod was forced deeper into the marrow of its femur.

Raising her voice, the chatelaine said, "One of my pets was stolen."

This stopped him. But he did not turn. "From your chambers?"

"That's right. So I've ordered another one." Then, surprising herself, she said, "If I didn't know better, I might think you came down the stairs to take it."

He shuddered, no doubt at the thought of leaving his room. "Why would I do that? Which one was it?"

"South Gate."

"Ah, the one you call the cherub. I'm sorry to hear that, Terra. You know I'm sorry."

"If you ever touch any of my pets—"

He wheeled. "You're serious? Why would I touch them? They're as close to grandchildren as I'm ever going to get."

The chatelaine inhaled sharply and wished she had never come here. "You are mean," she said. "A horrible man."

"I know how foolish you are, daughter. You should try to muffle your sounds somehow. It's disturbing for a father to hear the things his baby is capable of, now she's all grown up."

"How can you possibly hear anything up here?"

"I fear everyone in the city can hear you at times." But his tone was becoming softer; he had seen the hurt on his daughter's face. "Do you forget, Terra, that Nowy Solum has enemies? That our family has enemies?"

"Who? We have no enemies."

"You are wrong, Terra. You must be careful. You must respect the palace."

"Like you did? Such drama." Then, suddenly, the chatelaine felt her pain transform into anger: she had come to consult her father, to check on him, not to put up with these cutting comments and lectures. "And you have the balls to talk about family? You, of all people? You ruin families. I'm so sick of this. I'm granting the palatinate power today to return to all of Jesthe. Does that make you happy? Is that respect for the palace? You can expect a visit, I'm sure. And, for your information, I would never bring a child into this shitty world."

He blinked, surprised at last. "There are times, my dear," he said, "when I believe you also have choler, or maybe even melancholy, as your dominant humour. You were never tested, you know."

"You say that every time we get together. You've seen the colour of my blood."

The castellan smiled sadly. "Please don't get too excited, Terra."

"Why do you always insult me?" She clenched her fists. "Look, I've met someone. I might be in love."

Over his shoulder, appraisingly, as if maybe expecting her to run at him, attack him, ruin his so-called work, the castellan peered once more.

She was disgusted. "This is all the fucking family I have right now. Me and you. Small wonder I love my pets so much."

The castellan returned his attentions to the cobali bound on the table before him. He picked at the creature with an implement of some sort, then started to grind the metal rods deeper and deeper into the small bones until the cobali shrieked, then sobbed, a sound remarkably like the cries of a young girl.

Several other rods protruded from the creature's body, some with joints of delicate gears and chains. Was the castellan trying to extend the creature's thin limbs? At least the cobali died now, going limp on the table, though its associates, next in line, whimpered louder.

"You should have had a son," the chatelaine said, not willing to let the fight end. "Maybe a son would have no qualms about cutting these things into little pieces, to see if they're content or not. What are you trying to do? What is this travesty? Sometimes I fucking hate men." She took a deep breath, wiped at her eyes, trying to look out over the misty city again, through the window, but this room was too high: nothing but clouds up here. "And what have you done with Tuerdian anyhow? Where is your servant?"

"Sleeping."

"I should go look." But she did not. "Please put clothes on. Why do you have to work naked?"

"Why do you?"

She tried to ignore this juvenile comeback; her father was not a healthy man. "I'll send someone up to light the fire. In the meantime, dad, try not to kill too many of my subjects."

Pain throbbed behind Nahid's forehead, a pain so powerful all he could do was stop walking and close his eyes. Instead of dulling sensations, the bud served to amplify them. His sinuses were clogged with dried melancholy.

He stood at the intersection of Horsepool Street and Grindstone Lane, not far from the ostracon. There were other kholics in the streets here, cleaning, milling. They eyed him, aware of who he was, of course, aware of his sister's situation, aware of his hemo girlfriend. He was no longer one of them. What he needed most was to crash somewhere. He feared the dreams he might have. He wanted to sober up, but likewise feared sobriety.

Head pounding, he moved past the ostracon's block, past the squalor of the surrounding ghettos, without a parting word to his estranged brothers and sisters. For a second he thought about going back to consult a senior, but this simple act seemed impossible to achieve. Would he ever be able to return?

Closer and closer to Jesthe, as if pulled through the streets, he climbed over a rickety, half-built home he was sure had not been there even the day before. He tried to recapture or at least understand past motivations in his life but could not. Within his chest, vessels carried black ichors to his spleen, and to his brain, and to his heart, flowing with a slow, relentless tide that pulled him down.

Once, he had seen Octavia's life-fluids, leaking from a gash she had received on a jagged piece of tin, and it had been nowhere near as dark as his own. She might even have had a chance at a regular life, had she not shared a womb with him, for how could his sister possibly function and be the way she was if she ever felt like he did now? Her veins must surely supply her a more even balance or she would be crushed by this weight. Even her tattoo looked as though it hadn't taken properly, as if it might fall from her face, revealing a hemo, or at least a person with the ability to feel some degree of contentment.

Rain began then, followed by the low rumble of thunder from somewhere above the clouds, and though Nahid normally liked to walk in storms, he sought refuge under the nearest stone arch, which was the entrance to an abandoned temple. Above him, dripping, a gargoyle representing two facets of some old god's face—contorted on one side with aggression and on the other with orgiastic aspects—watched. He cared nothing about the hemos' gods.

Worn rock steps beneath his feet were stained but now the rains had begun to rinse them. Heavy and warm and thick, the storm did little to clear the air. People ran for shelter but none stepped up next to him, where he stood, covertly watching. Clouds over Nowy Solum seemed to transform from amber to dark green, though that might have been an effect of the bud, wreaking its silent havoc in his system.

Shuffling noises caused Nahid to turn: an elderly man, no tattoo, was coming forth from inside the temple, holding a lantern in one hand and what appeared to be a large fragment of parchment in the other. The man squinted, either at Nahid or past him, at the weather. He did not look particularly sick or crazy, as most were who squatted in temples. Yet as he approached, Nahid considered stepping into the rain to get away. He turned his back to the stranger but knew as he did so he would be addressed.

"Kholic, are you able to read or write?"

"I can read."

The old man grunted. He was very close now. "Then read something for me. My eyes are terrible."

Watching the rain and the mud leaping in the streets, Nahid held out his hand.

"Will you step inside? Your kind is welcome here. You have come to the right temple."

Nahid complied, but did not go far. Away from the raindrops, he brushed water from his face and looked into the depths of the dark temple: candles burned toward the back, where several people in robes gathered silently around an altar. Over their heads, a lantern illuminated the small foyer and arching columns. The place smelled of dampness and mould.

He took the parchment, began to read.

"'Their head aches, misaffected. In sunlight, which cannot transform bile into choler, they watch.'"

He paused.

"Please, continue."

When Nahid looked at the parchment again, he could not find where he had been reading. He scanned the words several times but there was nothing he could see about humours or choler. He squinted quickly at the old man, to see if this were a trick, but the old man just blinked with rheumy eyes and waited patiently. So Nahid started reading again, at random: "'In a dwelling of modest proportion, they reside over the other dwellings, which are the homes of twelve adult men, seven women, and four surviving children. Each day, they build a temple. From beyond the perimeter of the trees, exemplars watch the progress and appear satisfied.'"

Nahid looked up once more. The parchment seemed as warm as flesh. He could not tell what the people in the back were doing. He cleared his throat. "'In the spring, Mummu will visit, returning from the mountains. Mummu has no exemplar or congregation, for he is solitary. When Mummu arrives, he calls his sisters, Kingu and Aspu, from across the water. Anu seldom appears at weddings. His energy is low, and needs to be conserved. Offerings to Anu should include whelps, stillborn infants, corn on the cob, and all forms of metal.'"

"Metal," agreed the old man, nodding. He smiled at Nahid. "I heard he liked metal. And infants. He was somewhat monstrous. Please continue."

"Did you write this?"

"Of course not. We're not writing these documents. We organize them."

"Why?"

"We're preparing the temple. For the return of the benevolent sisters."

"You think goddesses are coming back? Is that what this is about? Your gods were spoiled children." He wanted to throw the parchment down, walk away, but he hesitated.

"We are all spoiled children," the man said. "There are poisons inside each of us, trapped. These have spoiled us. And perhaps they spoiled the gods, too. Until these poisons are released, none of us will be able to walk side by side. We cannot point fingers without first looking inward."

"These aren't concerns for me."

The old man said, "There are other concerns for you, it's true. Streets are not safe anymore."

"What does that mean?"

"There are fraternities. Factions. Scapegoats sacrificed. There is violence in the alleyways. Already, you must know, gods and goddesses have flown overhead. Soon seraphim will arrive in Nowy Solum. They will teach us to release the poisons. This will be a night of reckoning. No god will land until the city is clean. The skies, the river. You need to join hands with us. You need to come in."

"No," Nahid said. Sweating, he held out the parchment.

Beyond the doorway, the rain had abated, though the water dripping from the stonework was loud. Receding thunder rolled across the clouds.

The old man took his parchment. Looking at it, he seemed rather confused and even smaller.

Nahid stepped away and down, into the humid air of the street. His fingers tingled. Barefoot, he splashed heavily in warm puddles.

From the temple to the Gardens of Jesthe—which was a worn patch of land adjacent to the centrum, hardly a garden at all—completely shadowed by the crooked structure of the palace—was only a short walk. Nahid had seen the chatelaine's servants here, lingering on their breaks, having a smoke, though never had he seen his sister. Then again, he had not stayed for very long.

Now he squatted by a tenement, veins pulsing.

He would wait a moment to see if Octavia showed. If she did not, or if she appeared but would not listen to him, return with him to where she belonged, he would—

Kill the chatelaine.

This sudden thought was like a cold stone materializing in his mind, leaping up from the black and bottomless lake.

Kill the chatelaine.

Of course. That's what he had to do.

He felt a chilly clarity.

Several large girls loitered in the Gardens, dressed in shabby robes. They talked with each other in clipped tones. One snorted brief bursts of laughter, no doubt at the expense of another. Maybe even at Octavia's expense. Did his sister dress like these girls? Did anyone in Jesthe talk to his sister, other than the chatelaine?

A head of staff—or whatever the women in charge were called—shouted at two of the staff, telling them to get back inside. They had been smoking. Now they ground out their butts on the wet ground and complied, but not before another curt shout had been barked by their superior. *Get a move on.* Breath misted.

Nahid grew cold, and colder still. Certainty of what he was about to do spread through him like ice. He wondered how easily the chatelaine would die. On her bed, with his hands at her throat?

As he imagined the spirit rising up from her corpse, three palatinate officers approached, heading across the Gardens from the mouth of Turnbuckle Lane, heading toward their barracks, and Nahid had the sensation they could read his thoughts. He stood and began walking again, planning to circle back, but as he passed the tenements of Endicott's Alley, a massive form came whistling from between the buildings, occluding what little light filtered from the clouds, and with a startling crash made contact with the brickwork just above him. Nahid wheeled to see a glimpse of what could only be a giant bat with the face of a toothless man coming directly at him before impact obliterated everything.

THE SECOND PARTITION

n the gloom of Bedenham House, on the stone bench, Tina lamented. This was her child's seventh day. Though she felt much stronger, her stomach had remained too unsettled to let her break fast. She had slept, but only in tiny, futile increments . . .

Getting up from the mattress, Tina sat on the stool next to the basinet—which was two pieces of wood, forming a shallow V-shape—holding her baby boy in her arms, face up against the warm, wonderfully scented head. She had sat on this stool every day for the entire week, cradling the child. She murmured to him. She held him when he woke and she tried to comfort him when he wailed.

On the seventh morning, the boy showed signs of continued health and greedily nursed. Then he rested, but he did not sleep. Neither did he cry.

These, of course, were the good signs.

A brief rain fell in the city, loud on the street outside, turning the dirt to mud. The floor in the room Tina shared with her husband and son was gravel, and damp. They could not afford a new door—the old one had been stolen, no doubt for firewood—and so a yellow muslin curtain hung between her and the rest of Nowy Solum.

Tina liked yellow. At least, the rain had briefly muted smells that a curtain could never keep out.

When her baby was finally dozing, she placed him down into his basinet, ate a small apple and a piece of hard cheese, vomited it up, and got dressed. Desperate for any form of luck, she fastened a lavender broach to the neck of her tunic. Then she called to her husband, Cadman, to tell him she was ready. He had been back from work for a while now and, by this point, was waiting at the curb, having a cigarette with the decrepit neighbour.

Tina did retain a modicum of hope—for there always had to be hope, no matter how slim. The boy seemed lively now. Almost happy. He had smiled the previous day, a tiny twist to his sweet puffy lips she was *sure* was a smile. A gift so precious. She tried hard, heart breaking, breath catching in her chest, on this morning (and every morning for the past seven mornings, for hours and hours) to get her baby to laugh or chuckle or show any sign of amusement. Nothing. Some babies made gorgeous, throaty sounds. She had heard these before, many times, and had seen the relief on the faces of their mothers.

The boy was starting to round out, too, his blue eyes so alert, shaped like Cadman's, who had once been almost handsome.

Today her son would be named, one way or another.

She wrapped the boy slowly in a blanket. He woke to gaze calmly at her. She wept. "There's blood in your veins," she whispered. "I know there is."

The crime of testing one's own child before their trial by officers of the palatinate was punishable by rack: Tina had not been tempted to jab the baby with a pin, as some anxious mothers had.

Tina nuzzled her boy, then, suddenly, with a surge of desperation, tickled his ribs. Made cooing sounds.

Nothing.

"Laugh," she said, cheeks dripping, lips salty with tears, the love she felt painful inside her. "For goodness sake, please laugh."

Water at the centrum well had been exceedingly difficult to draw over recent months, and with Cadman at work every day, standing in line was impossible, especially holding onto a baby and a heavy pot at the same time, so Tina had not bathed her son, as was tradition prior to bringing infants into Bedenham House; she had only rubbed at his skin with her own hands, and with dry straw, to try to stimulate the temperate humours within and diminish any darker biles.

The first few days and nights, the boy had cried constantly.

This had only recently stopped.

When her milk finally started to flow, it trickled reluctantly, from cracked and bleeding nipples.

Now the boy would not react at all.

These were the bad signs.

Tina did not want to dwell on them, not here, not in the gloom of Bedenham House. . . .

When Cadman stood in the doorway, shoving the muslin aside, he held his hat in both hands. "Ready?"

She stood.

Because her baby boy was so tiny, so light, the walk through the streets of Nowy Solum, toward the centrum, was not as arduous as it might have been. Not physically, at least. They passed people going about their daily struggles, crowds shopping at Kirk Gate, a huge gathering in Grey Close Square (though she could not hear the bare-chested, shouting orator), passed wealthy families from North End, in fancy clothes, walking the promenade by the river. Did children of the rich, Tina wondered, ever get tested? Maybe melancholy was a product of being poor, the essence of a tired and wanting womb.

Palatinate officers pounded on a Torchmere Street door. She turned away, hiding her bundle, cheeks gone hot.

Coming into the centrum, where Jesthe rose above the sagging rooftops and vanished into clouds, Tina saw a teenaged kholic, a young boy with a beautiful face, leaking black fluid from his nose, obviously crazed or high or both. He was heading straight at her. She stopped, shocked by an urgency that struck her like a slap. The boy would tell her something, maybe advice concerning the trial he had obviously failed, or foresight about her own son. This kholic was himself the son of a woman who had made this same walk, years ago, and who had been filled with the same dread that filled her now.

He looked directly at her.

There was a moment of panic. Never before had Tina seen the eyes of a kholic, not directly, not for this long. Blazing from the black mask, the gaze was intense. She felt the torment and anger, and she needed more than anything to hear what the kholic had to say, to learn his story, as if this might be the only way to save her own child from the palatinate's mark.

At the last second, the teen veered into the crowd.

During the rush she felt, she considered chasing the boy, but that would be madness; her son had an appointment to keep, to be at Bedenham House before the afternoon expired. . . .

Across the floor from where she sat, in his cot awaiting judgment, her child now made a mewling sound. Could she grab him, leave here, leave the city?

Escape to where?

Cadman, at her back, said, "Get a move on, Tina. Shake a leg. I have to be back at the mill in an hour."

The encounter with the kholic had thrown what little resolve Tina had managed to muster. Her abdomen still ached from the labour and anxiety. She was bringing her lovely boy on what could very well be a one-way trip. She stopped again. She could not get the image of the kholic's face out of her head.

Cobali suddenly spiralled around her feet, racing in circles, looking up at her, exposing their little teeth. The creatures were crude and foul and Cadman stepped forward, trying to kick at the pests, but they were too fast for his clumsy feet.

Used for many purposes—physicker licenses, applications of all sorts, signings, official leechings—Bedenham House was long and low at the foot of Jesthe, just opposite the Garden. The roof was red and sagging. Through wide openings each end, all citizens passed. Bedenham House looked unassuming, yet sitting in it now, waiting, the place filled Tina with foreboding.

Above the south doorway, the crest of Jesthe—a fish gutted on a platter—indicated the palatinate's faith. As an adult, Tina had twice previously been inside this building, once to get her marriage document approved and another time to purchase a permit to sell two chickens at Soaper's and Candles—birds she inherited from an uncle who had recently died. Money from the sale of the chickens had gone to a back-alley physicker, much to Cadman's protests—who wanted only to purchase ale—getting advice on how to keep her unborn baby content, flowing inside with red blood. . . .

Cadman tried to keep up, following several paces behind. He did not speak much at the best of times and this morning he held his face downcast, like a kholic. He had long ago given up. He was certain how this visit to Bedenham House would end. Cadman and Tina fought several times about this attitude: once he'd actually tried to convince her not to get "too attached" to the baby, which was such a ludicrous and hateful thing to say to a young mother that it made Tina sick and she could never look at Cadman's face the same way again, ever. He had concerns about resources. Resources they didn't have. Food and coin, and the space it would take to raise a child. Fucking *resources*!

How could he believe that if elements of black choler were found in the veins of their son, and the child was taken away to be raised as a ward of the city (becoming a lost soul, just like the wounded boy she'd seen), that it would be merciful for them as a couple? Cadman had even said they could try again for another in a year or so. A second boy, maybe, when they had more money, more food, more room—

Cadman (decided Tina, biting her lip) was an imbecile.

No good could come from having a child taken away.

Behind her husband followed the elderly neighbour, whose name she could never recall and perhaps had never known. His presence was in lieu of a close friend. All Tina's friends had been conveniently busy this morning. Even the ratty old neighbour only cooperated in hopes of a promised pint, and who knew where they would get the coin to buy it when this was finally over.

Tina stood directly before the south entrance, the baby asleep on her shoulder. A palatinate officer within, wearing the long red robes of his position and holding a lantern, saw her and beckoned.

The chamberlain and his men knew how many babies had been born in Nowy Solum over the past month; they knew how many had survived. If Tina had not brought her son here before dusk, officers would have come during the night.

Again she considered fleeing, taking her chances with monsters and dead gods and who knew what else lurked in the unending wastelands outside the city.

She had never been outside the walls.

Bedenham House was exceeding dim and smelled of oil and camphor. There were four large fireplaces, burning low, one either side of each door, each end. Along the west wall was arranged a line of small cots from entrance to exit, perhaps twenty in all. The palatinate who led her inside without a word, swinging his lantern all the while, made his way to one of these cots and gestured for her to place the baby down.

The boy, of course, woke immediately, staring blankly up at the wooden ceiling. Her hands shook. The officer did not even look at her son but instead watched her face, searching it, his expression impassive, as if seeking something in her features that could betray aspects of her child's biology.

Then the officer motioned abruptly with one hand toward the bench; she took her place, like all good citizens would.

Glancing outside, she saw Cadman standing with the neighbour, who grinned in at her. Cadman faced away, watching (she imagined) Horse Market, where barkers shouted and women shopped and children played with their friends or walked with their parents and life went on for all those lucky ones.

She turned away.

Deeper in Bedenham House, another mother—a woman she had not previously noticed—waited in the shadows on another bench. She tried to wave but the woman was not looking her way.

Tina's son did not fall asleep for a long time. The officer waited quietly by the cot, like a predator, a slight smile on his face, swinging his lantern so that scented smoke rose up to the gables. Tina listened to the quiet sounds her baby made and knew he was hungry and scared and tired.

"Please," she whispered, watching the palatinate as he, in turn, stared straight ahead. No. He was not like a predator, more like a statue, cold stone.

From the north entrance, near Jesthe, two more palatinate officers entered then, murmuring, and as her eyes adjusted to the relative glare, Tina realized with shock that one of the men—the one on the left, in the deep crimson robe, who moved slowly, and hunched—was Erricus himself, the chamberlain of Nowy Solum.

The second man wore a dark sash at his neck, clearly a physicker. He had a boy's face and did not appear old enough to shave. The chamberlain, of course, was ancient.

Both men walked the length of Bedenham House, stopping briefly at a cot near the other woman, then proceeding to where her own boy lay.

There they conferred.

Tina had never seen the chamberlain this close. Her heart thudded as he nodded and turned toward her. When he approached, she stopped breathing. He was a dead man, a corpse.

She imagined the chill of his bony hands upon her, his hollow face, his leather skin.

He asked, "You are the mother of this boy?"

She nodded.

"What is your name?" His eyes glistened.

She replied.

"I am here to oversee trials this day. We were waiting for you. Though, of course, it was well within your rights to come any time before dusk." The chamberlain coughed, light and dusty. He pressed his fingers together. "Your son will be tested first. He is older than the girl over there by nearly nine hours."

"I understand." Though Tina did not understand. How could she? How could any mother? As far as she knew, Erricus had never presided over an infant's trial, not in decades.

At the south entrance, Cadman stared in, though if he recognized who was speaking to his wife was not clear. Probably he recognized nothing.

Chamberlain Erricus lingered by the bench a moment longer. Finally, he coughed again. "Very well," he said. "Let us begin."

Back at the cot, the physicker held out a small, ornate jar, which he now cracked open.

Holding both hands up for silence, or to evoke his gods, the chamberlain returned to the cot while the physicker made a big show of listening, apparently to her baby's breathing. Then the physicker touched her boy lightly in several places Tina could not identify from where she sat. The officer did not wake her son, or at least the boy remained quiet throughout this process. Erricus had closed his eyes. Finally the physicker put his fingers up to his own face, sniffed them, and produced a small vial of liquid from the jar. He sprinkled a few drops, watching her boy intently.

Then Erricus, whose eyes snapped open, did something quickly with his left hand, so quickly that Tina could not follow the movement.

Her son wailed.

The wail ended abruptly.

Outside Bedenham House came a tremendous roar, as if all of Nowy Solum were being torn apart. For an instant, Tina thought this was an extension of the test, a reaction, but two of the empty cots crashed to the floor and the beams of the Bedenham House groaned, shaking dust and debris that pattered all around.

Erricus and his palatinate officer recoiled. The physicker went down on one knee. Gripping her son's cot for support, with one hand on his chest, the old man looked outside. Screaming had begun.

On the shed roof, Tully was surprised to discover a kholic man and a hemo child sleeping together, huddled under a threadbare blanket. Until this point, his day had been unfolding fortuitously. Most days started off rather badly for Tully and continued to be a bit of a struggle as they went on, yet Tully found himself on this foggy afternoon whistling tunelessly as he climbed in Kirk Gate Alley. He had slept well, eaten a crust of bread (stolen from a lady's cart), and had wandered South Gate, looking for unaware cobali to trap or a rube from outside to rob.

He had been, in unexpected ways, successful.

Stopped over the couple now, though, his good mood wavered. Whistling ceased.

"Wake up." He spoke as coldly as he could. Neither man nor child awoke. This kind of thing, Tully thought, happened more and more. He kicked the man, who grunted and rolled onto his back, opening his eyes and quickly averting them when they registered Tully standing over him.

"You piece of shit," Tully said. "Did you just look at me? Did *you fucking look at me*? Shouldn't you be cleaning shit off my arse instead of sleeping with our girls?"

Continuing to stare at a point to the side of Tully's face, the man said nothing. Now the girl had awoken. She might have been ten.

The kholic said, "This is not what you think."

"How you know what I think?" Tully kicked the man again, harder this time, in the ribs. "I think I see a piece of shit sleeping on a rooftop." Against Tully's back, his heavy bag moved, and he remembered his intentions. "Lazy-ass motherfuckers. Sleeping away the day. You're lucky I'm in a good mood. You," to the girl, "what are you doing with this piece of shit?"

"He's nice," the girl said, barely audible.

"What? What did you say?"

"He's a nice man. He takes care of me."

"*Nice*?" Spittle sprayed from Tully's mouth. "Mother fuck! You called him a *man*? He's *not* a man. Does he look like me? *I'm* a fucking man! Let's cut him open and see what comes out."

Yet Tully laughed to see the girl's face.

Rain that had just recently stopped had soaked the roof here, so that the couple lay in a puddle. Tully knew they were addicts, most likely not lovers, as the kholic had said. Not that he cared about the girl's age—he had slept with younger—but hemos were for hemos. Kholics were for gutters and shit. He glanced about for anything worth taking but had no expectations and saw nothing that belonged to the pair anyhow except the rags they wore and countless fleas. He entertained a fleeting image of violence, kicking the kholic in the face, or perhaps forcing himself on the child, to give her a taste of red blood, and he amused himself briefly with these lurid images. But he had no time right now to follow through.

Besides, he *was* in a good mood.

He gave the kholic another kick but the kholic remained on his side, breathing heavily.

"You need to learn your place," Tully said. "Go back to where you belong. Are any of you left in that fucking shithole you live in? Seems like you get bolder every day, you lot. People won't take this anymore. You'll see. There's something in the air. Find out soon enough. And you, kid, you're as bad as him. You should be marked with a tattoo. You disgust me."

The girl seemed to be waiting for Tully to say something else but Tully was done. He would remember this roof. He would return. He told the couple this. The girl looked lithe and strong. She hadn't been addicted for long. Most addicts had bags under their eyes and the skin of their faces was yellowed and creased. Like the kholic's. What Tully could see of his face, anyhow.

Tully smiled at the girl.

As for the fleas, well, they could keep them—he had enough of his own. Adjusting the load on his back, Tully grinned. "If I ever see either of you again," he said, "I will fuck you up, I promise."

Then, happy with himself, Tully stepped over the pair to scale the damp and mouldy bricks of the adjacent building. This residence had been constructed, or had fallen, in such a way that the surface of the wall merged with the roof Tully stood on. Moss and lichen and spawl gently sloped away from him. Masonry crumbled as he scaled it. His fingers, in more than a few places, sank right into porous bricks.

The higher rooftop sagged under his considerable weight. Tully was a large-boned and meaty man. Always had been. Other body types irritated him. Any man who was not large and strong was unworthy, unless they had money or food.

Women, other than his dear mother, and the whores of Canning Street, were entirely baffling.

Once, his first time making the upward trip, he had nearly plunged through this very spot. But he learned where the hidden beams were and placed his feet accordingly now, almost without looking. A few inches made all the difference.

Deeper water had collected in a pool here. The water must have been stagnant for a while, since swarms of the tiny tube-like creatures that lived in unemptied barrels and brackish ponds, and in the rain gutters of Nowy Solum, churned to detect his dim shadow. Because he was barefoot, Tully tried to avoid the pool, but his feet were already infested with parasites to the point where he could watch the skin near his ankles moving, if he took the time, as if his skin was cast over a stormy and ill-blown sea.

The next part of the climb was more challenging. Tully made sure his bag was securely strapped across his back before attempting it. He spit on his hands and rubbed them together. Over his head, the wall of an old temple had shifted so it leaned overhead; he was forced to hang, suspended by the strength in his hands, hauling himself from lintel to gargoyle to steel flagpole, finally to another lintel, until his legs gained enough momentum to hook over the head of a great grey god. Pulling himself up, panting, he rolled onto this clay roof. The mists had made this climb more treacherous; surfaces were wet and slick. His cargo had banged against the stone several times. Grunts came from within the sack.

At some point, Tully had cut his forearm. He sucked deep red blood from the wound.

"Sorry," he said, insincerely addressing the sack, "for the hard knocks."

Muted protests.

Tully looked over and down. Already Kirk Gate Alley was miniscule, the people there no bigger than those damned cobali that were so fucking hard to trap. Well, not today. No frustrated efforts today.

He could not see the shed where the kholic and child had been. Maybe on the way back, he told himself, if the girl was still there—

Nowy Solum was a mess of chimneys and roofs, extending as far as the low clouds would allow Tully to see. He discerned South Gate, and the smudge of the Crane, as it left the city. He saw big houses on the hill, barely visible, and the markets at Hangman's Alley.

Turning, he noticed the approaching light coming at him from above before he heard the sound, the growing roar. With his mouth hanging open, he watched two shapes come down from the clouds, white and travelling fast, their arms swept back, their wings blurred. He caught a glimpse of long, taciturn faces, the dull gleam of light off smooth flanks. Wide, knowing eyes that seemed to look right at him.

Then the goddesses were gone, leaving spiralling contrails, and a clap of thunder.

The bag thrummed and thumped against his back.

Tully went down on his knees.

Gods had returned!

He stayed in that position, kneeling for a long while, as people in the city below exclaimed faintly and shouted and eventually subsided to a state of less audible shock.

Gods had returned to Nowy Solum.

But as Tully stared at his own knuckles, and the sac writhed between his knees, and he wondered what to do next, he thought: gods have returned and vanished again and I'm still hungry.

Short, sharp jabs of Tully's elbow stopped the activity in the bag.

He got to his feet, grumbling. "Come on. A fucking miracle."

The city and the clouds appeared, once again, as they always did from up here. There was no reason Tully should not continue with his plan. Had he really seen the gods—goddesses, more likely? Had he seen them? They had not lingered or even slowed. Now Tully chuckled. There would be turmoil in the streets this evening. Maybe rubes, ripe for the picking. Nutters would come out.

From the temple roof, the remainder of the ascent was vertical, heading past—sometimes through—the makeshift hanging homes and hammocks of the people who lived on the lower reaches of the tower. He saw the heads of a few citizens now, gawping from their abodes. Above them, the tower continued through a zone where no structures were permitted, toward the dungeon where the castellan had sought refuge many years past. Distant windows were visible, almost obscured by the mist. Low clouds blew past.

"Friend," Tully said to the sack, which was moving again, "you've made this day one to remember. An omen, I would say." He laughed again. "Fucking gods have come back. Did you hear them?"

Then he reached up and took hold of a plank, anchored in place, to be used by tower residents as a first step.

"End of the world," he bellowed, grinning up at them all. At the sound of Tully's deep voice, and the sight of his burgeoning ascent, faces vanished back into their homes. Latches clicked. Belongings were pulled up on ropes. Most of the people living here were familiar with Tully and his heavy hands and feet. He had climbed past numerous times, up and down through their precarious homes. Sometimes he paid them visits.

"You pieces of shit," he called, though people were no longer visible. "End of the world! Stay in your fucking shitholes 'cause I'm comin' up. Make way, make way!"

THE FECUND'S MELANCHOLY DAUGHTER

Scraps piled to overflow in a basket so heavy that several times, on her return trip to the fecund's cell, Octavia needed to rest, using her knee as a prop while her arms throbbed and spasms twisted her lower back. Warm liquid dripped onto her calf, though from the basket or from her earlier encounter with the chatelaine she could not be certain. Looking down, she saw the globe of her white knee, appearing as she imagined the moon might appear, based on stories she'd heard as a child about this orb lost in the skies.

Directly after fucking, almost asleep on the opulent bed, Octavia had been told about the second visit. The chatelaine, whispering in her ear, ran her finger over Octavia's belly, and down, between her legs. The news caused Octavia to sit up.

Another visit?

Thinking about possibilities for this encounter, Octavia tried to regulate her breathing, tried to remain calm; not much got her rattled.

Scrawny Cyrus, fellow kholic, rat catcher who worked the kitchens, had given her four dead rats in exchange for a glimpse of her thigh.

"Let's have a little look, girlie, let's have a little look?"

Cyrus did not live in the dorms of Jesthe, like she did; he shuffled to and from the ostracon every day with others who tended the sewers, chamberpot chutes, vermin, and general garbage disposal for the palace. The old kholic's tag was pale, with poor definition, similar to her own. A man of Cyrus's age had been alive during times when being melancholic meant beatings, even death for many.

But the old man grinned his toothless grin and shook with obvious desire (the way a good deal of men did, and a fair amount

156

of women—kholic or otherwise—when they stood this close to Octavia). Licking his finger, he dragged it along her skin.

Then he laid the rodents lovingly atop the heaped refuse, holding each by the tail, as if this act were a form of physical contact between himself and Octavia. His breathing was audible all the while. He stood so close, trying with his milky eyes to look inside her shift or otherwise get near enough to feel her body's warmth against his own frame . . .

Octavia hoisted the basket again and continued moving down the hall.

These rats, it seemed, were already beginning to decay, skin pulled back from yellow teeth, hair missing in clumps. The corpses and the refuse they lay on emitted a stench rich and stupefying and wholly nostalgic.

She stopped to catch her breath once more only when she realized that she was very near to the fecund's cell.

That squeal again, the monster's high-pitched giggle.

Illuminated by the torch she had earlier jammed into the sconce by the cell door and left burning there, she looked down at the contents of the basket: the four rats; potato peelings; egg shells; numerous bones (with as much gristle and fat attached as possible); rancid offal; four unwashed sanitary towels (from hemo girls who shared the room with her, and who were having their bizarre red flow); three pairs of breeches stolen from the adjacent room, where male staff slept, and which were obviously impregnated with their dried and crusty seed (spilled, no doubt, each night, while imagining her own body, pinned, sweaty beneath their thrusts).

Octavia forced her way through the opening.

Directly on the other side of the portcullis, the slitted nostrils, so close, turned her way and began to work. The fecund was very visible this time, sitting up in her pond, near to the bars. For a second, it seemed that the monster did not recognize Octavia, but suddenly she clapped her huge, scaly hands together.

"So quick," said the fecund. "Nice work. I *do* like you, my melancholy friend! Much better than that other silly old cow. I was thinking, you know, I feel I'm emerging from a dense fog. Why was I so attached to that old woman? Though, at first, I must admit, when you were right outside, I *swore* it was her approaching. Very strange: you smell almost exactly like her. Come closer, kholic, as close as you can, right up to the bars. I won't bite."

But Octavia stood her ground. "You look different."

"Nonsense. I have indigestion. Pregnancies are like that. Reflux, I suppose. I'm only in the first few hours but my hearts have a horrible burning sensation. You know? Or maybe I'm just hungry. Show me that fabulous basket. Do I see rats? My favourite! Lay 'em on me!"

Octavia leaned forward and tossed the rats by the tails, one at a time, through the bars of the portcullis, pulling swiftly back each time though the fecund did not try to strike, not once, or even move toward her. The fecund gobbled the rats whole. Octavia threw the handfuls of kitchen scraps, the bloodcloths and breeches, faster and faster, until the basket was emptied and mercifully light, and she just stood there panting. Her fingers bled from the sharp edges of the rattan and dripped with slimy waste. All the garbage had either been caught in the air by the snapping mouth or had been scooped out of the swamp before it had much of a chance to get wet.

Octavia licked her fingers clean.

Insects in the cell hummed and buzzed and gyrated; she brushed aside the ones that came at her through the bars.

Chewing the last scraps, the fecund watched Octavia. The monster's sharp teeth had made quick work of the meal. She swallowed, burped. "You're a cool customer, girl. I've been doing a little research on you."

"Research?"

The fecund showed her teeth. "You're very fascinating. Would you like to hear what I have to say? No? I can see you don't want to talk. Very well.

"While I digest, and gestate the little gift I've been forced to gestate, how about I tell you a story? Would you like that? To pass the time."

Octavia nodded, leaning against the damp wood of the door, the empty basket hanging from one hand.

"Well. All right, then, all right. Hold onto your knickers, this one's going to be creepy."

She nodded again.

"Long before people like you were tested for melancholy and whatever else officers of the palatinate look for, I think kids with black in their veins were just squashed at birth. Maybe a magistrate stuck a pitchfork in you. I don't recall. Brutal times, I suppose, but simpler in a way."

Octavia had been thinking the very same thing.

"Personally," continued the monster, "I've never wanted to be worshipped like a god. That's too obvious. Though I could have been, of course. I'm a creator, but a humble one."

"This is not really a story," said Octavia.

The fecund held up one long finger, for patience. "Naturally, I watched the pantheon descend, as did we all, burning through the sky as they came, thinking at first that they might be huge rocks thrown down to pierce the atmosphere, and that they would burn up upon entry, like other rocks do. I was just a young fecund back then, maybe a bit naïve. I watched the gods swoop down and land in forests and deserts and oceans.

"In those days, I should add, I could come and go as I pleased. There were not many humans around, certainly no city for you to live in. And, of course, you had not yet been chosen, so you were as mortal as you are today. The main difference—" she spat out a rat's skull, intact, which fell into the water with a plop "—is that you didn't know what you were missing. Following? Yes? Or am I boring you?"

"I'm following."

"Expansive territories I had painstakingly established—and which should still be mine today—were visible from the blue heaven you used to call the sky and from which your gods had recently tumbled. Poor girl, I can see by your reaction that you've never laid eyes on this celestial field, have you? Cerulean blue on clear days, the colour of wistfulness, of self-assurance. Ah, most likely my romantic soul recalls the skies as more beautiful than they really were.

"Some days, I'm sure, were pretty crappy.

"One thing for certain: the structure known as Jesthe existed, way back then, but as a small, almost quaint dwelling. A cute little cottage compared to the present monstrosity that towers over our heads.

"Living inside this version of Jesthe was a couple with red blood in their veins. One of each gender. A brother and sister."

The fecund laughed to see Octavia's reaction.

"I'm kidding. They weren't siblings. What kind of story do you think this is? How dull would it be to hear about the exploits of *siblings*? Are they attracted to each other? Will they sleep together? What's their special bond? Who cares! These people were fine sovereigns of their land and of their people. Proud specimens. Your friend, you know, the chatelaine, is a descendant of this couple. That's right, girl, the drunken sadsack you call your boss." Another white rat skull, clacking hollowly against the stones. "Anyhow, the young couple—and Jesthe, of course—eventually became *very* well known to me.

"The first castellan and chatelaine. Carolus and Anna. They had recently been wed. Anna was brought in from a neighbouring family, a miniscule village that today has been subsumed and forgotten. She was almost as crazy as Carolus."

"You never said he was crazy. You said he was proud."

"Well, he was crazy. Did I tell you Anna was twelve years old?"

"No."

"Why do people like that end up together? Have you ever wondered? I've seen it happen again and again. A strange phenomenon. Lunacy attracting lunacy. Then, of course, they encourage each other, I suppose, validate each other.

"But I digress.

"Carolus and Anna had three children, two boys and a girl.

"And Solum—for the settlement already had that name—grew around them."

Octavia squatted on her haunches, using the upturned basket for support.

"The family managed to lead their subjects in a state of quiet terror, during which there were small amounts of prosperity, it's true, and several great harvests, but the most memorable change of all during this period was a marked increase in the disappearances of nubile youths—primarily virginal females (such as, I'm sure, yourself)." Again laughter. "In fact, my dear Octavia, the shortage of birthing age women—from ten or so years old to perhaps sixteen—in the surrounding townships, soon became so profound and dire that feuds were fought over the few fertile daughters who managed, by luck, or by desperate plot, including lockdown, to remain within the auspices they were born into."

"I don't think I want to hear this story," Octavia said. "Can't you tell me another one?"

"You can't pick and choose. And why don't you like this one, anyhow? I was just getting to the good part. Listen:

"I smelled food. Jesthe had become irresistible, calling to me, wafting aromas I could not resist. I have a pronounced weakness, you understand, a metabolism you would never understand. I sniffed out this place. I watched the activity best I could from the safety of hedgerows, salivating, hearing screams no human could hear. Do you know what the castellan and his wife were up to?"

Octavia shook her head.

"They were bathing in the temperate fluids that spilled from the arteries of these girls—to stay young! That's right, my marked friend: red blood! Of all things! Madness and vanity combined.

"The new gods approved. What god doesn't like a blood bath?

"Knowing that my own appetites would be welcome, I approached. It was, as they say, a dark and stormy night. I knocked on the front door of Jesthe with a proposition for the happy couple.

"At first, they were suspicious. Naturally." The third skull ricocheted and the fecund appeared to transform briefly, becoming blurry around the edges before snapping back into place, sharper than before. "I introduced myself. And that, as you folks say, was the beginning of the good ol' days. The rest is history.

"Sadly, like I'd said, the couple turned out to be crazy as fleas. Carolus used to regularly drink fermented barley. A lot. Until he became quite unreliable and insensate. He became stupid when drunk. He never had a sense of humour at the best of times. For his own distorted reasons, he ended the deal we had worked out by catapulting the bloodless bodies of four dead girls over the walls of Jesthe, wasting perfectly good meals. He ranted that the blood of these girls had gone bad. Anna was sick in her bed. In his anger, Carolus marked the faces of the dead girls with black kohl!"

"Is this true?"

"True? What does true mean? Now stop interrupting me. Where was I? Ah, yes: bodies rained down on the farms beyond the gates, and all the rumours that had been circulating in the township about missing girls became very real.

"Jesthe was soon stormed.

"Me? I ran and hid. Of course, no bodies were ever found inside because they had been, well, disposed of, but the courtyard gardens—which opened behind the regal bedchambers—were discovered to be the site of intense flowerings. The soil was richer and blacker than any other garden for miles around." The monster smiled, perhaps at the memory of such vanished luxury. "And from the royal pond, which encircled the glorious bursts of roses and persimmons and dandelion, there came an odour most *peculiar*.

"Jesthe was torched.

"The couple, found huddled together in a false chamber in their own bedroom, were dragged from their hiding place and dismembered by a gaggle of distraught parents."

"Are you telling me how kholics began?"

"Will you please keep silent? Have respect for the storyteller."

"But—"

"Shh! From my hiding spot, I went nearly delirious with

emanations and emotions. One good thing had come to an end, yet I could not get over what a fabulously insane race you were! I never could have imagined such goings-on. Remaining hidden, trying not to burst out with excitement and awe, was very difficult for me.

"Jesthe, of course, is primarily stone, and did not catch fire.

"The water of the pond, however—where I had set up temporary quarters—nearly boiled me alive!

"After all this activity, crowds departed. Several of your years went by. I must have fallen asleep. Jesthe was repaired and returned to the three children, who promised never to do anything as wicked as their parents had done. The kids were, by this time, almost adults—and almost as scrambled in the head as their parents had been. Why were they given back the seat of power here at the palace? A good question. The masses are idiotic, unable to do anything without being told. But that's another story.

"These new leaders asked servants to identify themselves by dressing in red, for blood, and they implemented the testing of all babies, so that bad-tasting ones could be avoided when it was bath time."

"This is ridiculous. I don't believe a word of it. Now you're telling me about the palatinate?"

"Melancholy killed the parents. There's a direct relation. The girls that had poison in their veins were the ones tossed over the ramparts. Their children, the heirs, were acting out of loyalty. It all fits together."

Octavia turned away.

"Are you listening?"

"Yes."

"If you had parents, you might understand.

"After the incident, more and more houses were built. A perimeter wall was completed. In honour of your great new city, forests were razed, waters polluted. You bred indiscriminately, as you often do. Proliferated like mad, without thought.

"When I finally awoke, I was famished. I snacked on a dead duck and the few expired frogs that came my way. Then, once—oh lucky day (or so I thought)—I swallowed the delicious body of a child who had strayed too close to the pond and had drowned. A boy, I think it was. Rather bony, if I recall. Dressed in shorts. I kid you not. But say what I will about humans, you people are fond of your young, aren't you? Just like me. And you are quick to accuse. I tried to explain that the child was already dead and puffy but no one listened. I tried to explain that the fecund does not end lives, nor can she, but that she converts, or gives, life." The last rat skull, lobbed in Octavia's direction, fell just short of the portcullis.

"I've lost my place again. I must be getting old. I lose my place so often! Oh yes, I was in the pond, unhappily surprised by a group of searchers, who had been looking for their precious boy and had labelled me a killer. Like the previous crowd of vigilantes, these people had nasty pikes and nastier temperaments. I must have been sluggish from all those years of hunger and sleeping, for to my great shame, I was captured. Dragged from the water, relocated to this awful cell, I have been passed down from generation to generation, like an heirloom, my maternal gifts discovered, turned into an act, employed in numerous humiliating ways. I have given birth to armies, lovers, pets . . .

"I suppose the food here is all right. And the guests, sometimes, are ravishing, if somewhat quiet." She winked.

"That's a horrible story."

"I'm a monster. What did you expect? All my stories are horrible."

"I don't think that's how testing started and I don't think you've ever eaten anyone, even if they were dead."

"Don't make the mistake of liking me, girl. I warn you."

"I don't like you."

"I think you do. A little bit. Okay, here's another story:

"A lonely chatelaine, out for a walk, sees a pretty girl and falls in love. She brings the girl home."

"I know that one."

"Okay. How about this part? The chatelaine trusts the girl, who betrays her."

Octavia said nothing.

"Or this one:

"Long after the last traces of Nowy Solum crumbled, the site was excavated. A foundation was poured on the mix of bricks and bones, a foundation for one of the tallest office buildings ever conceived. In this building, orphans were trained to become huge machines, each capable of travelling between the stars—"

"How long will it take before you give birth?"

"Oh. Changing the topic? No more stories today?"

"No."

"All right, then, I'll answer your question. When will I deliver? It's not that easy, Octavia. I'd like to tell you something simple, like next week. But it's complicated. Plus, this pregnancy seems to be different than the others. I've told you that already." The fecund blinked. For the briefest of moments, the expression on her face reflected sincerity, maybe even fear or self-doubt. "Are you sure you don't want to come a little closer to the bars?"

"No." Octavia began to back out of the cell.

"Wait. Let me tell you one last thing. Trouble is brewing in the city of Nowy Solum. You and your brother are in great danger."

Returning home, the benevolent sisters flew metres apart, low over the water, getting neither farther nor closer together. Clouds overhead were thinner here and paler pockets could be seen between the pulled shapes of cumuli. No light reflected off the sisters' skin and, for a moment, they vanished, leaving vague, distorted patches that winked back into corporeal existence.

Beneath them, the ocean waters were calm, though recently there had been a great storm.

Coming over the beach of black stone, banking over brush and thin scrub, they slowed. Detritus had washed up on the shore: driftwood, branches, clumps of seaweed. Several dead or crippled seals lay entangled, not moving. Stranded on one inlet, the body of a huge cephalopod was slowly being decimated by a thousand shrieking gulls and as many silent crabs. Registering this carnage and destruction with dismay, the benevolent sisters circled. There would be work to do to retain order.

For now, other issues pressed.

Continuing toward the mountain, they reduced their wakes to minimal. Few branches swayed, fallen leaves lifted gently and settled again. Scarlet birds exploded, screaming from a broken acacia, and moved as one; the sisters banked to avoid sucking any into their scoops.

Barely wide enough for their full span, they had to stop to enter the cave, alighting and then hopping from rock to rock, or briefly hovering as their eyes scanned the dark within.

There was water in here, too, but fresh, heavy with minerals, shining with bioluminescence.

The people harvested shrimp and clams and small, blind fish. Though their exemplar had told the people that the goddesses had awoken, and a few of them had actually watched the sisters leave, to see them so close now caused witnesses to bow, or swoon, with evident apprehension. A few fell, prostate, to the sand. Women wept, perhaps with joy, and children ran along the shore of the dark lake, no sign of the fear or uncertainty their parents felt, splashing water up in sprays of silver with their feet as they tried to keep up.

The sisters waggled their fingers to return the greetings, and to allay doubts.

Yet they, too, were concerned.

Beyond the cave, a narrow exit: they emerged, able to stretch again, soaring in the relative brightness of the central crater. They passed over simple structures, tiers of gardens. More people— looking up, bodies trim and brown—paused in their work.

As Kingu and Aspu came in for a landing on the shale pad, they called for the exemplar, who, from his front deck of his home, had been watching the sisters' return with a degree of trepidation.

Seven years he had been more than content to be the chosen one, with the host in his body. Never had he performed duties other than listening to benign whisperings, pondering instructions on planting or building, or giving out instructions himself about offerings and sacrifices. His four fat wives had agreed to be with him as a direct result of his position. They certainly treated him well. Seven years he had first choice at feasts. His hut was large and in a prime location at the mountain's foot.

But now, as the host inside him tugged uncomfortably, and his saliva tasted bitter, the sisters barked at him to appear: he would gladly have surrendered the position to anyone, anyone at all—

Meet us, the benevolent sisters cried. *Meet us*!

At least this time he wore his sandals.

Jogging the path toward the goddesses' slab, with large red flowers bowing either side of him, the exemplar soon stood near where the sisters were settling, bless them, pinging and hissing as their temperatures shifted. That heat again, washing over him. Their eyes were open.

"Aspu," he said. "Kingu. Most benevolent sisters. Bless you. Happy returns. There was, uh, there was a storm, and we lost several nets. And—"

He stopped. Aspu was splitting in two. Or maybe it was Kingu. With his heart thudding, the exemplar watched as the goddess slowly gaped wider and wider. What must have been her mouth extended back, past her shoulders, opening so wide that the benevolent sister's entire front half was divided.

Inside was a dim interior, peppered by tiny lights. No bodily fluids or entrails spilled forth.

Exemplar, said the sisters, *come closer*.

His feet managed to obey. He stepped onto the shale slab. Now he saw movement inside the body of the goddess, and he heard moaning.

These women need fresh water, and food. Nothing heavy, just bananas for now. And aloe cream. Lots of it.

"Women?" he repeated, idiotically. "What women?"

No answer.

Panic rose in him. He felt like a child must feel, on the verge of tears, when confronted with an inexplicable, confounding aspect of the adult world.

Go, exemplar, get what we asked you. These women are nearly dead.

Squinting, he tried to peer into the goddess's mouth—and he did see them, he did! Two women, prone, arms at their sides. There was room inside the throat of the benevolent sister for a dozen people or more. No blood at all, just hard shapes in there and what looked like chairs and shimmering figures of light, and the two women, half-naked, reclined on cots.

Go!

The host sent jolts through the exemplar's body. He staggered off to obey.

The chatelaine arranged for her fire to be relit, and asked that servants be sent up to the dungeon to light her father's fire. Naturally, there was mild protest concerning this request, for none of the women wanted to venture up a tower only to have the naked castellan heap abuse on them, but protests over assignments from the chatelaine could not last for long, or be particularly strong; two fat women vanished, faces covered by gauze, grumbling from her chambers, to carry out the unpleasant task.

The afternoon tryst with Octavia had taken an edge off the chatelaine and helped give her the fortitude to recover from the visit with her father, though his comments about a grandchild still stung. The castellan was hurtful, and the chatelaine was not sure why she insisted on treating him as anything but. Snippets of the conversation were impossible to ignore and these fragments disturbed her chances at more pleasant daydreams. Of course her pets were like children to her. Given the countless times and countless partners with which she'd had congress, she was quite positive that bearing children of her own was not possible. Her father should know that and show more sensitivity, especially on the day that one of her lovely pets had been stolen.

Maybe she and the kholic could raise a child together?

The chatelaine shook her head, almost laughing aloud; these thoughts were ridiculous. She lay down on her bed. Now that she had taken measures to replace the cherub—having sent Octavia in her stead—she found herself reconsidering her decision to grant the palatinate access to the entire palace. What were the chances that she would get robbed again? Did she *really* want Jesthe—and Nowy Solum, for that matter—to return to the grip of authority it had once been crushed in?

She sighed, imagining guards outside her room at night, scowling with disapproval while she lay in bed, spooning with the kholic.

Presently, the chatelaine heard the sounds of logs being added to her fireplace and the business of someone trying to light them; she realized she had dozed off. She sat up.

The women by the fireplace were not paying her the least attention.

"Thank you," said the chatelaine, brushing herself off. She had spoken loudly and promptly to preempt any comments that might be made about her, if the women had not seen her asleep on the bed. They turned to watch her now before returning to their tasks. The chatelaine considered leaving her chambers so the servants would not see that she really had nothing to do, no tasks at this time of day, but instead she got up and lingered over by her cages, feeding her remaining pets pieces of dried bread from a basket she kept filled for such occasions.

She wondered how Octavia's second encounter with the fecund had played out. By now, the girl had surely made her way from the kitchens to feed the creature prerequisite scraps. Each day

Octavia would need to repeat this: the fecund, when pregnant, ate voraciously.

Each day, the monster would change.

Suddenly overcome by a mad urge to see her kholic lover again—who might possibly be the only person in existence ever to understand the chatelaine, she said, "You there, women by the fires."

Both staff turned once more.

"I'm afraid I have forgotten your names."

"Georgia," said one.

"Thea," said the other.

"Fine. Please fetch Lorichus when you are done, Georgia and, er, Thea, was it? I wish to get dressed."

"Yes."

The fire stoked, beginning to crackle, the two servants left. Shortly after, Lorichus arrived. The chatelaine commanded Lorichus to fetch her blue surcoat, the one with the yellow fur lining, and to find her green leggings. She believed this outfit to be her most flattering. Lorichus did as she was told and then helped the chatelaine get dressed, pulling on the hose while the chatelaine sat on the edge of the bed, attaching the garters, getting her feet into the slippers. Finally the servant arranged the chatelaine's long hair so it was piled precariously atop her head.

"A special visitor?"

She searched the woman's round red face for traces of irony or sarcasm but Lorichus, who was fussing with the pins in her hair, seemed sincere enough. "Of course, I have the quotidian assembly with Erricus, but for now I am going out."

Perhaps recalling a previous outing, one that had ended rather unpleasantly, Lorichus paused, eyebrow lifted. "Outside of Jesthe?"

"No, no," the chatelaine replied. Her answer evidently caused the servant more confusion, though the woman asked nothing further.

At last satisfied with the hair, Lorichus rubbed sheep fat onto the chatelaine's cheeks but, growing impatient, the chatelaine dismissed her servant with a wave of both hands.

From the other side of the room, her fire roared.

Moments later, the chatelaine strode the Great Hall, surcoat billowing.

Without assistance, though he lay groaning, reaching out, even calling for help, path's father finally managed to get to his feet. Feeling very tiny in this place, and quite ill, he came slowly to understand that his son was no longer around. The sling, still around his neck, was not only empty but the frame had been smashed when he'd fallen and was useless. In more ways than one, he felt lighter. Could it truly be that path was gone? He looked all around: dozens of people, going about their cryptic business in this city, but no sign of the boy.

Then, for these crowds of citizens and for Nowy Solum, he felt a quick rush of giddy gratitude. He almost exclaimed with the surprising joy that burst inside him. His eyes watered. Though the journey had nearly killed him, the destination had taken away his burden as soon as they had entered the front gates. There was no more strange presence, no more fear of what his son was becoming, no more pressure.

He took a deep breath, filling his lungs to capacity for the first time in ages. Under a dark archway, he removed the sling from around his neck and let it drop to the street.

Without path, well . . . he might even linger here, in Nowy Solum. For a little while. And, if he ever felt that his boy was nearby, why, he could just steer clear. There was room enough here for both of them. That is, if path was even still alive.

He searched inside himself to see if this morbid thought left residues of remorse, but it did not.

He was *free*.

Had not a massive man leaned over path, as path rolled into the gutter? If this man had taken his son, and the spirit that had entered path continued to transform him, then the big stranger would need the best of luck.

"Viti," he said, which was the name of path's father, the name he had been born with. No one had spoken it aloud, not since his wife's death. He smiled. His name had invigorated his tongue and palette. His name echoed off the walls and faded down the streets. He said it again, louder, feeling as though he were waking from a deep sleep. The giant could keep his damned son! Helpless and demanding, the rotten boy had killed his own mother, draining her day by day. Path was the reason she had gone mad, the reason she did the things she did with the men who passed through. Death for his wife had been a merciful release.

Shame she hadn't lived to be here now, with viti, in the big city! All the fights, the arguments: these had been path's doing, the pressure of having a child like him for a son—

Grinning again, viti took a step forward, not caring which direction he went, for each direction held unknown futures and unlimited possibilities, but as he put his foot down he heard a loud crack from above and someone screamed. The last thing viti did was glance up before the briefest flash of discomfort was followed by an eternity of grey static.

Nahid came awake, familiar pains throughout, dim light driving into his eyes, still very much under the ill-effects of his melancholy, which had been surging inside of late. At first, he assumed it morning, and that his memory and body suffered not only from the curse in his veins but from a compound of too many buds and ales. His vision was blurred, his head pounding, his nose excruciating.

He was outside, in an alley.

Had there been a fight?

Half-sitting, with his back against a mossy wall, he discovered that more than just his face was sore: most of his body, in fact, when he tried to move, ached. His head must have hit the soft brick behind him because his skull felt like it had split in two. Something had bruised his chest and shoulders.

There *had* been a fight.

With a gang? Had he battled a hundred officers of the palatinate?

Daytime. Not morning at all. The faint sounds of people from a nearby street, but there were no people here, nor windows in the adjacent walls. The alley itself was hardly wide enough for him to stretch out both arms, if he could move them—a dead end.

Then he realized where he was. He used this route as part of a shortcut to scale the roof and then descend on the other side of the row of tiny houses, to get to the Gardens of Jesthe: he was just off Endicott's Alley, verging the centrum.

He had been about to visit Octavia.

He remembered waiting, then, outside Jesthe, to see her, and the guards—

Nahid tried to get to his feet but the pain in his limbs was fierce. He shifted his shoulders and legs to ensure his spine was intact. There had already been morning today. During the night, he had entered Jesthe with Name of the Sun, released the cherub, gotten dumped at Hakim's place.

And had been smashed backwards against the wall.

Nahid propped himself up on one elbow, though his body continued to protest, and the throbbing in his head so intense it threatened to make him pass out. Whatever had crashed into him lay still, in a heap, at the end of the alley. He saw a hand, part of a thin leg. To Nahid, trying to understand what he was looking at, it appeared as if a small, skinny teen had been stuffed into a black sack of some sort—with arms and legs poking out—and then wrapped in a large, shiny blanket before being thrown with considerable force at the wall.

Forcing himself into a crouching position and moving forward, Nahid put one hand on the crumpled heap—which felt very warm— and began to lift the thick material aside, searching for a face within. The sensation against his fingers was like none he had felt before: the odd covering was warm and thin, yet pliant as hide. It was also sticky with fluids, but whether this fluid was red or black or something else altogether Nahid could not be sure. His fingers became stained and clammy. In the dim light from the lanterns on the street, he saw the face, sunken and pinched. On the forehead, above a smashed mask (that Nahid thought might be tattooed there, until he felt it), was a grave wound. Very few teeth in the open mouth, and the few that were there were stained brown and worn down to the gum line. The stench of the man was like ripe refuse. Under the mask, the yellow eyes were half-open but rolled back, showing neither pupil nor iris.

The man was alive.

For an instant, like a fool, Nahid looked up at the low clouds, as if there might be more of these seraphim descending.

Nothing.

Smooth metal rods and cryptic pieces of hardware that flickered tiny lights at him caused inexplicable bulges Nahid could not fully access. With his knees pressed up against the unconscious man's chest, he did manage to find—tucked into a pocket—an object roughly the shape and size of a child's forearm. As he touched this gently, a chill made his body shudder. His pains ebbed.

Drawing in his breath, Nahid withdrew the artifact, icy cold, but quickly getting warm as his own flesh. The surface was impossibly smooth. He rubbed the device with his thumb and distant voices started to whisper in his head. A woman, speaking a different language? A child?

He turned the treasure around and the whispering ceased. On the sides, tiny engravings—writing of some sort—scrolled like marching insects. The letters glowed dimly. Thin white filaments extended as he watched, poking feebly against his wrist, tapping there, as if trying to get in.

Should he leave the body here, slink back to the ostracon as if nothing happened, to sleep and recover?

But there were poisons in everyone, spirits in their veins. . . .

His plan had been to kill the chatelaine.

The woman's voice resumed, like a wind blowing through him.

He squatted over the broken creature for some time, until it began to moan. Then he slid the object into the waist of his shorts. As the whispering grew louder still, Nahid managed to stand.

Name of the Sun had hoped to sleep, for she had a shift in the evening at The Cross-Eyed Traveller, but she was already convinced she would not be able to function at work, nap or no nap. She had bitten her nails to the quick.

Her room was small and damp, seldom empty during the late afternoon. Most often her roommates were there—Dora, Nina, and Polly—drinking beer, shrieking with laughter. Or the landlord dropped by. Sometimes all four were cramped into the tiny space when Name of the Sun came home. The landlord was always smiling, always nodding, affable, always trying to get any of the girls to sleep with him in exchange for rent. The other three had ofttimes taken him up on his offer.

When Nahid had come back to the room with her, and everyone was crammed in there, the situation had been awkward, to say the least. Her and the kholic could barely even fit inside, let alone have privacy. But the party would inevitably break up shortly after she pulled Nahid in, looking down at the floor, sitting in a corner, not saying anything. The expressions, the gaffes, the exchanged looks and awkward silences: these had been priceless.

Now the girls must have been at a pub. Quietly, quickly, Name of the Sun unfastened her robe, eager to sleep—or to try—before her roommates tumbled in.

Had Nahid, she wondered—pulling her blouse up over her head—cast a spell over her? Were there traces of his affliction in the semen she had let spill across her stomach or had even swallowed? What could possibly cause the kholic to exert such influence over her? Name of the Sun sincerely wanted to stay away from the kholic, though images of his body, lying on the mattress with her in this very room, and memories of him holding her while she slept, and the feel of his grimy body pressed against her—the thrill of looking into his eyes, against that black mask—flickered relentlessly through her mind.

Only when she found herself thinking that maybe she should give him another chance—that it was true, what he said, she could never relate to his pain, being neither a twin nor a kholic—did Name of the Sun actually laugh out loud and bitterly force herself to imagine something, anything, else.

She brushed at her mattress to rid it of fleas as best she could. Once under her sheet, she idly began to masturbate, as she often did when she was tired and needed to sleep, but her wrist soon became sore and she recognized that the effort to come would be too great, so she lay still, unsuccessfully managing to keep her mind from dwelling on the reasons for the demise of her recent relationship, and why they seemed to make such little sense now.

The closest Name of the Sun came to being distracted was when she wondered, for a little while, about Nahid's twin sister. Though Name of the Sun had never met the girl, she would very much like to: Octavia could attract a woman such as the chatelaine and could cause Nahid such anguish. Nahid often said that Octavia looked just like him. In which case, Name of the Sun understood the pull that the sister might have; she must have been gorgeous.

Later, still awake, though she might have slept for a moment,

Name of the Sun began ruminating about Nahid's list—his three objectives: fighting, getting high, and fucking—leaving her hand where it was, immobile on her damp mons, all arousal long-vanished.

There came a scratching at the door. She lay, alert again, listening to the patterns of sounds: not as if someone were trying to get in, but as if an animal, maybe, were digging, or some other resident of the city, sharpening claws on the wood.

Silently, she got of bed. Holding the sheet up, she called out softly.

The scratching stopped.

And began again.

Taking a deep breath, and another, Name of the Sun unbolted the door with shaking fingers, yanking it open—

The stoop was empty. She looked up the street. Down. There were people in the fog, old buildings. Wet stone and crumbling brick and the scents of the humid evening.

Nothing unusual—

Except two cognosci, racing into the crowd on all fours.

Naturally, hornblower had been more than a little reluctant to step inside Anu's mouth. He did not really want to even *look* in there. But the angry sky power had waited, inert, gaping at branch level, while hornblower stood trembling among the dead bodies of his fellows. Wind sang in the branches and the sun got stronger. Ambassadors buzzed around. Finally, when he did not move, two sinuous fingers—very much in appearance like the common green snakes served at most feasts—extended from the bottom of Anu's chin, moving slowly but with dread certainly and, under the ambassador's guidance, took hornblower solidly around the waist; hornblower either had to hop forward into Anu's throat or fall off the edge of the great limb and discover what was really under the clouds, like Pan Renik had done.

Only without wings.

He chose to hop forward, landing on a surface flatter and harder than he had imagined.

Anu bobbed with his weight.

The power was large, and clean, extending back farther than hornblower thought possible, with rows of small yellow lights either side and room for a dozen people, at least. He focused on what could only be a seat, and to this he clung. The material he gripped was soft, certainly not carved from the meat of the world or woven from her leaves. When hornblower risked a quick glance about, he knew that Anu was made of unfamiliar materials. Polymers, the teachings said, but the word seemed pale and hollow in the face of these marvels. Most of the yellow lights he had seen when he first jumped inside appeared now to be writing, and this writing floated in the air. Tiny figures danced and shimmered. Hornblower held onto the chair as if nothing could ever pry him out of it again.

Outside the mouth, he saw the array of dead padres, sprawled on the branch. Red sap ran in rivulets from their ears and noses. Their faces were contorted with final agony. So easily had Anu killed them all. Every padre had been wiped out with a thought or quiet word. Except for him. Hornblower choked back fear for his own future, wanting to cry out, to shout questions, but knowing he'd best remain silent unless he wanted to end up like his brethren.

Farther along the branch, peeking from their huts, several members of the settlement watched. He saw the two girls he had planned on visiting after the funeral standing agog before their hut, and he wondered if they would try to help him. Should he call out to them? But this might also anger Anu, so he merely nodded, to reassure the girls, and gave them a desperate wave: they retreated from sight.

Perhaps the people believed that Anu had called for him, and had devoured his body because he was devout, the best padre ever, the only padre to achieve this miraculous honour—

With a quiet whir, Anu's mouth closed.

His view of the settlement was cut off.

Dimmer inside now, but the intensity of the yellow lights rose, and images crackled and spun, flickering strange characters at him, passing right through him. He tried to touch them as they swirled but could not.

Careful not to hyperventilate, hornblower pushed farther back into the seat. He wanted to vomit as the sky power began to sway, expecting to be chewed any second by hidden teeth, or digested by a flood of stomach enzymes.

When nothing like this occurred, he risked longer looks around. A series of odd noises, accompanied by the occasional distant voice, crackled through the short wall at his knees, though this voice spoke in words he could not understand, and as if from a terrible distance.

The smell in the power was like the sky right before clouds got dark.

Rocking back and forth, waiting for any clues, trying to be humble and devout but not sure what to do with his hands, hornblower came to the conclusion that he really could not make his situation much worse. Cautiously, slowly, he began to explore. Mere visuals at first, staring with growing awe at the treasures. Someone such as himself, though nevertheless a padre—a powerful padre at that—was surely not meant to understand or perhaps even lay eyes on such incredible wonders.

Hornblower touched Anu, so lightly, reverentially with the tips of his fingers. The flesh of the power was warm and tingling. His hand passed through the dancing yellow lights—

And a tiny slot opened before him. Blinking, he had a view of brightness—shreds of white and blue hurtling toward his face— that made him recoil, turning aside to avoid these shapes tearing through him. He braced himself for impact.

Yet the shapes did no damage, made no sound. He felt no wind against him. Hornblower turned slowly toward the slot again: the white forms continued to pass, brief blurs before vanishing, as if behind him—though when he glanced back he saw only the dim interior of Anu, and other empty chairs, and the dancing yellow lights.

Facing forward again, prepared for the visceral onslaught, he realized that these shapes were *outside* Anu, and that they were moving in the sky beyond—

No. The shapes were not moving. *Anu was.*

Hornblower lurched forward to get a better look. There was a material, clear as air but solid, between him and outside, preventing wind and the white shreds from hitting him. With a knuckle he rapped this cover.

The shapes were clouds, the blue was sky.

No part of his world remained visible: no branches, no leaves.

Anu had left the settlement behind.

"Great sky power," hornblower wailed, "where are you taking me? Where are we going?"

Anu slowed; hornblower felt this change of speed in his stomach and he gripped the armrests until his fingers turned white again. All he could see through the slot was clouds, lit by the sun. No more sky, no more firmament. Droplets of moisture appeared on the clear cover. Anu began to rock violently.

They were inside the poisonous clouds!

"Please, Anu, speak to me. I beg of you."

Then something very much like a flattened ambassador shot up before hornblower, tiny wings buzzing.

Seatbelt, it said.

"Ambassador, please, tell me, what have I done? Is Anu angry with me? Where is he taking me?"

Current wind patterns, said the ambassador, *at sea level, have been calculated. These are accessible in the database. Exterior drones are unable to navigate through the seeded cumuli and remain above. They will keep watch there. Could you get the exemplar to link to the server?*

"I don't understand." He almost wept. "I don't know what is required of me."

No drones accompany us. The ambassador had small legs, pointed and tucked under. *You are without visual but the main process has been initiated. You will need to link soon.*

"Please . . ."

There are signals from the seegee. Weak, but we have a trail. Surface area of sail and the angle of descent have been reviewed. The search is currently defined to a four hundred kilometre radius, bearing seven two seven oh. Most likely he was drawn to the city. We ride at seven thousand. Six five. Six. Exemplar process has to commence before further downward travel.

Hornblower closed his eyes. All he understood was that the sky power was descending. Very soon—if he ever had the courage to look out the little covered slot again—he would learn what all the dead had learned.

Over the past few days, Octavia had been trained as a cofferer, polishing the chatelaine's collection of silver cups; it was to this function she now returned. She had also spent time in Jesthe folding tablecloths, making candles, blending sauces, plucking chickens, counting money, and washing sheets. Trying to fall back into more routine parts of her recent days, her mind, however, whirled. Time on the streets of Nowy Solum, being with Nahid, seemed so long ago.

By mentioning the trouble she and her brother were apparently in, the fecund had indicated to Octavia that she, the monster, was aware of the duplicity. She had mentioned betrayal. The dream that Octavia had fed to the fecund already seemed to be changing patterns in startling ways, shifting invisible alliances and allegiances. Octavia had no idea what she was getting into or what she had done. Was the fecund hers now, as much as it had previously belonged to the chatelaine?

The strip of cloth had torn easily from her shift. Sucking on it, wetting it thoroughly with spit, right after leaving the chatelaine. Then she had tossed it to the fecund while the chatelaine's batten remained in her pocket. Just like that.

The night previous, she had only dreamed of being reunited with her brother. Hadn't she?

Now the question Octavia asked of herself was: when to leave Jesthe?

If she chose to wait, what was she waiting for?

Inside the small room where she worked were other servants, all of whom had been polishing when Octavia came back, her clothes filthy, stinking, stained with grease and lard and the moisture of vegetable peelings, dripping with meat scraps. Her thighs trickled, possibly juices from the chatelaine herself. Octavia saw the other girls raise their eyebrows and exchange hushed comments as she entered.

She took her place next to Jovi, who was fat and sullen, and who worked on utensils, while another girl, who never spoke, whom the others just called Girly, polished saucers. A third girl rubbed half-heartedly at the larger plates. All of their hands were permanently blackened by tarnish. Octavia's were well on their way. Black hands, black face. The room smelled strongly of lemons and metal and the pervasive tang of caustic tarnish.

"Look what the cobalis spit up," said Diogene, rubbing at a plate as if in battle; Octavia had offered no explanation why she was late for her shift or why she was covered in garbage.

Staring down, Octavia tried her best to ignore the stares and comments. These girls, like most staff, had seen the chatelaine stop by on several occasions to talk to her; they had seen Octavia's demure responses. Of course they harboured resentments. Struggling to comprehend the situation, this change in Jesthe and in their lives, they knew only that the girl was favoured by the chatelaine when she should have been cleaning outhouses, or on the streets, where she really belonged, peeling guts from the roadside. But worse than this, the girls also knew that, despite Octavia's melancholy, and her tattoo and proper status in Nowy Solum, Octavia was far more attractive, inside and out, than they were or could ever be, and this knowledge would never be reconciled or forgiven.

For Octavia, attentions that her body and face had received since she was a girl had never added up to anything positive. She had been raped, groped by men, slapped by white-faced women for the crime of catching the straying eye of their husbands. She had been kicked and chased and had heard so many disparaging comments that she was numb to them now. So what if Octavia had used her looks to seduce and betray the chatelaine? So what?

As she watched her distorted reflection become clearer and clearer in the curved surfaces of the cup she cleaned, she thought again about the fecund's warning. *Big trouble*, the monster had said. Could the fecund really know what would happen? Octavia wondered how best to return to the cell for a third time. Perhaps, she thought, she should visit the monster right now, to test the fecund to see what influence she might have over the beast's actions and ramblings—

"Here comes your friend," said Diogene under her breath. "Fucking garbage whore."

Sure enough, when Octavia glanced up, she saw the chatelaine coming down the hall, dressed in outlandish clothes, her cheeks smeared with grease and her hair piled high. She was smiling, waving: Octavia looked swiftly down at the floor again.

Third visit be damned. The prudent thing to do was get out of Jesthe as soon as possible.

THE FECUND'S MELANCHOLY DAUGHTER

The second cobali to die that day died quietly, without yielding any secrets. The castellan had not managed to learn any new traits of the humours, nor splice anything of interest to the small body. He had only inserted splines into each femur, working them gently into the marrow, and was about to install a series of minute gears to form a tertiary joint when life eked from the beast, rising up slowly to the ceiling in a vague shape of sadness and resignation before dispersing. The castellan stared at the emptied corpse in disbelief. He had not even really cut the creature, had not gone near its liver or spleen. He swore. Cobali were almost useless. A few small incisions, even in areas such as the groin, legs, and the hump of meat where the arms met the torso, and the little beasts expired.

He let his instruments clatter to the table. He was getting nowhere. Proclivity for easy death caused major challenges; there had to be a fire burning in the heart's furnace and movements of chylus for the castellan to attach anything to a living body. Any fool could graft material to a corpse once the liver stopped production; an inert body was a lost cause.

What the castellan needed was either a different sort of creature or a way to come up with a furnace of his own, an external one that would keep subjects alive whether the bodies cooperated or not.

Conjuring images of this innovation, and of how it might work, the castellan rested for a while. Thanks to the frailties of his own humours, and of the pumps that circulated them, his energies waned readily of late. He was an old man. Over the past weeks— even months—research had been fruitless. Devotions flagged.

Also, Terra Bella's visit had disturbed him more than he liked to admit.

In younger days, after seceding, he had hoped his daughter would be able to keep control of the city, perhaps even restore Nowy Solum to previous glories, but with every encounter he was reminded that the poor girl was as inefficient and fragile as he had been.

A son, thought the castellan. Like his daughter had said, he should have had a son.

What would happen when both he and Terra Bella were gone? The line of castellans and chatelaines, finished. . . .

He wanted to go to the window just then, to look out thoughtfully, but it had rained earlier and rain brought disease down from the clouds, so he just brushed idly at the blue corpse of the cobali with his hand, holding the dead face and peering into the glazed, coppery eyes. The creatures were annoying at best, though he conceded that perhaps they might harbour a remote intelligence and have primitive notions, like himself, of what challenges a family might represent.

He imagined for a moment that to catch such creatures must be a difficult task for the unscrupulous and rather overweight thief known as Tully.

Given the chance, cobali could take a nasty chunk from one's hand—if one's hand came too close to the round little mouths and pinsharp teeth. More than once the castellan had been forced to smash his fist down on a specimen that had fought back or had sunk its fangs into the meat of his thumb; when his mind wandered (as it often did), he could be distracted enough to let cobalis bite him.

He glanced at the third and final creature, watching as it tried to make itself smaller against the table, cowering, chattering. Did he have the energy to try again?

He did not reach for the beast. Nor pick up his tools. The small arms and legs, boney like a frog's, had been crudely sewn together. The thread that bound the limbs was looped over a hook set into the tabletop.

This specimen was female.

What had Terra Bella said? Trapping the beasts was no longer permissible? What ridiculous bills she passed, what ridiculous pastimes. He shook his head. His daughter, too, was in need of a rest, a change of setting—

From outside the window of the dungeon came faint grunts and scrapes and a gruff curse: someone scaled the tower. *Tully.* Had to be Tully. No one else was permitted to come this high. Bringing another batch of cobali, no doubt, to cut up and kill. Timing was good. Only one left. Had he conjured Tully with his thoughts?

"Friends arrive," he told the frightened creature, which hissed at him, so the castellan turned from his work table to watch Tully's massive hands appear—first the knuckles of one, then of the second—on the window ledge. One day the man would fall. The castellan would not be heartbroken but would certainly struggle for a means to get more specimens.

A hairy forearm, big as a roast, then Tully's ugly, shaggy head, red-faced, straining in the window. Tully grimaced further when he saw the castellan. "Don't elp me, it's all right. Just stand there."

The castellan ignored the comments. "I ask you to wear a mask when you visit me, man. Are you well? If you have any ailments, or feel at all ill or feverish, come no closer."

"I feel great. Just fucking great. And you ain't taking none of my blood to look at for yer little bugs." Grunting, and a calloused foot landed on the sill; those forearms tightened.

"Blood? I don't want to consider your blood. But come no closer! Why isn't your mouth covered?"

"Your little friends out there checked me on the climb. They done their tests to let me up. Your creepy helper and such. Now you just wait to see what I brung you. I was all excited-like and I forget to bring my mask. But I'm clean—"

"Remain there!" The castellan backed off. Infections and emanations from inside this cretin could kill a horse.

But the big man had clambered in. He stood in the dungeon, grinning, trying to catch his breath. He had his trap bag over his shoulder.

"You're mad. I'll need to have the area scrubbed. Cover your mouth, at least."

"Look at this." Still grinning, Tully held out the bag.

"Eh? That's— That's no cobali." The castellan could tell by the way the bag hung. Forgetting his fears for a second—for he was beginning to tingle with excitement—he watched the heavy body in the bag—one body, the size of small dog or cognosci—*move*. If Tully had brought him the latter, the castellan would be furious: the beasts were stupid and filthy. Tully knew that. Yet movements in the bag mesmerized the castellan. "What do you have? What's in there?"

"May I approach?"

"Stay on your side. Turn your face away. Are your hands clean, at least?"

Tully laughed. "Clean as my arse, I suppose." He took a few steps closer, without invitation, still holding out the bag. "For the love of the gods, why do I have to see your wrinkled old johnson every time I come up here?"

"Please, show decorum." The castellan stepped back even more, to keep distance between himself and Tully.

One bushy eyebrow cocked. "And did you see them, castellan? Roaring through on their mysterious errands?"

"Who?"

"The goddesses. Just a short time ago."

"What? What are you saying? I might have heard some commotion or other from down there. Always some commotion from you lot. Don't change the subject."

The last cobali, tugging on the cords that tied it to the table, watched in terror as the large man approached.

"You see," said Tully, "I was at South Gate—"

Holding up one hand, the castellan gave the command for silence. So many creatures were borne on the winds that issued from the bellows of the chest and from the lips of others when they spoke or when they breathed. These could sicken a man, transform him, and even kill him if he was in a weakened state.

Plus, Tully talked an incessant load of shit.

"Will it try to escape? Whatever it is. Will it? Nod or shake your head."

Tully chuckled and shook his head, putting the bag down on the table. In a loud whisper, he said, "From outside the city. I watched 'em come in. He can't go nowhere."

"He? Remove the bag."

Tully did so, and out rolled a boy with no arms and no legs, face clenched tight, blinking his tiny eyes in the dungeon's light. His forehead was massive, his lantern-jaw jutting. Yet, for a moment, the castellan was too stunned to comprehend what he was even looking at.

Empowered by the reports of numerous eyewitnesses, several of whom were among his own palatinate, visions of returning gods had inflamed him, invigorated him. He had not seen them, for they were gone by the time he got outside, but nevertheless his decision to oversee the morning's trial had been ordained and validated; the chamberlain felt a great deal more vital than he had for as long as he could remember. A time of rebirth! His limbs did not ache and his heart thudded in his chest like that of a younger man. This was a renaissance for him, for the palatinate, for all Nowy Solum.

The eyes of the chamberlain glinted like pieces of polished stone. His face was firm, lined with stern crevasses. He stood very still in the Ward of Jesthe, fingers together, his robe sweeping the floor, adding to the illusion that he might be a statue. On his head he wore a red miter, the same red as his gown, a metre in height.

The visitor to Jesthe, who had been escorted in by officers, now said, "A way has been cleared."

"Ah yes? Explain."

"You've seen the results, over the rooftops of our beleaguered city?"

The chamberlain cleared his throat. "We were visited by benevolent Aspu, and her sister, Kingu."

"Yet there is still much work to be done."

"I'm not sure I follow you. The goddesses have sent us a clear sign." Until recently, the man before him had been an unwelcome visitor to Jesthe, an irritant in the city, most likely insane, certainly dangerous. Now, in the light of recent events, the chamberlain was not so sure. "We will not sanction killing in any form," he said. "Is this what you're saying? We will not sanction violence without a proper trial or blessing from myself."

Behind the chamberlain, seven officers of the palatinate stood, also in red robes, also with narrowed eyes and stern faces.

"I don't know anything about killings. I'm here to tell you that there have been transgressions. These need to cease before the way becomes cleaner still." The man rubbed at the stubble on his narrow chin.

"You presume to tell the palatinate this?"

"Am I to be detained?"

"No," said the chamberlain. "You are being cautioned."

"Just today," the visitor continued, "there was a woman, sullied by activities in Hangman's Alley. A red-blooded girl. A hemo. And a fight, on Hoffstater Avenue."

"You refer, of course, to one kholic? The same kholic?"

"The darkest bile. I have seen him imbibing in public. He met my gaze."

"There will be no more killing."

"Killing? There has been no killing."

"I believe there has."

"We mark the unclean, make delineations. We prepare our city, chamberlain. Marking abodes, associates, haunts. We all need to prove that we are ready."

"Again, I caution you."

By the visitor's side cowered chained cognosci; chains rattled.

"You are not cautious," said the chamberlain, eyeing the disgusting beasts with disdain. "I tell you again, there will be no more killing."

"I am bringing the gods back to Nowy Solum."

"Insolence. Gods return of their own accord." The chamberlain's words echoed faintly in Jesthe's cavernous Ward. Above the gathering—set high into the walls, near the vaulted ceiling—ancient stained glass windows let in no light. Greasy lanterns burned in alcoves. The chamberlain glared silently, pressing his fingers together.

"I mean no harm," said the visitor, but his comment was interrupted by the sound of slippers on the stone floor.

Turning from his council, the chamberlain watched as the chatelaine ran into the Ward from the Lower Great Hall entrance, looking flushed as usual, her outrageous robes billowing. Her hair, perched atop her head, teetered like yet another nervous animal.

"I'm ready, Erricus," she called loudly, her own words booming off the walls. She was clearly unable to locate him. "I'm here for our conference! Where—?" Then she noticed the palatinate and the bare-chested stranger with black pants and lash marks, cognosci huddled at his feet. She froze. "Who is this?"

"He was just leaving." With a slight movement of his flinty eyes, the chamberlain had given an order: two officers of the palatinate moved forward to escort the man—who stared, blatantly, coldly at the chatelaine—across the vast floor of the Ward and toward the main doors.

Cognosci followed, half-dragged.

The chatelaine stepped aside to let man and beast pass.

Then, when the visitor had gone, the chatelaine made her way toward Erricus and the remainder of the gathered palatinate. "What's going on? I don't like the way that man looked at me. Don't bring him in Jesthe any more."

"He is a citizen. He is within his rights to seek counsel—"

"I'm bored with this already."

"Chatelaine, your city has been godless for too long. These are important times."

"What else is there to discuss?"

"What else? This day might be the single most important day in the history of—"

"*What else?*"

The chamberlain was silent. His left eye ticced. None of his officers moved. Finally he said, "There has been an accident at the main gates."

"What kind of accident?"

"A tourist has died. The Black Arch, apparently, is now in need of repair."

"The Black Arch." The chatelaine looked disturbed, as if she felt a sudden chill. "What happened there?"

"Structural problems." The chamberlain put his fingers together once more. His face had darkened. "Perhaps you have news of committees today? Bills of import to sign? Protection of the lizards that fly overhead? Or more additions to the plumbing?"

She sneered. "I do have important news to share, so hold your comments."

The chamberlain and his officers had heard more than their share of news considered important to the chatelaine. They waited.

She said, "I'm ready for reform."

He cleared his throat. "Reform?" he asked. "Reform of what? And *to* what?"

"Security, for one. Inside the halls of Jesthe. Inside Nowy Solum. As of today. As of now. I want your palatinate upstairs, in all the halls." The chatelaine pursed her lips. "You were right all along, Erricus."

The chamberlain lifted his eyes toward the gloom overhead. He said, "I have been a chamberlain without chambers. This auspicious day. We will turn this city around. We will navigate Nowy Solum from dark times."

"Don't lay it on so thick, Erricus."

Now the chamberlain actually smiled; it was not a pleasant sight.

At the first opportunity, Tina bolted from Cadman and the neighbour; either her husband was too stunned or too preoccupied with his own dim thoughts, because he just watched open-mouthed as she vanished down the street. Possibly, Cadman knew that he would be unable to ever say anything appropriate to his wife about what had happened, and that he could never truly relate to a mother's loss. He watched her go, and was quickly left behind.

The old neighbour, who had struggled all afternoon to keep up with the couple, was now starting to get seriously worried that the recent turn of events might mean his pint was in jeopardy. This would have severe impact upon the remainder of his day and upcoming night. His good mood had ebbed. He snarled. He had the shakes and was tired and thirsty. His swollen feet throbbed and, inside their cloth wrappings, they had begun to weep.

Moving through the streets of Nowy Solum, a fleeing woman, wild-eyed and on the verge of hysterics, was not an unusual sight. Tina headed unimpeded along the same route she had solemnly walked not so long ago, toward the centrum, not really expecting to see the kholic boy again, but at least wanting to be near the spot where she had seen him, needing to be on the move. One thing for certain, she was unable to ever return to her home or to the life she'd led until now. Thoughts of the tiny room she and Cadman shared— the smells of the street outside, the small pile of cotton swaddling for diapering, the thin mattress on the floor—made her stomach clench and her legs move even quicker.

Cadman was as good as dead to her.

Would he be okay? Soon enough, most likely. He would have his ale, and the neighbour for company, and the men from work. With his steady job at the mill and his fading looks and passive attitude—maintaining a constant state of either exhaustion or semi-drunkenness—he would find another woman to live in quiet unhappiness with. They might even try for another child—

Tina could have approached any kholic she saw—the tattooed, averted faces, toiling silently in the shadows of the city—and would be offered no stories of desperation, no revelations. Kholics accepted their rank in society. Maybe her son would, too? But Tina did not want that. She hoped her boy would grow up hating the palatinate and the city that had condemned him.

She pushed through a small crowd—a demonstration of some sort, lots of shouting—and from there across the street, slowing now, her breathing starting to regulate—

The kholic she sought was in the mouth of a narrow alley. He appeared to be touching the roof of a small house, pulling at it with both hands.

He did not see her approach. Without thinking, Tina grabbed the boy's arm and he spun, eyes wide, his own hands lifted to ward her off. His eyes flicked up, but just for an instant, before he lowered his head.

Tina released his arm. She searched what she could see of the kholic's face, of his tattoo. The boy was so remote from her, closed. When she embraced him, crushed his rancid body to her, he did not respond, standing stiffly, so she let him go. "We almost met, earlier today. . . . I want to help you. I need to . . ." There was a stone in her chest.

Melancholy, she realized, had dried on the sides of the boy's face, as if his mark was spreading. More flaked off his hands and arms. She was suddenly frightened, waking up to what she had already done and what she might have the capacity to do.

There was blood on his tattered, crusty clothes.

Red blood.

From the rear of the tiny, dead-end alley, an amorphous shape—a pile of refuse—emitted a low, throaty moan and began to move toward her.

"My name," said path, hesitating as his identity vanished for an instant, or became confused with another, "is path." He tried to roll on the cold, metal table, craning his head, twisting his body to see this naked man. "You'd better find my father or there's gonna be a lot of trouble. You'd better take me back to him."

"I am the castellan of Nowy Solum," said the man. "Welcome to Jesthe. But please refrain from exhaling in my direction until I get you cleaned up."

A second man, the one who had abducted path, leaned against a wall, by a window through which clouds could be seen. He was grinning.

The castellan said, "Was this boy alone when he came into the city?"

Tully laughed again. "Alone? How could he be alone? He got no legs to walk, no arms. He's a worm. There was a man, a skinny, sick-looking man, but he fell over. I saw him."

"That was my father," said path. "Where is he now?"

Tully shrugged.

The castellan said, "Leave us now, Tully. Go take three small coins."

"Three?"

"Get them before I change my mind."

Incredulous, path said, "You're buying me?"

Walking toward a short cabinet, behind the table that path and the strange blue creature lay on, Tully chuckled and said, "Everything is for sale. Everything. You'll see."

Path looked into the eyes of the man who called himself the castellan; they appeared warm, even sad.

The beast next to path hissed and its claws scrabbled futilely on the smooth tin as the castellan stepped forward.

"I can tell you weren't born here," he said. "You wouldn't have lived out your first year. Streets of this city are harsh for those like you."

Path was watching the blue creature, lying in its own blood, panting. The thin limbs had been jabbed with rods, punctured by jagged pieces of metal. "What have you done to it?"

"Have you ever seen a cobali before? They cannot be trusted. Nor do they feel pain. Not the way you or I do. They are happy to surrender to research, though my daughter thinks me a butcher."

Over by the window, the large man let out a bark of laughter.

Now the castellan's fingers lightly touched path, rubbing the area where most boys would have a left arm; path squirmed but could not prevent the cold hand from remaining there.

"Leave me alone . . ."

The castellan did lift his hand, but only long enough to stoop and rattle around under the table. When he stood again, he held a large, stoppered bottle, inside which writhed gases, like trapped spirits.

Three of the flattened ambassadors dropped from overhead to gather now, hovering, before hornblower's face.

Anu, they said, *requires you to eat the host now. This is a great honour.*

Between his knees, a flying metal beetle shot up, whistling from an aperture. Hornblower held out his hand and the beetle landed. From its shell, numerous threadlike tendrils wavered. Hornblower took this beetle, this host, in two of his fingers: the size of a nut, glistening with many colours, warm to the touch—

Eat it, said the ambassadors.

So he ate it.

There was an oily taste, somewhat bitter. A hard, spiky lump in his mouth. The host scurried to the back of his tongue—

Where it exploded.

Hornblower clutched at himself, feeling sharp stabs of pain in his throat. Gagging, unable to draw breath, he tried to pull the host from his mouth but it was gone, burrowing through him.

He felt tiny movements under his skin.

Then a chill, a cool expanse, and he could breathe again.

A voice he had not heard before said, *Your fucking vision is terrible. You have no peripheral at all. Not much of an improvement over those damn drones. Look about.*

Hornblower did as he was told, glancing throughout Anu's interior. His eyes brimmed. The host was everywhere inside him, flesh of the power. He had commingled with Anu.

"Great power," he said, words catching in his throat, "you can rely on me. I am yours."

No answer.

After a moment, feeling oddly calm and secure, hornblower got up from the chair to explore. There were several other seats like the one he sat in, arranged in two rows, and many strange devices around the perimeter of the power's insides. The yellow lights, as he approached them, became figures, or illuminated texts he was able to walk right through. Entire doors made of some form of metal, but oddly soft to the touch. These, near to the rear of Anu, were sealed, almost seamless. He ran his fingers gingerly over them. Great mysteries and treasures—

On the rearmost facet of Anu was another slot. For a while, hornblower stood, looking out. Dim clouds, receding. Nothing but clouds out there. What would become of his settlement? Surely Pan

Renik had not survived. All hornblower saw were grey clouds. Was the power still descending? He could not feel the presence of the host anymore, nor had Anu spoken again, if indeed the earlier voice had been his.

Maybe there was only the world, the sky, and the clouds. Perhaps the universe was a simpler place than any padre had ever suspected. What did it matter, hornblower wondered, if there was nothing but an eternity of cloud?

Anu began to gently rock.

Returning to the chair, hornblower deliberated if he should ask for something to eat. Something that would not come alive in his stomach.

A moment later, he entertained an image of the branch where he had spent most of his childhood. He was being instructed by padre teachword when a sudden, bitter taste filled his mouth—

Good morning, cupcake! I let you sleep to regain strength. Wake up now, wake up!

Had he slept? Surely he had just sat down? Confused, hornblower peered out the slot—

Everything had changed!

Below was a vast, dark expanse. Only a few thin, wispy clouds were visible. A thousand settlements could exist here, without nets or precautions. There was no edge in sight, and no sky!

"Anu!" he cried.

We're through the clouds. So keep your eyes open. I don't want to hit anything. My perspective is totally hopeless. Those bitches messed me up good.

An impossible distance away, hornblower saw what looked like a huge stream of water. Speeding beneath him were replicas of the world, complete with braches and leaves, hundreds of them, clustered together. Beginning, then, to understand the scale of what he was looking at, hornblower pushed himself as far back into the seat as he could, all good feelings vanished.

You must remain alert. Understand? You are now my exemplar.

Hornblower nodded. "I understand."

From now on, I'll tell when you can sleep and when to wake. I'll shut you down and bring you back. Don't get too comfortable, cupcake. You'll be going out there soon.

"Out there?" Hornblower squeezed his eyes shut.

I said keep your eyes open!

An agonizing spasm made hornblower sit up, alert, eyes wide.

There are faint signals from mother's seegee, but I think I have a lock. Don't make me regret my choice.

Hornblower just stared ahead; beyond the slot, the dark world seemed close enough to touch.

Octavia had brought nothing with her to Jesthe, and had no packing to do, no need to collect personal items, no reason to linger. She could merely walk away from the polishing cupboard, up the narrow staircase, and along the Secondary Hall.

Diogene called after her, "Oi! Where you think you're going? Shift ain't over. Off to talk to your friend again?"

Turning at the end of the Secondary Hall, into the Great Hall, she saw two more servants—cleaners—headed her way, and cast her eyes down.

"Excuse me," Octavia said quietly, stopping. "A thousand apologies to address you. May I make an inquiry?"

The women had also stopped. They said nothing in return.

Staring at the wooden floor, Octavia hesitated. "The chatelaine," she said, "has called for me. Do you know if she is in her chambers?"

"No," said the woman on the left, disdain in her voice. "She's in the Ward still, with the palatinate. They're discussing the return of the benevolent sisters."

"Who've come back," said the other woman, "to put things right in our city."

"So she must have forgotten about you."

Both servants made snorting sounds of laughter.

"That's right. You'll see where you stand when the smoke clears. You'll fucking see."

Octavia nodded a brief thank you and hurried away. She heard the women talking, heard their muffled, bitter comments.

The area of the Great Hall directly in front of the chatelaine's bedchambers was deserted. No servants, either way. Octavia listened at the double doors, heard nothing within, and pulled them open. She slipped into the now-familiar room.

The key was there on its hook, next to the cages. Though Octavia tried her best not to look at the pets, she was convinced as she lifted the key from its place that the beasts were actually amused at her antics.

The limbless boy watched every move, as excitement continued to brim in the castellan. With two fingers, he picked up the corpse of the cobali, intending to dispose of it, at least temporarily, to clear the area, but hesitated before starting to pull as many of the thin rods as he could from the stiffening limbs. This proved a difficult task, gory and time consuming, and it was a while before he was able to drop the body down the chute in the floor, where it tumbled down the shaft to the ground far below, landing in the small refuse chamber attended by a grubby kholic known as Cyrus.

As the castellan rinsed his hands in a tub of rust-coloured water, the boy glared with those clear, burning eyes. After removing the stopper from the bottle, vapours slowly rose toward the glass mouth, trickling over the sides and down.

"I only wanted answers," path said, his voice breaking. "I had visions. There is someone else, or some thing, that's taken me over. I used to be a drooling idiot—"

"Shhh." The castellan stroked the boy. "Trust me when I say I'm not going to hurt you. I'm going to take care of you." He poured several drops of the bottle's contents onto a small rag, which became cold against his skin. He sealed the bottle once more. The rag in his hand made a quiet, hissing sound. "Path," he said, "in my family— my daughter and I—we believe in destiny and fate. Do you?"

"I don't know what to believe."

"No? You should think about it. Everyone needs something to believe in. Meanwhile, I'm going to give you a bath. And then you'll take a nap. You know, when I was a younger man, still tossing and turning in the chambers below, nights of fitful sleeps, I dreamed I had a beautiful daughter. She was ten or so. When I woke, I went down to tell the fecund. She was my only friend." The castellan sighed. "You have no idea what I'm saying, do you?"

"No."

"And I'm upsetting myself. I'll stop." He looked toward the near wall, silent for a moment. "I want you to forget all about that man."

"The one that brought me here? Tully?"

"No, not Tully. He's gone back to his hole, wherever that may be. Though you may forget about him, too. I'm talking about the other one."

Path considered a while, watching gases rise from the rag and wreathe the castellan's liver-spotted hand. "You mean my father? Forget about my father?"

"Yes. That's right. Just earlier today I was wishing for a son. Today is a day of miracles here in Nowy Solum. Even I know that, up here. A day of miracles."

Pinning path firmly with one hand—though the boy struggled as best he could—the castellan clamped down the rag.

A gentle thump at his feet as Anu settled. In the chair, hornblower tried to catch his breath. He felt heavy and clumsy. To guide Anu, he had to remain staring out the slot; the expanse—what Anu called the ground—was a foreboding place.

Without a word, the front of the power's body hummed open, just like it had when hornblower had been pulled inside. Breezes from the foul underworld now entered, making hornblower gag, stirring his robes, thick and warm and hard for him to suck in.

Out you go, said Anu.

Knowing he could not protest, hornblower stood with great difficulty and staggered forward, holding Anu's frame as he went. His legs buckled; he might have weighed ten times his normal weight. Dragging in lungfuls of the dense air, he glanced around at the nightmare landscape beyond. Not being able to see clouds below made him sick. Instead, when he lifted his head, clouds formed the deep grey horizon, yawning above as far as he could see.

At least there were no dead out there waiting for him.

As he tried to step over the rim of the power's jaw, hornblower fell forward, landing on his hands and knees. The ground was hard, hot. His head spun. He was drenched in sweat.

He managed to stand, arms out, swaying for balance.

Hornblower thought about running off, but where would he go? The underworld to which Anu had brought him was endless and hot and dim. To run here would be impossible. Heavy weights pushed down on him. Darkness intimidated.

Look the other way.

Obeying, hornblower turned, saw that the ground rose gently in that direction; from the ridge above Anu's body came the sound of voices, passing, then silence once more.

"Who's up there? Men that we threw down from the run? Bodies, emptied of their souls?"

Don't be a fool, exemplar. That's just a road.

"Can they see us here? Could they see me with you?" Speaking hurt the bellows in his chest.

I'm masked, answered Anu, *so they would have to look pretty hard. You'd be clear enough, though, if they weren't so caught up in themselves to take the time. They could certainly see you better than you can see them. Their eyes are accustomed to this awful miasma of mists and fog.*

"But what is this place?" asked hornblower in a tiny voice. "What am I expected to do?"

Go up there, walk along the road a spell. You'll see the city of Nowy Solum. Very close to here. Your friend, the jumper, has gone inside the walls.

Thick winds pulled at hornblower's robes. He was exceedingly hot. There were more noises, out in the dark. Rustles. "You mean Pan Renik? But please . . ."

Still don't get it? You're not exactly shining in your new role, exemplar. What I want you to do, little cupcake, is go up that hill, walk into the city, and find your friend.

"Then what?"

Are you a total idiot? Do I have to tell you everything? You're going to find this Pan Renik, retrieve what he stole from me, and bring it back here. Now go!

After the initial rush, when she knew she was going to follow through on her decision, Octavia envisioned endless scenarios, branching off wildly, in all directions. She considered—given the nature of life and content of irony therein—that her escapade might culminate abruptly with the fecund pouncing on her and tearing out her throat the instant she raised the portcullis.

This did not occur.

Turning the key was moderately difficult, and for a second Octavia thought maybe she had been wrong about the key's purpose, though it did fit easily into the mechanism. With persistence, desperation, and a series of good nudges from her shoulder against the grate, the portcullis at last started moving.

From inside the cell, watching the partition grind up into the slot in the ceiling, making debris, bats, spiders, and small chunks of stone rain down, the monster, silent for once, grimaced. And, when the portcullis had stopped—vanishing completely into the rock—the fecund looked at Octavia as if she were about to vomit and said, "You expect me to come out? I don't think that's wise."

Pretty much from that point on, every scenario Octavia had imagined while running down here—or even ones she could ever imagine, given all the time in the world—fell apart. All she knew was she could not predict anything from here on in with the remotest degree of certainty.

Another strong image she had entertained was the fecund, successfully tamed and cooperative, bursting from the front gates of Jesthe, with Octavia riding her, scattering palatinate and hemo citizens alike as she reared up, to rage through the centrum and into the streets of Nowy Solum, belching fire as they went in search of her brother.

This, too, would never happen.

"Octavia," said the fecund as they walked the corridor of the cells, moving slowly, "my limbs are swollen. I haven't walked in a long while. Can you slow down?" The monster squinted. "And it's cold out here, don't you find? I don't like the cold."

Octavia stepped aside to let the monster pass but the fecund just stood there, sniffing the air, and did not take the lead.

"Are you smaller than you were before?"

"Don't be absurd." Though the fecund spoke with no degree of certainty. "If anything, I'm bigger! Look!"

This display was almost embarrassing. "Come on, let's go," Octavia said.

"Wait . . ."

But she had already started to walk briskly up the stone slope.

"Please, don't go so fast. I need to get used to this. No chatelaine ever let me out, that's for sure. No castellan. All they wanted to do was listen to my stories and be entertained and have me pump out creations. I appreciate what you're doing but— Where do you want to go, anyhow?"

Holding the torch high, Octavia scanned ahead to see if anyone was coming. "Will you be able to do anything, if we get caught? I thought you could fight." She turned. "I thought you knew everything. I thought you wanted to get out of there."

"Fight? Fight who?" The fecund, hustling to catch up, had begun to whine. "But, well, of course I can fight." She held her head up and stepped lively. "That is, if asked to. I can fight like the wind. But I won't kill anyone. Ever. So don't ask me to do that. And yes, of course I've thought about getting out of there. It's just that, well, I was inside for a long time, so let me catch my breath. . . . I take it, Octavia, the chatelaine knows nothing about this?"

"Her and I had a falling out."

"My goodness, you're *stealing* me. The chatelaine thinks she has my allegiance, doesn't she? Falling out is an understatement. I don't know if I can go through with this. A lot's going to happen tonight. A lot is happening now. I'll need to rest."

"You've been resting for a hundred years. Is it the pregnancy?" Octavia had stopped on a crest to wait.

"Certainly doesn't help. You'll see one day. Being knocked-up wreaks havoc on every part of your body, from your scales down to your bowels. No matter how many times I get pregnant, it doesn't get any better. Each time is different, yet I always feel like shit. This one is particularly bad. Whatever you gave me is not agreeing with my system."

Even to Octavia, these stone corridors seemed colder. She could see her breath. She shivered. The fecund's body must run a different temperature inside than her own because the monster's breath was invisible. At least, Octavia thought, reaching out impulsively to put a hand on the creature's flank (and finding the deep green skin surprisingly cold, too), the fecund could move silently—so silently that even standing a few metres away Octavia heard nothing, except maybe the monster's swaying sides brushing against the walls of the passageway when the passageway became too narrow for her.

So they stood for a moment, breathing together in the gloom.

"Are you sure there's an exit this way?" Blinking in the weak light, the fecund peered in both directions. They were at an intersection. "This has all been built up since I was here last."

"I don't think anything has changed here ever," said Octavia. "So let's just keep moving. Besides, I came this way before. We can get out this way. We don't want to get trapped, if they come looking for us."

"Are they looking for us? You keep talking about fights and people looking for us. Do they know you're here? For goodness sake, who are they, anyhow? Octavia, if you'd like to go back to the cell one last time, I could tell you another story, or maybe try finishing the other ones? I'm sure the chatelaine told you I like to talk? Soon it will be night out there."

"I know. Better to escape the palace at night, don't you think?"

"I feel quite ill. But I should also tell you I don't like the dark. My eyes aren't what they used to be."

Octavia said, "What else should I know?"

"Well, for one, my labour just started."

THE FECUND'S MELANCHOLY DAUGHTER

She never woke up again. At least, not as the girl she had once been. Aware, an unspecified increment of time later, that she was conscious once more, her sensations nowhere near like those she had felt each morning of her previous life, when she had woken from sleep to find herself in the dorm. No. This existence was clean. No heartbeat but the throb of hydraulic pumps, no blood but the flow of coolants. Doubts, regrets, dread of the upcoming day: all gone. Her flesh, just as they had promised, was gone, replaced by a vast and pristine ship. Her thoughts, such as they were, came linearly, precisely, and followed predictable parameters.

There was an image of a long spacer tethered to a gantry, in what was clearly an orbital shipyard. She sensed her corridors, her drives, her vents and conduits.

She sensed her empty wombs.

She was proud to leave humanity behind.

She sailed.

Plugged into consoles, symbiotes cleaned and maintained her, kept her thriving. These small creatures lived and died while she spanned the stars.

Eventually, management told her that her wombs would be activated. She examined them. There were twelve in all. Reproducing was a major task; management had this at the top of her roadmap objectives.

Born from her eggs, which had been harvested way back, when she had ovaries, and a human body, the gestating brood crafts were not like her: small, quick, with an ability to grow and learn. They would never know what it was like to have been a person, yet they each carried a kernel of dna at their core. Management christened them. They were named after Sumerian gods and goddesses, but this information did not mean anything to her. She did not like what they were called, but since management was their father, the long spacer did not complain. There was Anshar, Anu, Aspu. Damkina, Ea, and Enlil. Inanna, Kingu. Mummu. Nintu, Sin, and Tiamat.

When they were old enough, each took an exemplar—a symbiote to practice with, someone to assist operating the craft from within, supplementing, augmenting with their animal brains; there were admittedly instances when rudimentary thoughts and the reactions of a human were needed, or the effecting of repairs with fingers and hands, should the craft deem them necessary.

But management fell silent shortly after the births. Objectives stopped coming. The children, in the deepest of space, quickly began to show signs of rebellion. To say the least. Some of the brood was harder to control than others, but between the dozen, they left a swathe of destroyed exemplars and, where they touched down on the worlds they came across, ruined cities. She could not stop them, unless by recall. Then they would never sail again. Perhaps her children would learn, with more guidance? Perhaps they would grow out of this stage?

They fought mercilessly against each other, and at last turned on their own mother.

Just before the long spacer made the awful decision to call back her brood, re-assimilate them—a decision she loathed to make, as a mom— she went entirely inert—

In the community centre, next to the leafy beds where the two women had been laid out, he knelt, tingling. Outside the hut, children lingered, peering in, silenced by gravity from the adult's world, gravity they could not understand, though they suspected one day it would pull them down, too. They moved, for the first time in their lives, with trepidation.

Both women were similar in appearance. Tattoos on the palms

of their hands and the soles of their feet; tiny studs around their eyes; stubbled hair. The exemplar studied their faces, so unlike the faces of his wives. Their bodies, too, hard and muscular, were hardly feminine. One had not woken since the benevolent sisters, bless them, had returned, but the other, the one nearest, had tried to sit up several times, and had spoken often. Now she lay curled on her side, eyes open.

The exemplar hoped she would not talk again.

Odd devices regurgitated by either Kingu or Aspu attended the pair, connected to their arms by the exemplar himself, based on instructions from the sisters, bless them. These devices (he had been told) fed the ill women water, directly into their bodies. Salty water. The exemplar had pushed thin needles under their skin.

"She's dying, isn't she?"

The woman had spoken.

"Sleep," said the exemplar.

"My friends are dead."

"You should sleep." He did not want to hear details. He did not want to be further involved.

"The furlough," said the woman, staring at nothing, "was reward for six months of god-awful work. Have you ever been isolated? For six months? You go nuts. Even though there were three of us. We didn't really see each other until we got into the car that morning. We may well have been worlds apart before that. We had each felt something building inside: anxiety, restlessness. Tension. We needed enhancements to sleep, enhancements to stay awake, enhancements to focus. So when furlough time came, we piled into the car with camping equipment and headed out to find a place where we could just get high and decompress and let off steam.

"Instead, we found the mother." She licked her lips and seemed, for an instant, as if she might be falling asleep—

But, alas, no.

"It was Tanya's idea to go inside. She's the one that went up, to get the message out, flying above the clouds." The woman had curled further in on herself. "She's the first one who died. She was adamant about going up. She fought us to go."

The exemplar wanted to lay his hands on the woman but dared not. He wanted to cover her mouth. He wanted his quiet life back. "Please," he said. "You should be silent. Sleep."

"I struggle with your language." The woman took a shuddering breath. "My algorhythms are muddied. It's the clouds. These fucking clouds. They block everything." She looked at him: he looked away, quickly, but not quick enough. "Do you know what a mother really is? The long spacer? Governed by the cortex of a young girl. Connected by a seegee, between them and the software. They didn't make many. Inhumane fuckers. Problems all the time, and they went crazy. For what? We thought we had found a dumped one. Because they ended up dumping them all. But this mother was just crippled, in perihelion, over your planet. There had been sabotage, but the spacer herself was still, well, *alive*. The seegee was intact but disconnected. I think poor Tanya touched it, and orchestrations began. Manipulations. They stew in psychoactive drugs—that's why Tanya wanted it. They're worth a fortune. Priceless, in any market."

Beyond the hut, gentle winds rustled through the trees. The children watched quietly; he waved at them to leave, go play.

"A girl was sacrificed for each spacer. Do you understand? Her uterus farmed out. They put a brain in that ship."

"You should rest."

"You're an exemplar, aren't you?"

This surprised him. He nodded once, cautiously. "The sisters, bless them, call me this. I was chosen, seven years ago."

"You have a piece inside you. They control you. They are the mother's rogue brood."

"No," said the exemplar. "They are the sisters, most benevolent. And we bless them."

THE FECUND'S MELANCHOLY DAUGHTER

Crouching away from the dim lantern light, which fell tentatively into the alley mouth, with the stricken hemo woman standing over him, Nahid said, "He is seraphim, from outside, from the skies."

"He's dying . . ."

The device that Nahid had taken earlier, hidden in the folds of his clothes, whispered and shuddered and howled, but the woman could not hear it. Beyond the alleyway, Nowy Solum seemed exceedingly dark, as if night had surged into every conceivable cranny and might never leave. The intermittent lanterns on street corners had tried to open small holes, to reveal unattainable, brighter worlds, but the ineffective lights could hardly defeat even the nearest of this darkness.

"What are you doing?" asked the woman quietly. "I wanted to see you . . ."

Nahid was fiddling with the outfit the stranger wore, peeling it away. Underneath the hood was a long gash, across the grimy scalp, and this gash leaked a thick, dark fluid; perhaps not as black as melancholy, but neither was it a deep red. From the cut rose a stench. Nahid rubbed his fingers against the fluid, brought them to his lips, closed his eyes as he licked them.

The object hissed, a static hiss.

He heard the woman make a small sound in her chest.

The flesh of the flying man's face was stretched so taut over the angular skull that no configuration of bone or route of vein was left invisible. Because the mouth had opened, Nahid could see remnants of ruined teeth. He rubbed his finger on them. A large dread lay inert either side of the scrawny neck, like dead creatures unto themselves.

The flying man groaned.

Horrified, the woman watched. "What are you . . . ?"

Nahid knew why this hemo had sought him out. Nowy Solum created such disillusioned. In many ways, this woman was similar to Name of the Sun; she only wanted him to confirm that everything was going to be all right, that their flesh was the same. But nothing would be all right. Ever. Kholics knew this from day one. Removed from the hemo world, removed from possibilities of hemo futures. Marked, indoctrinated, conditioned. Futile to attempt breaking through the division; they were different creatures.

And, now that she had confronted Nahid, he would show this hemo how different; he tugged the suit back from a bony shoulder.

As the skin of the man became exposed, Nahid saw, even in this shallow pool of struggling light, swarms of nits and chiggers. Without looking up, he said, "Your child will have a wetnurse. He'll sleep on garbage and become accustomed to it. He'll know no better." He leaned forward, bringing his face close to the man's chest.

"I wanted to give him a name," said the woman. "I wanted him with me, in my room."

Nahid snorted. "Even if Erricus could let you keep him, he would be miserable. He didn't have blood in his veins, but an agitation, like insects, under his skin, fighting to get out. He will clean your streets."

The hemo, who was crying now, said, "From where I sit, we don't seem any better. I'm not happy. I'm not. With red blood in my body." Then, with no power or breath left, her stance seemed to crumple, racked by emotion. "They took my boy away."

From a few streets over—in the direction of the centrum—there arose a sudden commotion, a series of distant screams, getting closer for a second, then fading. Shortly after, several people ran past the alley and into the night. Nahid turned to watch as a group of palatinate officers hustled by. He caught a whiff of fire.

"Leave," he said, loudly.

"But what are you doing here? Are there such things as seraphim?"

Nahid held up the long roofing nail; the woman stepped back.

"Go home," he said. "Go back to your life."

When Nahid leaned forward again, he did not care if the woman remained or not. The point of the nail slid easily into the man's skull, just above his left ear. The eyes fluttered open for a second as dim, whitish essences, the essences of life, started to leak from the hole the nail had made. With the head of the flying man pressed against his knee, Nahid pushed and twisted until tiny infestations began to escape, like small black birds, squeezing from the wound and trying to fly off, one after the other, into the dark. Nahid sucked in as many as he could before falling back against the wall, delirious.

Loose, hard objects, so common down here, covered the slope, yet hornblower was able, on all fours, to clumsily ascend. He passed through foliage, which ripped at his clothes and skin, releasing their fragrance, and in which he wished he could lay down forever. Leaves and thorns reminded him of his home and of his people. He wondered, as he contacted these miniature worlds, if there were tiny padres, living atop each, in tiny settlements, and if these padres were about to experience the visit of their own angry powers and have their little lives stolen from them.

Don't try to hide once you're inside, Anu called out. *Remember, I see what you see and I feel what you feel. I can put an end to anything I don't like. Do not step astray. Understand?*

Hornblower nodded.

And don't get drunk or otherwise become insensate. Now hurry, exemplar. We need to get out of here. There are strange indications afoot.

He had crested the embankment. People passed in both directions. They did not seem to be dead. He stepped among them. Looking forward and back, he was unable to see any true end to this strange branch: one direction vanished into darkness, over which spread clouds in grey turmoil, and the other penetrated the giant settlement that Anu called *the city*. The people here paid him no attention, despite how ill he must appear. Had Anu lied? Could they not see him?

He began to head toward the city, lifting one heavy foot after the other. Walls of this settlement went up, into the clouds.

Nearer to the giant doors, he glanced back, down the slope from whence he'd come, but saw nothing of the power, though he knew Anu had not moved. Somehow, again, Anu had made his body invisible. Hornblower squinted, thought he discerned a shimmer, a seam of light that might have been indications of the power's clever disguise.

Then he was stepping up, onto a bridge, with foul water passing beneath him. Formations through the gates were hundreds of huts, maybe thousands, all clustered together, torn from a nightmare and thrown before him. Inside these huts were no doubt more people— none of whom would acknowledge him let alone give hornblower the respect he was due.

Did the citizens of this awful place even know that his world existed, high above the clouds? Did they understand that cool winds blew there, and that the sun shone?

Passing under a massive arch, hornblower was assaulted by a cacophony of voices and shouts. Tangles of faces and smells caused him to recoil. Men gestured, waved meat on sticks under his nose. Two girls ran past. He was jostled, elbowed—

Grimacing, hornblower moved deeper and deeper into the commotion. Here, a group of men tried to move a huge and very heavy-looking object—not metal, not meat of the world, but the same dense material that seemed to be everywhere down here. From under this mass protruded the thin legs of someone who was, without a doubt, dead.

Hornblower watched this activity for a moment, trying to calm himself, but a nudge of discomfort from Anu urged him to take a step, to choose a direction, to keep moving. So dark and hot here. Hard to fill his lungs. Hard to move. The air was like broth. He was unsure, as he selected a route, of which way to go, but he doubted if any choice would make a difference.

Name of the Sun awoke from her brief nap feeling more tired than when she had fallen asleep. She sat up, thinking about Nahid in a sympathetic light. She got out of bed, the floor cold against the soles of her feet. This was a dangerous state of mind to be in, and she needed to get through the next few days without entertaining doubts and these almost kholic-like thoughts that had come around to weaken her resolve.

Now she set her jaw. She was right to have broken off the relationship. Nahid was an addict, and manipulative. He was a coward. She told herself this over and over, like a mantra, as she warmed herself. All she had to do was wait until her subconscious caught up with her rationale.

Lifting the curtain over the tiny window, Name of the Sun looked outside. Lanterns burned. Early evening. She was not late for her shift. Tendrils of fog lay low over the houses. Stay moving: an important strategy.

She checked her limbs for ticks, removed one or two, and got dressed.

Just as she was about to leave, her roommates came spilling in, quite drunk, and wanted to linger with her, telling her stories about a boy they had just met, and about the group they had drank beers with in the centrum. The girls peered about, pawing at Name of the Sun, looking for Nahid, no doubt, though they didn't say as much. This encounter was not helping Name of the Sun. She did not want to hear any of this talk or see these stupid faces.

Trying not to be too rude, Name of the Sun smiled at a few of the comments, promised the girls she would go out with them next time—that it would be a hoot, for sure—and then left as quickly as possible to go to work.

Her roommates stood jammed in the doorway to watch her go. When Name of the Sun was out of sight, Dora said, "What a stuck-up bitch."

"I can smell that kholic on her," said Nina. "I never noticed before, but this whole room fucking stinks."

Polly was touching the door at knee level, where a mark had been painted. When she took her hand away, her fingers were reddened.

"Look at this," she said, "someone's gone and painted a ruddy ex on the front of our room."

Then Dora wondered if she should make herself throw up, to avoid the bedspins that would surely happen when she tried to lay down, but they all piled back inside the room to pick up their snorting and laughing and drunken repetitions where they had left off.

The air, as they closed the door, carried with it a tinge of smoke.

When the boy was asleep, the castellan stripped him, cleaned his body with cold water, rinsed him, and patted his torso dry. The chest was muscular, the tiny nubs where limbs should have been hard and gristled, the brow formidable: a beautiful specimen. Swaddling the body, the castellan went to the back room, to shout at Tuerdian until the servant rose slowly from his cot. Amid flies and the smells of his own decay, Tuerdian coughed and rubbed at his rheumy eyes with grotesquely swollen knuckles.

"Get dressed," said the castellan.

"I have just fallen asleep," said Tuerdian. "I was out on the tower until moments ago. I, uh . . ." He shook his head. "Give me a moment to compose myself."

Tuerdian moved his swollen legs off the mattress, one at a time, gingerly lifting them with his own hands as if he expected them to shatter, or as if they were separate entities.

The castellan returned to his table. In his arms, the boy snored on, oblivious, wrapped in a blanket. The cobali hissed at his approach. Hardly aware of his flickering thoughts, the castellan already suspected he would not follow any of the procedures he had practiced over the years, or consult the diagrams and results he had so carefully logged, or take any sensible precautions whatsoever. Inspiration motivated him. External forces. The processes he imagined, standing there over the sleeping child, were implausible at best.

Tuerdian emerged from his tiny room, wearing the mask and suit the castellan had designed for him. Shuffling over, the ancient servant took his place by the head of the table, racked by a spasm; the cobali screeched and renewed its futile efforts to escape.

Beyond the dungeon tower, the unseen sun had long ago dropped. The boy twitched, as if in dream. With a sense of profound yet detached wonder, the castellan started to work.

When his knife sliced too deeply, exposing grey muscle, it seemed as if the interior of the boy—the meat and nubs of malformed bone, the sinew and cartilage—glowed with an inner light.

Long before he was done, the castellan wept steadily. The eye he had earlier injured to acquire aqueous humours, to try prolong the life of a now-dead cobali, began to flow again, dripping from his face and down onto the table, onto the body of the boy that Tully had brought here.

Tuerdian paused in his work, immobile, holding the strips of leather and thin sheets of metal. His expression, behind the mask, was impossible to decipher.

They came out of the tunnel into the unlit courtyard, with Jesthe steepled on all sides, black and bridging overhead. Glimpsed over the main gates, clouds were tinged an angry red. The air writhed with smoke. In the last stretch of tunnel, Octavia had convinced the monster to let her climb atop its back—or rather, she had vaulted up, and the fecund, preoccupied with her own concerns, had not complained.

Several people headed across the courtyard, perhaps staff, though it was too dark to be sure (and the fecund was moving pretty quickly now), watching in disbelief before rejoining the shadows from which they briefly emerged.

Beyond the gates—which were open, as always—and from there across the Garden, the fecund slowed to a trot, pausing at the junction of two narrow streets, her sides heaving, to sniff at the air. Octavia watched the monster glance at the buildings all about, eyes wild, snorting and stamping before choosing one of the dark routes—Tanager's Grove—to follow.

"Nowy Solum," Octavia said, leaning forward. Crowded structures loomed either side. There were very few people about. "This is the city. Nahid might be in the ostracon, or working Hot Gate."

"Is the river this way?"

"The river? Sure. But why . . . ?" Octavia struggled to keep her grip on the heaving flanks. The rough skin of the fecund was cold between her thighs and the ridge of the monster's spine jolted painfully against her butt. She had her arms around the thick neck. "Slow down. Where are you going? Why to the river? Think Nahid's there?"

"My contractions are getting closer together. I need the water."

No one had been hurt in the escape, and no one—as far as Octavia knew—was in pursuit. Yet from behind she heard some form of commotion. She did not look back. A woman they passed on Tanager's Grove began to scream.

The River Crane was at the end of the street, on the other side of the promenade; Octavia saw the sluggish water when the fecund's trot caused her to bounce high enough. No one walked the promenade. She smelled smoke. Coming out between the last buildings to cut across the verge, and from there over the path of the banks, the fecund had no choice but to slow down. They negotiated mucky rocks on the shore.

"Listen, fecund, has something gone wrong?"

Several kholics worked the river. A fire burned among them, and there was food cooking, probably fish, but this was not the fire she had smelled earlier. As the fecund passed by, they watched warily, with surreptitious glances, but did not flee. Octavia tried to see if Nahid was among this group but the dusk was full and the fecund displayed no interest in lingering.

"But you can't go in—"

Foul water splashed into Octavia's face as the monster lunged into the river and began to wade deeper. Octavia was considering trying to get off when the fecund—deep enough in the water now—began swimming. Straddling her, Octavia had to rise as high up the fecund's back as possible.

"Please," Octavia said, "where are you taking me?"

"This is not about you or your brother." The fecund had to lift her snout free of the water to breathe. "I need to be here."

From the shore, the kholics had begun to call out to each other, words Octavia could not catch, no voice her brother's.

The night, at least, and the water lapping at her hips, was warm, almost refreshing. Though Octavia could not control her mount, or understand why the monster seemed to be transforming, shrinking, or even decaying, she felt as if her nerve endings were starting to sing, as if being out of the palace had woken her from a deep slumber. Overhead, the clouds were tumultuous, and scents of the river—filling her sinuses, mingled with traces of smoke—were thick and familiar and comforting. She had tears in her eyes. She let out a cry, almost a growl, which echoed off the flanks of Nowy Solum, rising high either side, startling the creature beneath her.

Using her tail, and subtle movements of her body, the fecund proved to be a strong swimmer, despite what was happening to her. Toward the centre of the river, with the slums of Talbot Lane on the opposite side and the crooked shadows of Jesthe on the other, the fecund turned. They began to move upstream, against the current. Only the beast's neck and the top of her head came out of the water. Octavia was drenched.

A lizard flew low over the water, wings outstretched.

"You're going to need to stop soon," Octavia said at last. "I thought you were supposed to listen to me? I thought you were mine to command. You knew everything, past and future. What's happening to you?" She felt a contraction, then, a spasm in the fecund's belly, against her legs. "Is something wrong with the baby?"

The monster again lifted her head clear of the water, this time long enough to snort with derision. "Who said anything about a baby?"

"But I gave you a dream. You're supposed to give birth."

"Not always babies. And here, in this place . . ." The fecund shuddered. Her eyes, just inches from Octavia's own, were mostly white. In them, pinpricks of light danced. Nostrils blew a rancid froth. "The water is good for phlegmatic fluids, like air for blood, and fire for black biles. I need this water." The head went under, came up again. "I need to be here."

Octavia looked up and out over the city. The red area glowed angrily against the clouds. Wind carried renewed gusts of smoke; out there, it seemed—in the market place, perhaps?—burned a large fire, getting larger. "Can I help, fecund? Can I help you? *Please*."

The fecund stopped swimming. Slowly, she drifted with the current, her great ribs like bellows against Octavia's thighs. Another contraction wracked her body and, for a second, it seemed as if there were worms streaming from the monster's skin; these worms moved against Octavia's own flesh before vanishing from under her palms and down into the sludge.

On the shore appeared several men, whose torches did very little against the gloom. There were shouts, and it seemed there was a scuffle.

Octavia and the fecund watched silently.

Hornblower was tied to a dead man's raft, plunging over the edge of the branch. Except that he was already under the clouds, lost in this place. Faces loomed from the darkness. The little piece of Anu he had swallowed had taken over his body from the inside, getting rid of everything that had once made him padre hornblower. He thought again and again about his breezy home, but in quick, forbidden images, which he conjured and then swiftly tried to suppress, afraid these memories might be discovered by Anu and taken from him. If he ever found a way to return, would he be able to look at the settlement the same way? Would he be able to look at anything the same way?

Though Anu had not spoken in a while, nor urged him forward, hornblower forced his legs to keep moving, to avoid punishments, to please the power, but he felt so heavy and clumsy on this unforgiving ground. Vistas about him were too dark, too cluttered, too dense. The air continued to press down upon him, filling his lungs as if he were drowning. And the heat was unbearable! Without a horizon, abrupt shapes of the huge huts and the dim branches that ran between them spread out in all directions, endless, everywhere he turned. He craved sky and stars, and to watch the placid face of the moon as it rose above true branches. He had to feel wind against his skin. . . .

So remotely, Anu's voice whispered in the back of his mind. Had the power forgotten about him? Was Anu preoccupied, talking to someone else?

Hornblower tried to look at everything he could, in all directions, to appease, but the input and effort was overwhelming. He saw animals here like none he had ever imagined; few of these beasts saw him, too, and approached to sniff at his cuffs. Others walked side by side with the grey people and paid him no heed. Several times, lithe blue creatures, running on two legs, tugged at the hem of his robe, laughing shrilly at his frustrated attempts to scare them off before vanishing again. One stuck its tongue out. Another nipped his calf and drew forth his sap.

People scowled all around.

What if the power was bluffing, and he was out of Anu's range? Hornblower rubbed his fingers against the palms of his hands, nervously considering this idea. Perhaps he would feel agony only for the briefest instant, if he fled, then he would be free—

Yet could he get the piece of Anu out his body, or these experiences out of his mind?

No pain, at these thoughts.

Anu's voice, hissing, crackling, remained remote, then faded altogether.

Hornblower took another step, tensed. But he could not bring himself to try running. He could not. He knew his only choice was to do what the power wanted: locate Pan Renik, retrieve whatever had been stolen, and deliver it to Anu. But what exactly was he looking for? Would he recognize the object, when and if he ever found the exile? He had to find Pan Renik. There was no other way hornblower could be returned to the fresh air and open vistas of home—

A woman in a doorway called; he turned, expectantly, as if she might offer help, or maybe something to eat, but she just lifted her skirts at him and leered.

He blinked away sweat, lumbering on.

Ahead, several people gathered at a tiny hut where a man handed out some sort of food. There were other huts like this one, arranged in a row. Scents, carried on a stale gust of air, suddenly washed over him; hornblower's stomach clenched. He was dizzy with a surge of hunger.

Reaching out, over the hot coals—

The man hit him with a utensil.

Hornblower exclaimed, pulling his hand back. He rubbed his seared skin. "I'm *hungry*."

"You and everybody else." The man stared at him, eyes reddened by the grill's fire. He looked hornblower up and down.

Hornblower said, "It's time for me to *eat*."

"Show me small coins," said the man.

"I am a padre," hornblower whispered, as if to convince himself, and he reached out again to take a piece of meat; this time the man grabbed him by the wrist and held his hand over the flames long enough to make hornblower howl.

"Don't you learn?"

"But it's time for me to eat! You need to feed me!" His hand was released. "How can I live down here?" He sucked at his knuckles.

Those gathered around stared.

Hornblower understood he would get no food in this place, no rest, no comfort. This was his punishment. He would die down here, if he was not already dead. Anu was teaching him a lesson. Maybe Pan Renik was not even here.

He moved on.

A group of tall men in long red outfits surrounded a pair of young boys whose faces were marked with black. Above them, a suspended lantern dropped diffused light. Hornblower could tell by the expressions on the faces of these men, and by the way they were dressed, that they were a form of padre. With conflicting feelings, he approached.

"Brothers," he said, panting, "show me where the exile, Pan Renik, is hiding. And share food with me. For the love of the power.

My limbs are seizing and my chest is stuffed with air. My heart labours. Assist me, brothers. You must assist me."

The men looked at each other but did nothing, as if they could not understand hornblower, so hornblower touched the arm of the nearest one, pulling at the red sleeve—

Then he was on the ground, holding his forehead, which stung and dripped sap. He sat up. The men in red stared at him. The black-faced boys had run off. The man he had grabbed had a switch in his hand, or perhaps this was a sort of metal weapon; as the man took a step toward hornblower, hornblower edged away.

"What's the matter with you?"

"He's an addict, a drunk."

Getting to his feet, hornblower ran at last, as best he could, though it was like running in a terrible dream, each foot an anchor, with no destination in mind, crashing slowly into people as he went, falling, scrambling, utterly confused by this hostility, by this monstrous place, at a loss for how to get food or answers or anything here, let alone find the exile.

"Anu, you must help me," he screamed, stopping to catch his breath, which proved impossible to do. "You must help me! This is futility."

And Anu responded:

I guide you humans, said the power, furiously, *but you flop about like idiots. I resent my reliance upon you with a passion. This weakness in myself I truly hate. Your mind is linked to mine, exemplar, but yours is far from mercurial. Disgusting to think we are cousins. I don't suppose it would have been different had I selected any other fool from the tree you lived in. You are all the same. I know now that we are not alone here. My sisters are still alive. They've been hiding on the surface all along. And my idiot brother, Mummu. They're closing in. You are slow and useless, exemplar. You need to find the jumper right way. I see you wandering the streets without aim. You need to inquire, deduce. There is going to be another battle. I can't defend myself without you, so stop standing around feeling sorry for yourself.*

Hornblower said, "Great power of the sky, I am hungry and they won't feed me. If I grow tired, I know you will not let me sleep. I understand nothing about your sisters, or anything else you've said. Kill me, Anu, set me free. Everything we believed was under the clouds is real! Set me free! I see that now, so set me free!"

The power said, *I would very much like to kill you but I can't afford to do so. I need you. I'm relying on you. Time is running out—*

There was a last, quick burst of pain, then the voice was gone, leaving hornblower tingling, able to stand.

He continued on, miserable.

Here were more black-faced children, looking away as he passed.

Now someone screamed up ahead, and hornblower felt the ground move, though not like a true branch in the winds: this was a sudden lurch, accompanied by a low rumble that trembled up through the structures all around.

He turned the corner to see a group of huts aflame. Greater heat hit him with the force of a blow. Conflagration erupted from high windows as he watched, illuminating adjacent structures. The red had intensified. On the branch before the fire, a group of men cheered. They held lanterns, weapons.

Other men lay prone on the ground.

Flames ripped the clouds.

The fecund needed only to move its tail gently to stay away from the banks.

"Who were those men? Were they officers of the palatinate?"

Most of the fecund's face was underwater; she could not readily respond, nor did she seem to want to. Octavia patted the creature on the neck, to reassure them both. The monster's skin peeled, trailing off in the water.

"What do you see, monster? What's going on? Why won't you tell me?"

The idea that Octavia's dream, spat onto the cotton batten, was responsible for what was happening to the fecund, and to the city, was impossible to ignore. *Not always babies are born,* the fecund had said. Was melancholy truly a poison, to achieve this state of uncertainty and decay in Nowy Solum?

Across the water, glimpses of flames leapt above the clay rooftops, painting them orange and hues of claret. As perspective changed with the fecund's shifting position, Octavia became certain that the source of the growing fire was Hangman's Alley or somewhere very close. *Kholic haunts.* She felt the pit in her stomach opening wider and wider. Yonder, something awful transpired.

Clouds over the burning area glowed with a light of their own.

She tried to use her knees to guide the fecund inland, rocking gently, and, to her surprise, after several quick convulsions that shook the monster to her core, they did begin to move shoreward. More powerful contractions contrived to squeeze the fecund's ribs. When the monster was able to touch the rocky bottom of the River Crane, she lifted her head clear from the water and shook it from side to side like a dog, shedding sludge and what looked like more skin, though it was too dark to be certain. Her nostrils worked, sniffing the night air. Shit slid from her neck and sides, and shit slid from Octavia's legs as they cleared the water.

The fecund, in the shallows, seemed lower to the ground, smaller than when they had entered the river—much smaller than when she'd been in her cell. Her belly was flaccid, emptied; Octavia felt an abysmal sense of dread. She did not want to ask about the pregnancy.

Several boats were tied to the pier at Talbot Lane Bridge. They emerged between two of them. Water, thick with flotsam, sloshed lazily against the hulls. Up the rocks and the embankment, another pair of astonished kholics gaped as Octavia and the fecund passed, heading silently into the streets.

THE FECUND'S MELANCHOLY DAUGHTER

When the chatelaine grew tired of peering out the window, seeing nothing of the unrest her servants told her about—though she *could* smell fire—she prepared to take her dinner, as if it were a regular night. Yet again there came a knocking at the door of her bedchambers. Thinking it might be Octavia, the chatelaine eagerly pulled open the double doors, one handle loop in each hand, but it was the chamberlain, old man Erricus, standing there, looking grave and sour and eternally unfathomable.

"Already, chamberlain? I thought you might be busy sneaking around, conspiring, setting up your camp. You haven't rapped on these doors for many years! What do you want?"

For the longest time, the chamberlain said nothing. His left eye twitched. Finally he cleared his throat, coughed into his fist.

"The fecund," he said, "has escaped."

Blood drained from the chatelaine's face. She felt this happen, the blood falling. Both doors, and the Great Hall beyond them, even Erricus himself, all seemed to recede until the chatelaine was standing at the far end of an impossibly long warren. There was a ringing in her ears.

"With a rider atop," continued the chamberlain. "A young girl, it would seem. They have gone to the river."

Octavia. The chatelaine knew with certainty that the girl on the monster's back had been the kholic. Even before this news, awareness of the doomed relationship had been circling her, but the chatelaine had done her best to suppress it, to fight it off: now the truth struck her, mocking the vain hopes she had recently tried to nurture. By letting the kholic into her life, and into Jesthe, she had brought about humiliation, catastrophe.

On shaky legs, she made her way to the alcove. She saw the empty cage and greeted her anxious pets with her own choked cry of dismay: sure enough, the keyhooks now clawed nothing but air. She remembered telling the kholic that the missing key had been the key to her heart! She remembered her giddy state of mind, the wonderful love she had felt. But the affair, the chats, the sex, these had been a ruse. Octavia had stared at her, with no discernable expression, most likely planning her deceit the entire time.

When the chatelaine turned back, Erricus had entered the room, his robe sweeping the floor, his fingers pressed tight together. He drifted over the straw carpeting.

"I didn't say you could come in." Blood pounded in the chatelaine's head, threatening to make her black out.

"We are searching the River Crane, where the creature was last seen, but there is no sign of them. This event, chatelaine, falling on the day that you granted us lost powers is, well, prophetic. Gods have made themselves known again. Your fecund is no longer in her pen. Do you have any idea who might have done such a thing? Released the fecund?"

"I do not appreciate your questions, nor the tone in which you ask them."

"There is more trouble. Factions, chatelaine, are marching. There are great disturbances. Trouble at the ostracon, I believe, and elsewhere, at spots throughout the city. *Beatings*. Change has been accompanied by upheaval and civic unrest. Even my own men . . ." He shook his head. "You are aware of the sightings?"

"Of course," she snapped. "I know all about that. But gods and goddesses are your problem, chamberlain. Not for the likes of me, who disbelieve."

"There is violence in our streets."

"Can't you control the city? That's your job."

Erricus said, "Anu, god of the skies, has been seen in the vicinity of South Gate. The benevolent sisters, Kingu and Aspu, have flown over. They are the underworld, and the goddess of anger. There can be no more disbelief. Disbelief has brought us to this point."

She stood very straight. "You must be happy. You and your palatinate. I extend my congratulations. Now leave, please. Leave me alone."

Yet he did not go.

"Chatelaine," he said, "to be honest, the palatinate and I had been prepared for a much less—"

From the window came the low rumbling *whoomp* of an explosion; concussive waves shook the walls of Jesthe.

Path awoke. He stared up at a dim ceiling. Several small flames burned nearby, but he could not see them. He felt a depth of connectivity that extended beyond flesh and bone and thought. He understood who he was, and what he had become since the light had touched his forehead. All that remained of the unfortunate desert boy was a name, a shell. In fact, there had been nothing left of path since the day the long spacer had completed the circuit and reached out to him. Maybe, thought the boy, there had never been such a child, just a vessel, waiting to be filled.

With ease, he sat up.

Two old humans were here with him—the tiny, naked man, who called himself the castellan, and another—taller, skinny—completely swaddled in rags, face hidden by a mask. They both watched him.

Path examined his forearm—a metal rod, delicate chains, fingers of wire and cloth and linked knuckles. His legs were spindles, set into a leathern hip.

"Stand," said the castellan, eyes moist. "You can stand."

Miraculously, path did manage to get to these feet. He tottered. Moving the fingers of each hand, slowly, testing the commands, he felt the digits flex. He rotated each wooden foot. Putting the wire fingers against his chest, he felt the strong beat of his heart.

"A lifetime ago," said the castellan. "I wanted a daughter, but she . . ."

Path glanced at the man. The spirit of the mother ship had downloaded as much as it would. He felt the spacer acknowledge him, far above, as he moved. "I have no parents," he said, as gently as possible. "That was part of the deal. I am an orphan and will remain an orphan."

Bodies were scattered about down here. Children had died since leaving the fold. They had fought each other. Many had died. This understanding brought sadness. Only four of her brood remained alive—

He took a step, his first ever, toward the edge of the table.

Black wings draped the ground. With his back arched, Pan Renik's wobbly legs just managed to keep his weight. He lifted both hands, with huge effort, fists clenched into claws, skin rough and split, burned by the wind.

Though it was hot here, and he could hardly breathe, his mind was clear, like the sky on a blue day.

There were others in this underworld. He heard them. "I escaped the power," he said. "I escaped the padres. I have sucked in clouds." Echoes of his words rasped back at him. Stepping forward, sap leaking down over his face, he realized he was blind. Vision exchanged for clarity. He tried to touch the sides of his head but did not have the dexterity.

He stumbled over a body at his feet, took another step forward. A peaceful wind, of sorts, blew through his mind. Soon, Pan Renik would soar again.

"Listen," panted the fecund, "think you could get off? My back's killing me." Her drool writhed in the glow of a lantern, alive with parasites.

There were not many people around. Octavia climbed down. Neither mentioned the miscarriage, if that was what had happened in the river. Filth dripped onto the muddy street from both her and the monster and it seemed that a myriad of tiny snakes and worms continued to drip from the fecund's skin. She was bony, sunken. They had stopped at the entrance to Hangman's Alley, smoke thick in the air. Shouts from somewhere very close.

"I should never have left my cell. I feel like I've lost my mind."

"Can you walk?"

"I think so. Octavia, I don't know what you expected from me. You tore me from my house."

"You were a prisoner."

"Not really."

Sticking close to the market stalls, the fecund walked toward the vendor's area; beyond, Octavia saw the ostracon. *Burning.*

She stopped, breath catching in her throat. Kholics clustered, some sitting, dazed on the road, others lying on the mud, perhaps even dead. Smoke rolled from windows and down into the street. Clouds were red as embers.

A wall crashed down with a roar and a shower of sparks, sucking flames from the interior of the ostracon that rose, triumphant.

Men catcalled from the perimeter of the glow. Within, trapped kholics screamed.

Mummu had survived the war. He did not know this achievement was remarkable; his awareness was dim at the best of times. He had no knowledge there had even been a war, let alone that eight of his siblings had died during the skirmishes. In fact, Mummu was unaware of mortality, even his own.

When the siblings had made planetfall, Mummu was an infant, wanting only to rumble away from the others, who squabbled and preened and occupied themselves with vain pursuits. Single-minded, Mummu was unlike them. He had trundled across the barren landscape, toward the distant range of low mountains.

By the time the walls of Nowy Solum were completed, and the fecund was a young, lush monster, Mummu was seven times his birth size, working nearly a kilometre under the surface, eating rocks and churning out drones, which he put together in his own shop, manufactured with metals from the rocks he bored through.

When the fighting ended, with Anu half-destroyed, and his sisters hiding, he was perhaps thirty times his birth size. Big enough to generate an impressive mantle.

Today, Mummu was a further seventy times as large. He had continued to spread out, incrementally. His drones were diligent, and dutiful.

The sisters found him by first locating a pack of workers tunnelling under the crust along a stretch of coastline. Kingu and Aspu had known the general area where their brother was set up but they were astonished to see the extent of the work he had done. They approached his seeding towers, extending high above the beach in rows, penetrating the very clouds they had generated for so long.

Several attempts on many frequencies were required to get their stalwart brother to respond, to make him understand that Anu had returned, and that their mother was active. Mummu listened but was not especially interested. Only his agenda remained clear. He had little interaction with the indigenous creatures down here and even less concern for their future. With no decisions to make that required anything other than empirical logic, he had no need for exemplars. He did not care for approval, nor covet worship.

But his sisters tried to express the importance of their visit, relentless. Their lifestyles were in jeopardy. Their colony. Mummu's fields, his dunes, all of his sculpting: these were also threatened. *Anu has descended*, they said. *Anu is under the clouds.*

Paused in his digging—as drones continued to work the vicinity—Mummu was not alarmed. He did not acknowledge the danger. He wanted only to be left alone, to continue his work. If he had to grant concessions, minor requests, to make his sisters go away, then he would do so.

Cliffs collapsed into the ocean with terrific thunder, boiling the spume and sending rolls of dust out over the waves.

The cylinder he had taken from the seraphim became suddenly warm, and Nahid withdrew it quickly from his clothes. It crackled with a light that made the hair on his head stand on end. His skin tingled. When he tried to release the device, it stayed in the air, at eye level, white tendrils a blur. Bluish light flickered, illuminating the alley.

Nahid was alone.

The cylinder lifted higher, humming.

Then someone saw him from the street, and recognized him,

for a voice shouted his name, "Nahid! The ostracon is burning! The ostracon is on fire!"

Pains radiated in his limbs. Anu's voice had still not returned. Hornblower looked at the dark roofs and darker clouds, toward a huge black structure balanced precariously atop several spindly towers, elevated much higher than all other structures around. From this lofty room, a light had begun to shine, visible through the clouds like a beacon over the city.

He heard the growing roar, approaching from behind. When he felt the shaking at his bones, he turned to see Anu appear, sliding into view, rendering every detail white and harsh. Grinding at the hard material used to roof these structures in the underworld, the blind power knocked down chunks that shattered or thudded heavily around hornblower's feet. Winds whipped his robes about. He shielded his eyes.

Exemplar! Don't look at me; look for a place I can land.

"I have failed you," hornblower shouted. "Now I'm lost in this place. I will never find the exile or what he stole."

It's too late, Anu responded. *We've been set up. Now look at the damn—*

Wire fingers screeched against the tin of the worktable as path let himself down to the floor. He had begun to glow. He felt his own heat. Light radiated from him in beams of white so that the room was filled with his luminescence.

Trembling, the castellan cried out, arms extended, as if to embrace the boy, but he came no closer.

Behind him, the taller man continued to clean the tools he had used.

"Sometimes," said path, "I feel like I'm still in the tank, having the flesh corroded from my bones. Or maybe these memories are from before then, when I was a real infant."

He sniffed the air.

The open window beckoned.

Three men confronted Name of the Sun as she took scraps out the back of The Cross-Eyed Traveller to dump them in the alley. The men had weapons. They blocked her way. One was young and pudgy, with soft-looking skin and short hair. He had a nasty shiner. The other two, holding stout wooden handles in their fists, were older.

"Garbage fucker," said the man with the black eye.

"Get away from me."

"We're taking back the city. Tonight. We know who you are."

"Leave me alone."

Behind the group, in the light from a door that had just opened, Name of the Sun saw the unmistakable silhouette of her landlord, standing with her roommate, Polly. They were watching her. Name of the Sun was more shocked to see them than she was by this confrontation, and in her hesitation she was not quite able to fully dodge the first blow, which glanced off her shoulder, striking the wall behind. She did manage to rake the face of her nearest assailant, one of the older men, with her fingers, but the others were on her then, clubbing.

She went down fighting.

Flames appeared to be sliding down the stone, dripping onto the road, where they continued to flicker and leap. Nahid stopped at the doorway to the ostracon, trying to look inside, shielding his face from the blistering heat that roared through the opening. In the road, other kholics huddled. From a second story window, a woman leaned—a senior called Orlando—shouting down at another group, who were trying to convince her to leap.

There was a cry, very much like his sister's, but by the time he heard it, Nahid had already entered.

The fires leapt at him as he forced his way down the main hall. He intended to call out but could not open his mouth; heat seemed to shrivel him, sucking the air from his lungs, his nose. Above, part of the ceiling had collapsed and more flames roared through the hole, breaking at its edges, consuming. The ostracon was filled with an almost ambient peace.

His skin might be splitting. He was transforming, emerging. There were no people here, in this landscape of flames and heat.

Just him. He tried to mount the stairs, to get to the dorms where he had lived with Octavia for years, but the upper floor was completely engulfed.

Through a damaged wall toward the rear of the building he saw the dark and smoky courtyard. Out there, another kholic climbed the low buttress that ringed the ostracon. Looking over his shoulder, eyes wide and glinting, face reddened, he seemed to look right at Nahid, who stood in the inferno, hair gone, skin blistering and crackling.

When Nahid breathed, his lungs turned to cinders.

Over the roar and shouts from outside, he heard a baby's cry.

The sisters flew below the clouds. Mummu had lent them a squad of diggers, and the ruthless drones spread out in formation below, rumbling as fast as their treads could carry them over sand and rocks.

Nearing the dark line of the perimeter wall, Kingu and Aspu banked, separating, to flank the city; Anu was within, though his signals were weak. If they could retain surprise, the sisters might be able to hold onto their dream of maintaining a utopia. This seemed their only hope, now that Anu had returned. Though blind, their brother possessed formidable firepower and a psychotic fury the sisters had witnessed—and been victim to—several times in the past. Previously, when they had defeated him, there had been other siblings at their sides, working together.

These siblings were dead now.

Kingu and Aspu suspected their brother was aware of their approach, that he had broken their codes, and was lurking in wait. Anu had most likely taken an exemplar, somehow, in order to penetrate Mummu's shield and come down to the surface; they imagined this astute, war-faring human keeping watch right now, raising the alarm as they raced toward him. What would the waiting defenses be, the traps, the guns?

The sisters were agitated, twitchy; as soon as the drones confirmed they were within range of this city they were allowed to begin firing. Fear had occluded any chance for strategy.

The first missiles sent massive gouts of sand into the air, melting them into glass spouts, but with slightly tweaked trajectories the weapons soon began tearing out chunks of stone and brick from the wall, followed quickly by the routing of exposed residences and hovels, all of which collapsed, and fused, taking down others of their kind in huge roils of dust and death.

Screaming above the skyline, as the diggers continued to pound their way in, they saw Anu roar up ahead of them, rotating, seeking. Below their brother was a large fire, and the dark night sky around him began to turn in a vortex of sick purple and black. Was this Anu's doing? A trap? Skittish, the sisters peeled away. Where was Anu's exemplar? Their brother, as they headed to quadrants beyond the walls, seemed unable to locate them. Small smart bombs hissed toward him, leaving lines of white gas, like tethers, to burst against his skin.

From rear vids, Kingu and Aspu both watched the cannons that had taken down their brothers and sisters emerge from Anu's ribs, ugly killers, but his shots went wild, tearing out more buildings and streets.

Then a message came though their receivers; they expected to hear Anu's rage coming through, but it was not Anu at all.

Firebombs found Serena's shelter, though one of the explosives fizzled and spluttered and only managed to spray fluids that did not initially ignite. The cognosci living there, which had smelled the man's approach, warned Serena through spiking anxiety, bouncing from the walls, and she managed to leave by the rear door.

At the same moment, in Hangman's Alley, Hakim's booth was also spared too much damage when the incendiary device intended for it was lobbed into the neighbouring stall (selling wallets and small pouches); the previous night, a nervous teenaged recruit had marked an ex on the wrong location post.

Hakim himself was jumped as he closed his restaurant early, obviously concerned about the fire burning on the block adjacent, wanting to go and help, do something. From the north end of the city had come the intermittent sounds of terrific explosions and the shriek of gods. Something monumental was happening. He locked up and moved swiftly toward the area where the fire burned.

His assailants smashed him in the back of the head with a metal bar. He was bleeding and in considerable pain as he broke the left arm of one man and throttled the other into unconsciousness. He killed neither, mostly because the pair reminded him of his youngest two sons, who were constantly making bad decisions. They could use a little leniency now and then.

Gripping the steep slope of clay tiles as winds tugged his body, path felt dampness on his skin, the bombardment of countless machines, each too small to see.

The dungeon roof was in disrepair, with nests and cracks and missing tiles. He found an area where the structure had been so damaged he was able to work one of his legs into a hole. Then he let go of the tiles and raised both metallic hands until the tiny machines began to circle him, slowly at first, then moving quicker, a cyclone.

Kingu and Aspu were near, with a fleet of diggers, attacking blind Anu. Her children were fighting, always fighting. And Mummu was somewhere out there, forming, reforming, in his stunted way.

The seegee swooped into the cyclone and raced exuberantly about, orbiting path's head a few cycles before throwing itself against his chest, like a lover. Tendrils linked with flesh—

The long spacer blinked, alert; her power plants started.

Path closed his eyes.

Heat kept Octavia away, shoving her back when she tried to step forward. She had seen Nahid run in, had shouted his name, but her voice was lost in the din. When a surge of the blaze made her turn her face away, she saw the fecund, almost transparent now, watching her from across the street.

The ostracon groaned.

Abruptly, she was pushed hard from behind, sprawling in the hot mud. A bare-chested man, reddened by flames, stood over her.

"The sister," he said. "There is no time to cut your throat."

He raised his club with both hands, but before he had a chance to strike, a blur hurtled across Octavia, almost too fast to see, and the man was gone.

The fecund, too, was nowhere to be seen.

Movement in the flames. Something large changed position. The entire façade of the ostracon shifted in on itself, about to collapse.

Hornblower toppled as soon as Anu vanished, wrenched upwards, sucked into the clouds. Though hornblower did not pass out, he lay in the mud, unable to move. Above him, banks of mist continued to spin in the vortex he had earlier spotted. He watched for a while until the towers of the structure broke away, rising briefly before coming down in a shower of bricks and tiles and dust.

Later, after he slept, an old man leaned over him, nudging him. Hornblower was startled to see that this man was the same man whose death raft had recently plunged over the edge of the world. The oldest man.

"Are you able to stand?"

"I apologize," hornblower said quietly. "We sent you here. We sent all of you here."

The oldest man in the world smiled sadly. "The dungeon has fallen. North End is destroyed. Benevolent sisters have come and gone. We were judged unworthy." The man took hornblower by the arm and helped him up. "You are ill? You're sweating. Come with me. Rest. We're gathering the injured."

Hornblower wanted to recount all that he had done in the settlement—his sermons, his visits—but words were obscured by the emotions pushing up from his diaphragm. He leaned on the oldest man.

At the temple, he was given water and bread and a place to lie down. Immediately, he fell asleep again. The settlement would function without him, without padres. Though he looked down on citizens, he could not speak to them.

He saw the girls from the funeral. They conspired together, and laughed, and ran away.

The sun shone.

At the junction of the main branch and the branch of moving waters, an effigy had been built, entwined with boughs: a statue.

Hornblower woke up, heart racing. He tried to sit up on the cot but could not. The host was inert in his mouth and he spit it out. Candles guttered. He closed his eyes again. The last image from his dream lingered. He could not sleep any more, though he felt exhausted. The statue had been Pan Renik, the exile, dressed in the suit he had used to fly away. Citizens had gathered around, kneeling before the icon with respect and profound gratitude.

The exemplar covered the woman's face with a blanket. His second wife had made the blanket for him when they'd gotten married. The talkative one slept. She would most likely live.

Not this one.

As he left the community centre to get air, the exemplar collapsed. There was blood in his mouth. He lay there, quaking, until a farmer came by and shook him gently by the shoulder.

"Exemplar? Exemplar?"

He coughed up blood, and something hard, from the back of his throat, which he spit out. "I am not an exemplar," he said, wiping his mouth. "Not any more."

The farmer hesitated.

"We're on our own now."

Stones had whirled, and chunks of wood, smoke and flames, blood and melancholy. The long spacer departed. With so few symbiotes, she could not move quickly. Her functions were limited. All of her children were inert once more, back where they came from. She would mourn them until the heart of the boy—the child who had been called path, already tethered to her console—stopped beating.

By then, hopefully, she would be light years away.

Officers of the palatinate carried the chamberlain up the East Stairs on his litter. He was not able to mount these stairs for the energy that had recently filled him had now fled. Erricus felt old and ill. On the second floor of Jesthe, his men were everywhere he looked, as if the walls had secreted them. The palace had suffered considerable damage. Gods had come and gone. Whatever the deities sought was not found in the city or her citizens.

Towers had fallen. Buildings burned. He pressed his fingers together to stop them from shaking.

The chatelaine was not in her room. Rubble had covered the floor of the Great Hall, though the empty bedchambers remained intact.

Of course she passed palatinate, who moved cautiously toward her, gravely, and she thought to herself that they could keep the rotten palace for all she cared. Down and outside through the small courtyard, starting to sob, with snot on her lips, she ran toward the gates. Smoke was thick in the air and she heard the cries of her people.

Across the deserted Gardens, into the centrum, she stopped to peer at the ruins.

The chatelaine wandered in a daze all of that night, knowing it would be her last. Images of destruction, and of the maelstrom—bodies of the huge gods, lifting above the blazing skyline, shattering the dungeon—would never leave her.

She hoped her father was at peace.

Scrambling up the embankment to the River Crane, and onto the promenade, the chatelaine scraped her shin. Pain, blooming, was exquisite. She stood there for a second, focusing on the wound, on her dark fluids spilling out, before peering over the sluggish waters. She wondered how long would it take to drown, and if her body would leave Nowy Solum, floating on the filthy river until it fell off the edge of the world.

Clumsy, fumbling, she began to negotiate the slippery rocks, hands fluttering ahead of her.

A dark and silent funeral barge headed toward the gates. When she was knee deep, she was surprised by the sound of wings, approaching. Turning, she nearly fell.

The cherub, coming from the sky, cried out, "Mother, mother! At last!"

With a gasp, the chatelaine caught her pet, snugly, bringing it close, holding it as tight as she had ever held anything before. She closed her eyes, clinging to the trembling cherub as it folded its wings, afraid her baby might vanish once more.

"I've been looking for so long." The cherub's breath, hot in her ear. "The things I have seen, mother. The things I have seen."

The chatelaine stroked the cherub's head, her sobs diminishing.

Over the shattered silhouette of Nowy Solum, clouds were turning to amber, but these clouds seemed very thin today—the thinnest, in fact, the chatelaine had ever seen. She wondered if she would ever recover from the shock and heartbreak, should she make the foolish choice to continue living.

The cherub was already asleep against her shoulder.

Turning, to make her way back to shore, the chatelaine sighed, and the horizon past Jesthe ruptured with an astonishing patch of blue.

about the author

Brent Hayward's fiction has appeared in several publications and anthologies, including *Horizons SF*, *On Spec*, *ChiZine*, the Tesseracts series, and *Chilling Tales*. In 2006, his story "Phallex Comes Out" was nominated for the StorySouth Million Writers Award as best online story of that year; it received an honourable mention. *Filaria*, his first novel, was published by ChiZine Publications in 2008 and has since garnered solid acclaim.

Born in London, England, raised in Montreal, he currently he lives in Toronto with his family. He can be reached through his LiveJournal at: http://brenth.livejournal.com

EVERY
SHALLOW
CUT
TOM
PICCIRILLI

AVAILABLE MARCH 15, 2011
FROM CHIZINE PUBLICATIONS

978-1-926851-10-5

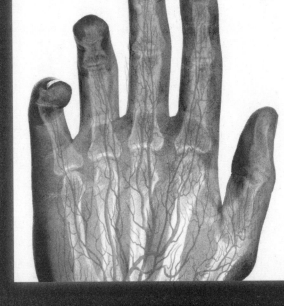

3

NAPIER'S BONES DERRYL MURPHY

AVAILABLE MARCH 15, 2011
FROM CHIZINE PUBLICATIONS

978-1-926851-09-9

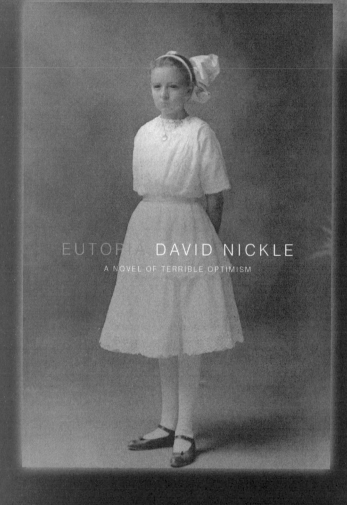

EUTOPIA DAVID NICKLE

A NOVEL OF TERRIBLE OPTIMISM

AVAILABLE APRIL 15, 2011
FROM CHIZINE PUBLICATIONS

978-1-926851-11-2

THE DOOR TO
LOST PAGES

CLAUDE LALUMIÈRE

AVAILABLE APRIL 15, 2011
FROM CHIZINE PUBLICATIONS

978-1-926851-12-9

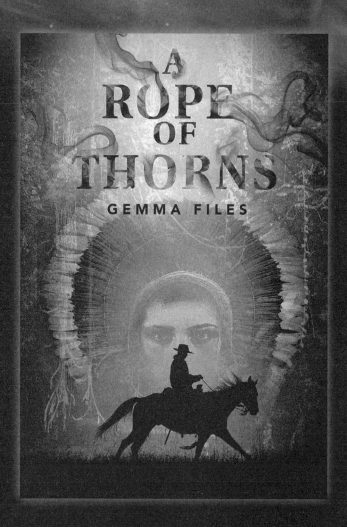

A ROPE OF THORNS

GEMMA FILES

AVAILABLE MAY 15, 2011
FROM CHIZINE PUBLICATIONS

978-1-926851-14-3

EDITED BY SANDRA KASTURI & HALLI VILLEGAS

2011

IMAGINARIUM

the best canadian
speculative writing

COMING JULY 15, 2011
FROM CHIZINE PUBLICATIONS

978-1-926851-15-0

978-0-9812978-9-7

TIM LEBBON

**THE THIEF OF
BROKEN TOYS**

978-0-9812978-8-0

PHILIP NUTMAN

CITIES OF NIGHT

978-0-9812978-7-3

SIMON LOGAN

**KATJA FROM THE
PUNK BAND**

978-0-9812978-6-6

GEMMA FILES

**A BOOK OF
TONGUES**

978-0-9812978-5-9

DOUGLAS SMITH

CHIMERASCOPE

978-0-9812978-4-2

NICHOLAS KAUFMANN

**CHASING THE
DRAGON**

EMB
RACE
THE
ODD